RELATIVE EXPOSURES

Felling the Family Tree

RELATIVE EXPOSURES

Felling the Family Tree

◆

David Elkins and Torben Schiøler

Woodley & Watts

MONTREAL · SEDONA · TAOS

Woodley & Watts
400 McGill, 3rd Floor
Montreal, QC, Canada
H2Y 2G1

Canadian Cataloguing in Publication Data

Elkins, David   Schiøler, Torben
    Relative exposures: felling the family tree

ISBN 0-9698972-2-7

1. Ross, Wilhemina, 1874-1962—Diaries. 2. Ross,
Wilhemina, 1874-1962—Family. 3. Henniker, Karl—Family.
4. Ross family. 5. Henniker family. I. Title.

CS90.R664 1998   929'.2'0971   C98-900523-2

Design by Carston Schiøler
Layout and production by Dakshina Clark

Printed and bound in Canada

For all those who have relatives

Acknowledgments

◆ A large number of people helped with this book. Torben is grateful to Donna Vekteris for her many excellent suggestions and for her unending support of – and help with – the writing. She has an eye for the "right" photograph and provided invaluable assistance in the selection of those which appear among the TS-authored stories. Don Winkler's meticulous reading of the manuscript uncovered a plethora of potentially embarrassing inconsistencies which his good council corrected before this work was thrust on an unsuspecting public, and for that Mr. Schiøler is also grateful. Closer to home, sons Daniel and Marcus provided unstintingly of their time and energy whenever called upon to dig out an unwanted word or prop up a sagging photo. A thank you too goes to Sonia Grard for her efforts spent slaving over a hot computer.

David is grateful first and foremost to his wife, Valmai Howe, whose twenty-seven years of nurturing and support finally birthed this book. However odd, ugly and misshappen a child it may be, it lives and breathes and has set off to find its place in the world. Without Valmai it would certainly have been stillborn. Stepping back from the perilous cliffs of messy metaphor to the safety and charm of firm reality, daughter Tilke's unfailing enthusiasm proved a constant joy and encouragement.

Both authors are indebted to Madeleine Partous whose remarkable editing skills rescued the damp, pathetic manuscript from the dark, dried it off and, with her sharp red pen, dragged it screaming into the light. The job of proof-reading – a Herculean task given the authors' shaky punctuation and even shakier spelling – was provided by Leyla Harrison and the eagle-eyed Lin Stranberg. But for Carston Schiøler's handsome design and Dakshina Clark's skill and patience with the layouts, this might still be written in pencil on loose sheets of foolscap.

DAVID ELKINS, TORBEN SCHIØLER

Contents

Contents

Preface

Wilhemina "Willy" Ross-Henniker
1874-1962

◆ Great Aunt Wilhemina "Willy" Ross–Henniker, pictured here at the Governor's Ball on December 16, 1914, possibly in Albany, New York, lived a large and rambling life. She and her husband Karl moved house so frequently that exactly where the photograph was taken remains a subject of conjecture.

Of the three diaries she kept in 1914 – notebooks, actually, in which she would fill in the date but, for reasons of her own, never the place — we can be reasonably sure that one was completed while she lived either in Florida or California. Three pages are covered with awkward but sympathetic sketches of tropical trees and plants and no fewer than eleven entries make reference to palms and coconuts, the most notable, perhaps, being the entry for February 7: "We lay on the beach in the moonlight and I remarked on how the great trunk curved up in exactly the same way he did, though he did not have the same lovely leafy hat. How we both laughed." Miami? Malibu? We can only guess.

We do know that in 1914 they also spent at least part of the racing season in Saratoga. There are only eight entries for the whole of July and August and each is a list of horses with a dollar amount next to it. These are toted up with the sum circled and underlined several times. Her winnings? Did she lose on all the missing days? Who can tell?

These vagaries and the many, many dates which have no entries whatsoever, would be of little consequence were she an ordinary diarist. She was not. She never wasted a line on those mundane daily minutiae which render most journals so utterly boring, even to their author. You know the sort: "May 10, 19—. Sunny day. Woke at 7:30. Had corn flakes and eggs for breakfast. Mr. and Mrs. P. came to dinner. Played cards till 9:30 and took a walk. In bed by 11:00." Willy's diaries were not like that. Of the ninety-seven notebooks and three thousand four hundred and twenty-seven entries which she made between October 1941, when Karl died, and June 13, 1962 when she joined him, there is scarcely a single line that does not reveal something of interest about the author or far more often — and this is important to the present work — about her kith and kin. This meaty content, combined with the large number of omitted dates — there were two hundred and one entries in 1953, her busiest year, to a low of only forty-seven in 1959 when she was laid up with a broken hip — establish Aunt Willy as a woman who said nothing unless she had something to say. Like any good biographer, she was at her finest when she shone the light of her unique insight not on herself, but on others. It was for members of the family — living and dead — that she saved her most piquant thrusts, and it is these passages that formed the raw material of this book.

Relative Exposures is a collaboration between distant cousins related through marriage. Wilhemina Ross hailed from the American/Canadian side of the family. She met Karl Henniker, a Dane, at the International Exhibition at Lyon, France in May 1892. They were married in a small unnamed town a fortnight later.

Karl and Willy lived a wide and handsome life together. They loved big houses and bought, occupied and sold seventeen during their marriage. Each was furnished with antiques in the grand manner. When things got tight — which they frequently did — Karl would sell off the goods and chattels at twice what they'd paid for them, the proceeds of which would provide a grub stake for his next venture. Great Uncle Karl made and lost more money in his lifetime than most successful men might accomplish in ten. At the time of his death in March 1941, he was on the verge of yet another dazzling and highly profitable coup. But for the piece of filet mignon which lodged in his throat at New York's Stork Club where he was hosting the general in charge of "protein procurement" for the U.S. Army, he and Auntie might have gone on living lavishly together for another twenty years.

It was not to be. Aunt Willy spent the first three months after he died grieving right where he had left her, at the Plaza Hotel. On June 7, 1941, we know from her diary, she settled her account with the manager with the proceeds from the sale of "an emerald bracelet Karl won in some dice game" and, along with seven trunks, moved in with her nephew once removed, Scotty, his wife and three children, who lived in a modest walk-up in Milwaukee. She and Karl had helped them out when they were first married — and several times since — and they couldn't refuse. After a couple of months, sensing that her welcome was wearing thin, she made arrangements to stay with her sister Lulu's step-daughter,

Margaret, whose husband, the heir to a dog food fortune and an avid amateur aviator, had just enlisted in the Royal Canadian Air Force and was being trained near Lethbridge, Alberta.

This established a pattern she was to follow for the rest of her life. She'd select one of her vast number of relatives either by blood or by marriage — Karl had cousins the width and breadth of Europe — and arrange to stay for a few weeks or months before moving on. Some of the family members lived in mansions, others in tenements. Fine china and pheasant this month, beans around the kitchen table the next, it was all the same to Willy. And besides, she had her little project.

In June 1962, Aunt Willy went on to her eternal rest — or perhaps not quite eternal; she was a life-long Theosophist and believed unerringly in reincarnation. Five and a half years later, in November or December, 1967 we — the compilers of this book — received a notice from Canadian National Railways advising that a trunk, addressed to us, had arrived at Montreal's Central Station. To retrieve it, we were required to present ourselves, together, at the baggage claim office.

It was a large, well-built, round-topped, brass-fitted affair framed in mahogany. The handsome metal sides were heavily worked with a delicate pattern of small blue flowers and it was locked. We lugged it back to Torben's flat, hauled it up three flights of stairs and set at it with two screwdrivers and a hammer. After a frustrating half-hour during which we almost came to blows, we finally managed to pry the sturdy latch open and flung back the top, giddily imagining banknotes, jewelry, stocks and bonds. What we found were the ninety-seven notebooks and hundreds of photographs of the family. Some of the snapshots were neatly labeled and fixed in albums with dusty padded leather covers, the thick black pages inside scrawled with white ink captions: "Uncle Thomas at Big Falls," or "Sara You-Know-Who in front of the Paris Opera" and the like. Others were stuffed, helter-skelter, into ancient shoe boxes, always Italian, and chocolate boxes, always

Belgian. On the top was a cream-coloured envelope addressed in violet ink in Great Aunt Willy's round hand: To my dear nephews. Inside was a letter dated May 31, 1962. It read:

"Both:

Since your Uncle Karl died, I've been doing more than playing *Mah-jongg* and drinking gin, whatever you've heard to the contrary. In my travels, I've collected everything I could about this grand family of ours. What stories our relatives tell once they've had a glass or two of schnapps! Whenever I heard something choice, I wrote it down. I had plenty of time on my hands to root around in attics and basements for pictures and nobody seemed to care about them except me. My idea was to write everything up and put it in a big album along with the photographs so the family history would be in one place. I don't think I'm going to get the chance.

Uncle Karl and I were always fond of you both. You were such clever boys. We would be grateful if you would carry on.

Love,

Willy & Karl (in absentia)

P.S. Do it for the family.

P.P.S. Don't worry what people think."

We're not very clever, Auntie. It's taken us over three decades to get down to it and to manhandle the material, along with a couple of updates we thought you'd appreciate, into a more or less coherent form. We did it for the family. We're worried about what people will think.

David Elkins
Torben Schiøler
Montréal, Québec, May 1998

_____

5

Natasha. Taken by Prescott in Moscow, 1959.

Prescott's tract house. It was later sold to a religious cult who used it as an assembly hall.

Toast

◆ During the forties and fifties Uncle Prescott was gainfully employed as an engineer in the consumer products division of Northway Electric, a large manufacturing conglomerate located in upper New York state. Sadly, this once-proud symbol of American industrial might went belly-up in 1965 due to "fiscal malfeasance," with the result that the chairman and six underlings received a total of one hundred and forty-eight years in the slammer. The sentences were later overturned on appeal. In the end those gentlemen walked away with the obscene amounts of money they'd swindled from the company coffers over the years, leaving the local citizenry in a devastating economic slump which has lasted to this day. At any rate, during the company's heyday, Northway Electric turned out such diverse products as toasters, vacuum cleaners, electric lawn-mowers, air conditioners, washing machines, dryers, radios and TV's. Their crowning achievement was undoubtly the 1952 Regaleeze-Vue TV set. With its rounded screen and high-gloss beech veneer finish, this little marvel is not only an enduring classic but is still a hot collector's item. A working model sold recently at a New York auction for fifty-eight thousand dollars.

Besides their consumer products, Northway Electric also manufactured a line of top-secret electronic gear for the nuclear early warning system as well as submarine detection and communication gear, electronic gun sights, components for weather/spy planes and advanced tank turrets and treads. Uncle Prescott, of course, knew little about these hush-hush products. His line was toasters and vacuum cleaners, and he was good at it. In 1957 his department introduced the innovative four-slice, three-cycle "Toast-eeze" heavy-duty industrial model. With its built-in humidity and temperature thermostats it was able to "optimize the active toasting potential" of any slice of ordinary Wonder Bread. The contraption also featured a light mist of sucrose and chlorophyll which was sprayed onto the bread slices during the second cycle, "rendering the toast more savory, nutritious and golden while avoiding unsightly charring." This bit of promotional prose, incidentally, was concocted by a young genius from public relations who would later go on to win fame as a satirical novelist. As a further refinement, the toaster's conventional spring-loaded ejection mechanism had been replaced by a miniaturized air compressor. This innovation had come about as a result of consumer complaints of "stuck toast." The clever little device was so powerful that it could actually dislodge a brick. If improperly handled, the gadget could easily imbed all four slices of toast into the plaster of a ceiling or slam them clear across a large sunken conversation pit. (A Wisconsin branch of the National Rifle Association used the toaster for a time as a launching pad during skeet-shoot practices.) The "Toast-eeze" won several prestigious awards for innovative design, but despite these honours sold very poorly, no doubt due to its high retail price of one hundred and forty dollars. Keep in mind that this was at a time when you could buy a conventional Westinghouse toaster for about six dollars, or a brand new Volkswagen for eight hundred and fifty. Northway Electric eventually phased out the production of the "Toast-eeze" following a rash of consumer lawsuits.

The trouble started when a Moline, Illinois restaurateur who hadn't read the instruction manual, power-ejected four slices of whole wheat into an exposed fuse box which in turn caused an electrical short circuit, resulting in seventy-two thousand dollars worth of fire damage. On another occasion, this time in a Catholic retirement home in Davenport, Illinois, errant toast ricocheted off a lava lamp, shattering it into tiny fragments and seriously lacerating the arm of a former substitute school teacher on his way to lunch. The toast went on to crash through a large plate-glass window, finally knocking over and shattering a plaster statuette of the Virgin Mary on display in a hardware store across the street. But I'm getting ahead of the story. The lawsuits would come much later.

To all outward appearances Uncle Prescott was a pillar of the community, "the man in the grey flannel suit," member of the country club and the Kiwanis, who devoted his working life to making a better America, as least as far as toasters and vacuum cleaners were concerned. Yet deep in his heart he sensed there had to be more to life than making kitchenware. As a thirty-three-year-old bachelor, he lived in quiet desperation in a suburban Levittown-like housing development a few miles from the plant, and his private life was as arid and barren as a Spanish roadhouse. In frequent moments of existential crisis he toyed with the idea of moving to Greenwich Village, growing a goatee, sporting a beret, dressing in black and becoming a poet. On weekends he would drive down to New York City where he could mingle freely with the beatniks at the Figaro Café in Greenwich Village. Over time he developed a close friendship with Elmer Woodhouse, publisher of "Blast," an early beatnik poetry publication. It was in this magazine that Prescott first saw his work published, alongside the early verses of Ginsberg, Corso, Olson and Kerouac. This interest in poetry was of course kept well hidden from his colleagues at the plant — after all, he didn't want to be labelled a weirdo. But Prescott's prosaic existence would soon change dramatically.

It all started in 1959 during a brief thaw in the Cold War, when the State Department, in a flurry of reciprocal goodwill, managed to convince Soviet premier Nikita Khrushchev that it would be in his interest, as well as in the interest of world communism, to permit selected U.S. companies to set up a consumer products trade fair in Moscow. For the State Department this bit of business turned out to be a brilliant propaganda coup, since it offered a rare oppportunity to demonstrate, for the benefit of Ivan and Olga and those other godless bolsheviks, how superior "dog-eat-dog free enterprise" was to Marxist dialectics. The State Department, enlisting the help of then vice-president Richard Milhouse Nixon, succeeded in signing up a long list of the most powerful American industrial conglomerates, including Northway Electric. Prescott, as the head of the department, was put in charge of the Northway Electric's consumer products exhibit. Meetings were held daily with State Department personnel, CIA operatives and FBI background checkers as well as PR and engineering staff. During an early brainstorming session Prescott hit on the idea of featuring the "Toast-eeze" machine as it notably turned out golden slices of Wonder Bread for the Russian public. It was the general consensus that toasted white bread would not only be a fabulous luxury but a stark contrast to their humdrum diet of Lenin, borscht and potatoes. Then Prescott came up with the idea of sandwiches. Why not go whole hog? Frantic last-minute arrangements were made to have large quantities of mayonnaise, iceberg lettuce, cheese, spam, cold cuts, peanut butter and jams flown in to the Moscow airport and cleared through customs in time for the opening. Just to add a bit of dazzle to the proceedings, four shapely young models, "The Toast-eeze Girls," were hired from a smart agency in New York.

In July 1959 the fair opened in Moscow's Sokolniki Park amid a great deal of fanfare. As luck would have it, Northway Electric had been assigned a booth immediately adjacent to the now-famous model kitchen. On the afternoon of July 25th the crowds were cleared away and Khrushchev and Nixon came sweeping along trailing an army of reporters, interpreters and aides. The two leaders were arguing heatedly, Khrushchev flailing his massive arms about as he made his points, stabbing his fingers this way and that and sweating profusely. Now and again the entourage would stop as he took a large swig from a bottle of Pepsi-Cola. It was clear he was enjoying himself hugely. From Prescott's vantage point it seemed obvious that the premier's outlandish behaviour was designed to unnerve the American vice-president. Khrushchev was a world-class ham; he was putting on his act for the press. Nixon, in sharp contrast, had the tight self-righteous look of the injured party attempting to salvage what little self-respect he could from a disastrous situation. How could anyone hope to look statesman-like next to this squat, sweaty peasant? God, the indignity of it all. But far worse than that, it was all going to play on the newsreels back home. And there was going to be an election in the fall.

As luck would have it they paused in front of the Northway Electric booth, still arguing heatedly. It soon became clear that Khrushchev was fast losing interest in the debate. He had spotted the display of club sandwiches arrayed on the counter and he clearly liked what he saw. A gap-toothed grin spread over his chubby face as Nixon ranted on. "O.K. Mr. Premier, so maybe you make better rockets, maybe you can send a tiny helpless dog into space. So what? We have colour television."

Khrushchev waved him away with one hand and pointed with the other at the sandwich display while making loud smacking noises with his lips. Prescott lifted a plate towards the premier. "Please help yourself, Mr. Premier. We would be honoured if you would try one. These ones are the best. They're called club sandwiches." He pronounced the words with exaggerated care. Khrushchev's table manners, without doubt motivated by a desire to irritate Nixon, left a lot to be desired. But it was clear he relished the sandwich; as Nixon and the world press corps looked on, he wolfed down another four in quick succession, after making a big show of ripping off the decorative toothpick with the U.S. flag on it.

"*Ata ochiny haraso, klubbe sanovich, otchiny haraso,*" he repeated, stabbing his chubby fingers at the display case while leering at the

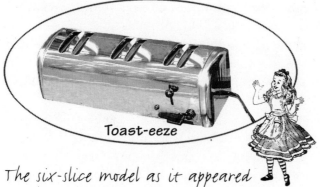

Toast-eeze

The six-slice model as it appeared
in the 1957 magazine ad campaign
that launched the innovative toaster.

Khrushchev and Nixon during the Moscow trade fair.
It is said that one of the figures in the background is
Prescott, and that the decoration in Khrushchev's
lapel is a Northway Electric friendship pin.

four tasty Toast-eeze girls. "Your sanveeches are good, very very good, much better than your colour TV."

Then Khrushchev leaned over the sandwich counter and waved at Prescott. "So tell me," he said. "What is this machine you use for making club sandwich?" He pointed at the Toast-eeze.

"That is a toaster, Mr. Premier. The Toast-eeze model, the very best money can buy, six slices at a time," said Prescott as the interpreters scratched their heads and tried to come up with a Russian word for toaster.

"Look at this, Mr. Premier," continued Prescott as he put six slices of whole-wheat into the slots. "It only takes a minute, and once the toast is done, this little gizmo here controls the ejection force." Prescott pointed. The Premier examined the machine with great interest. He ran his hands over the shiny chrome and fiddled with the dials.

"Please don't play with that knob, Mr. Premier," said Prescott. But it was already too late. The maximum "active toasting potential" of the bread had already been reached, causing the auto-trigger mechanism to release. Without warning all six slices shot out of the slots and ricocheted off the ceiling with a resounding thwack. For a man of his girth, Khrushchev was amazingly agile. He leapt back. Then he laughed, punching his fist into his palm. "Just like your rockets, eh?" He pointed at Nixon, who didn't seem amused. Everybody roared with laughter. Prescott held up the Toast-eeze.

"Mr. Premier, please accept this gift with the compliments of Northway Electric as a token of our esteem and friendship." Prescott handed the toaster to Khrushchev's aide. "And don't forget to read the instruction manual."

A flustered Nixon finally managed to have the party move on, the Russian premier waving to Prescott and winking at the Toast-eeze girls as he munched on a salami, bacon, ham and cheddar cheese triple-decker.

In the next booth a furious argument erupted. Prescott could quite clearly see and hear Khruschev loudly berating Nixon: "This whole exhibit is nothing but American lies. Nobody in America has a kitchen like this. It's absurd. And the stuff probably doesn't work anyway. Just look at your miserable rockets. You think you can come here and hoodwink us?"

"Mr. Premier, you think you know everything. Well, you don't. You're just filibustering." Nixon was getting visibly hot under the collar. This fat bolshevik was clearly winning brownie points in the verbal sparring and with the world press.

"This whole deal stinks," continued Khrushchev, waving away Nixon's objections. "And it stinks exactly like fresh horseshit. It's all horseshit, and nothing smells worse than horseshit."

"The chairman is mistaken," interrupted Nixon, gaining the upper hand in one brilliant stroke. "There is something that smells far worse than horseshit and that something is pigshit."

Well briefed as always, Nixon knew the premier had started out on his checkered career as a pig farmer. In the end a reluctant Khrushchev was forced to concede on this delicate point. It was at this critical moment that an alert news photographer snapped the now-famous picture of Nixon's finger poking into Khrushchev's chest. The wirephoto went around the world and helped lift Nixon's sagging ratings in the upcoming presidential elections. In the background you can spot a blurry Prescott — and the little emblem in Khrushchev's lapel is a Northway Electric friendship pin.

Later that afternoon, as things calmed down a bit, a delegation of Russian engineers toured the exhibition hall. They stopped at the Northway Electric booth, where they spent considerable time going over the various Toast-eeze models. By the time the exhibition closed for the day, the chief engineer, having skillfully negotiated a fifteen percent discount, signed a purchase order for eight hundred units of the DSV-37 industrial strength model. In their clumsy attempts to flirt with the Toast-eeze hostesses, however, the engineers got nowhere. The girls had been warned by the CIA about the dangers of this kind of fraternization.

That night, as Prescott was nursing a much-needed Moscow Mule at the bar of the Komisal Hotel, a peroxide blonde slid onto the bar stool next to him. Her name was Natasha, her English was flawless and so was her body language. They had a few drinks together and as so often happens in these matters, one thing led to the next. To make a long story short, they spent a memorable night together in Prescott's room. That might easily have been the end of it, but fate intervened and decided in its wisdom to throw a curve ball. They fell in love despite the fact that he knew, and she knew that he knew, that she was in the employ of the KGB. For the six remaining days of the trade fair they spent whatever time they could together.

On the final evening of the exhibit, as Prescott was about to enter the hotel, he was accosted by two beefy individuals. As to be expected, they had explicit photos of the previous nights. It was pure and simple blackmail. In they end they left him no choice but to co-operate. He was told to provide any and all photographic copies of blueprints from the Northway Electric engineering department. Of course he would be handsomely compensated. Upon his return to Albany he would be contacted by his future "handler" who would identify himself using the code words "What did Delaware?" to which Prescott was to reply: "She wore a brand New Jersey."

When Prescott landed at Idlewild Airport the following evening he resolved to spill the beans to the feds. It caused some consternation at the CIA headquarters in Langley but after some mulling over it was decided U.S. interests would be best served if Prescott played along. He was told to co-operate fully with the Soviets and provide whatever blueprints they wanted as long as it was limited to the innards of vacuum cleaners and toasters. From time to time the CIA would furnish altered documents designed to send the Soviets off on a goosechase. The folks at Langley were mighty pleased with themselves.

Prescott soon recieved a phone call from "Dimitri," who identi-

CIA photo of Prescott (right) and Pietrov Chernenko a.k.a. Dimitri near an IHOP in Watertown NY.

CIA archival photograph of the Toast-eeze air compressor.

fied himself using the pre-arranged code words. Prescott knew he was being shadowed as the two of them met in the International House of Pancakes in Watertown some days later. Over stacks of flapjacks *à la mode*, Dimitri handed over an East-German-made 35-mm Zeiss-Ikon camera with focal-plane shutter and six rolls of Agfa film. Prescott was instructed to deposit a roll of exposed film at a prearranged drop, a hollowed out tree stump in a field a few miles outside Albany, once a month. With each delivery he would receive an envelope containing eight hundred dollars in crisp new bills.

From then on, every few nights Prescott would bring home a roll of blueprints and photograph them on the kitchen table, and every few months he would get together with Dimitri for pancakes at the IHOP in Watertown. Over the months they worked their way through most of the menu and with time Prescott developed a preference for the German pfankuchen lathered with generous dollops of maple butter. For some reason, the matter of the monthly payment of eight hundred dollars in crisp new bills never came up when he was debriefed by the CIA. Being a practical man, Prescott salted the money away in a tin can which he buried among the forget-me-nots at the back of his garden. Something, perhaps, for a rainy day.

After about a year of this monkey business Prescott concluded he could no longer bear the pressure of being a double agent. Not only was he getting tired of pancakes but he increasingly felt his life was being manipulated by forces far beyond his control. For instance, he had recently been demoted to waffle irons and egg coddlers, a devastating drop from the glamour and excitement of toasters. Also, his membership in the Kiwanis club had mysteriously been cancelled. And just last week the mortgage on his tract house had come up for renewal and the bank was balking, something they'd never done before. Initially, of course, and against his better judgment, he had found the spy business not only exciting but also dashing. He had even gone so far as to acquire a British

Aquascutum raincoat with epaulets to get just the right look. But the whole enterprise was beginning to wear on him. He could no longer go to the grocery store without being shadowed by God knows which side, his mail was being tampered with, and he was certain his telephone calls were being tapped. And now he was afraid of going to Greenwich Village for his regular infusions of cappuccino and poetry for fear that this part of his private life would be tampered with as well.

But Prescott was not without resources. As a trained engineer, he had acquired a systematic and disciplined approach to problem solving, and when pushed to the wall he could summon up very lucid and practical responses to any number of predicaments. That's how he arrived at the catapult ejection system as a response to the problem of "stuck toast." In other words, clear logical thinking. Over the next little while Prescott spent whatever free time he had in his suburban tract house pondering and drawing up a blueprint designed to disentangle himself from the world of espionage.

He enlisted the aid of Elmer Woodhouse in Greenwich Village, who placed a small advertisement in the personal section of the *Bookbrowser Gazette*, a leftish literary review out of New York City. The ad read:

> Employed engineer, SWM, upper N.Y. state,
> seeks blonde SWF late 20s, willing to travel. Object:
> matrimony. Discretion guaranteed. Please send full
> description including recent photos to box 5668.

Granted, not a very romantic ad, but for some unfathomable reason very effective. In the next little while Elmer Woodhouse, using a numbered postal box, received fifty-one replies, a surprising number of them containing extremely revealing photos. In late April, Prescott started interviewing the candidates, using the pay phone in the men's toilet at Northway Electric. Later he narrowed his selection down to six candidates. In the end he met with one Sylvia Hendricks, a twenty-eight year old bookkeeper from Yonkers.

Their courtship, somewhat erratic and lacking a bit in romance, was short, robust and to the point. On a cold Saturday afternoon two weeks later they were married by a Unitarian minister in the village of Ipperwich in upper New York State. It was an economical ceremony, stripped of the usual frills. The wedding party consisted of Rita Gardener, a girlfriend of the bride, and Elmer Woodhouse acting as the best man. (Incidentally, Rita and Elmer hit it off like a house on fire. In no time at all they moved in together and have co-habited ever since. Today they lead a bohemian existence publishing left-wing tracts out of a mobile home at the Pinecrest Trailer Park in Norwood, New Jersey, half a mile down the road from the Meisner scrapyards.)

The night of their wedding, Prescott and his bride flew Pan-Am tourist class to Paris for an extended honeymoon. It caused quite a bit of consternation in Langley, in Moscow and at Northway Electric when Prescott went missing. Through some oversight he had failed to inform the various parties of his intentions. In fact he had been so successful at concealing his plans that none of them had the slightest idea that he was by this time married and touring Europe with his new bride.

Sylvia and Prescott spent a wonderful honeymoon travelling by train through the Continent. For both, it was their first trip to Western Europe and they were overwhelmed. In time the happy couple arrived in Berlin, which in those days was split into four military-occupation zones. The first night was spent at the Zeigler Hotel in the British zone, just off the Kurfürstendam. (This hotel, incidentally, ran a brisk business prior to and during the war as the hotel of choice for the dalliances of any number of high ranking Nazi officials, including Goebbels who was often spotted in the company of a well-known American actress.) The following night, Sylvia and Prescott decided, would be spent in the Russian-occupied eastern zone. It took all morning, part of the afternoon and a variety of dour East-German bureaucrats to obtain the necessary visas, stamps and permits. Late in the afternoon, after much checking and re-checking by heavily armed Soviet military border guards, they were permitted to cross at the Friederichstrasse U-Bahn checkpoint. Once in East Berlin, a uniformed tour guide sped them through the city to the threadbare Karl Marx International Friendship Hotel.

The following morning, as Sylvia awoke, she found that her recently acquired husband was missing. Since she was a late sleeper and somewhat groggy in the early hours anyway, she assumed he was having breakfast in the hotel restaurant and didn't pay it any mind. It was only when she emerged from the shower that she noticed most of her luggage and her passport had vanished as well. With a sudden shock she realized her desperate situation. She was alone in a shabby hotel room in East Berlin with hardly any clothes and just a New York State driver's license and a library card as identity papers. On the bedside table she found a note: "My dearest Sylvia. I have gone. Please find it in your heart to forgive me. In time I hope you will understand. I thank you for everything. Love, Prescott."

Underneath was an envelope containing three thousand dollars in crisp new hundred-dollar bills. The hotel staff was not cooperative in the least, and it was only after several hours of confusion that a couple of Soviet military intelligence types arrived to interrogate her. During the ensuing cross examination she did manage to persuade them, using what little I.D. she had, that she was in fact Sylvia Hendricks, bookkeeper from Yonkers, citizen of the United States of America, and wife of Prescott B. Fillmore. At that point the East German feds dropped a bomb. "Before coming here we checked with the border guards at Friederichsstrasse. They informed us that your husband crossed back into West Berlin this morning in the company of his wife, you, or rather, a woman who in every respect appears to be you, from your name right down to the green eyes and blonde hair. She was using your passport and visa, and even the name on the luggage tag matched."

It took several more hours before an American military escort arrived with temporary papers to bring the nearly hysterical Sylvia back across to West Berlin. The following day she was returned to the United States, where she eventually resumed her job as a bookkeeper in Yonkers. In time she married a fashionable Fifth Avenue proctologist and took up a profitable career as a marriage counsellor in Manhattan.

After leaving Berlin, Prescott and Natasha took up residence in a small mountain village on the Mediterranian island of Mallorca. They are still there today, living under assumed names. When questioned by Elmer Woodhouse about the events leading up to the Berlin incident, they had little to say. Natasha, however, was willing to admit that the plans for her defection originated with Prescott when they first met in Moscow. Neither the CIA, KGB nor Northway Electric ever caught up with them, and by now surely have lost all interest. Over the years Prescott has carved out a bit of a name for himself as a poet, and is frequently published in British and American literary journals. His most famous poem, "The Toast Machine" with its opening line, "Suppose a man worked in an office and had a heart as big as Africa," has been anthologized and translated into fourteen languages. The poem, in the form of a *bildungsroman*, covers twenty-eight densely packed pages and employs "The Toast Machine" as a metaphor for the regimented and conformist tendencies in a post-Orwellian industrialized society. Natasha, no longer a peroxide blonde, works as a teacher of English, Russian and Spanish. She has to her credit the perceptive Russian translation of "The Toast Machine," considered by some to be superior to the original. In 1986, an abridged Russian poem was set to music and recorded by the great Soviet actor Boris Kazalikov. It went on to become a phenomenal chart-topper in the USSR during the late '80's.

Prescott's short-lived career as a spy did produce one curious side-effect. In 1962 a Chinese air force captain defected to Formosa in a highly secret, Russian-built MIG 476 fighter plane. The CIA had a field day taking the plane apart. They swarmed

Mallorca 1964. Prescott and Natasha with
unidentified kid.

over every inch of this unexpected windfall. Each component was taken apart, studied, analyzed and classified by an army of experts. When the boys from Langley finally got down to checking the pilot emergency ejection system, it was discovered that the four miniaturized air compressors employed in the catapult mechanisms bore this label: Northway Electric. Toast-eeze.

TS

Narwin Cochise

Greatest love poet of the 1950's

◆ My third cousin, Narwin Cochise, told me when I was thirteen that he was "probably the greatest love poet of the 1950's." He was drunk at the time but I was impressed by his modesty and his precision. Then again, nearly everything about Cousin Narwin impressed me, including — actually, especially — the fact that everyone else in the family considered him a bum.

It's true he had certain bum-like characteristics. He was an unemployed alcoholic who specialized in sleeping with unloved and unlovely married women. He lived in a rooming house on rue St. Denis in Montreal with six other unemployed problem drinkers, each of whom, at Narwin's insistence, owned a mongrel dog obtained from the SPCA. He believed that dogs built self-esteem and were the world's most accomplished experts in unconditional love, two commodities in short supply among his fellow roomers. My parents didn't like it either that Narwin lived pretty much the way he pleased and yet had no visible means of support. It seemed immoral to them that one so undeserving should take so much latitude. What infuriated them so? Why was he such a threat? I didn't get it until a decade or so later when I first heard Bob Dylan sing that classic line in *Like a Rolling Stone*: "When you got nothin', you got nothin' to lose."

None of the roomers had anything to lose either — except their welfare payments and these they'd, in a sense, lost already. Narwin took them. Every other Thursday, when the government cheques arrived in the mail, Narwin would be there to meet the postman. Once countersigned, he'd deposit each and every one in his account. In return the roomers received room and board, clothing when they needed it and beer and smoke money — up to six quarts of beer and forty cigarettes a day. For these guys to whom, until Narwin took them under his wing, the bi-weekly infusion of the dole had meant twenty-four hours of copious boozing followed by thirteen days of begging on the streets and sleeping at the Sally Ann, this was some kind of paradise. As Narwin once told me, it was "an experiment in Utopian living."

During this phase of his life, my cousin was a creature of habit. He woke at the crack of noon, drank two cups of extraordinarily strong and sweet, "double-double" coffees — two heaping spoons of instant, two heaping spoons of sugar — while sitting at the kitchen table in his undershirt. He remained in the kitchen until almost three, kibitzing with his fellow roomers, offering a word of advice here and there, going over his accounts, cracking jokes and tossing tidbits to the dogs who lounged on the linoleum like Romans around the bath. He then dressed and headed down the street to the "Bridge Club," a tavern with Formica-topped tables where a draft of beer cost ten cents a glass. Here he played cards with a revolving group of habitues that included doctors, lawyers, stockbrokers and professors of literature, as well as bus drivers, door-to-door-salesmen, a famous former tightrope walker who suffered from a fear of heights, postmen, bank tellers, advertising copywriters and students. The game, at a penny a point, usually broke up around seven. After settling accounts — he was a canny bidder and usually won — and quaffing a final beer, he would cross the street to the local greasy spoon and have his only real meal of the day, most often meat pie, french fries and a sliced tomato on a bed of iceberg lettuce, with baked beans on the side.

Three waitresses worked in the joint; Solange, Ginette and

Narwin Cochise at 21 enjoying
a smoke in the alley behind his
basement apartment on Montreal's
rue St. Marc.

Jocelyne. Each wore identical white nylon short sleeve blouses with the collars and sleeves turned up and black nylon skirts so tight that, in the colder months, you could see the outlines of the seams of their underwear where it stretched around their generous thighs and up over their ample and much admired derrieres. None of the three wore undergarments in the summer.

His daily repast had become something of a ritual. As soon as he was presented with a menu, he asked, in a serious, almost doctor-ly manner, how their *oiseaux* were on that particular day. During inclement weather, he would express his approval of the decision to wear panties to protect the precious and delicate birds from contracting the sneezles and wheezles. During the fine months, he was full of congratulations at the good sense the women showed in releasing the little darlings from their binding rayon cages to bask in the mild, health-giving air. After the meal, it was his habit to take a post-prandial stroll which ended, six nights out of seven, at The Madeleine.

The Madeleine was a brown bar where even the whores, ac-cording to Narwin, would "rather drink than make love." Their customers, in a lather of desire and frustration, would often have to beg and plead to the point of whining to obtain what they paid for while the objects of their affection would coo, "Relax, darling. Calm down. Enjoy your drink. We've got plenty of time. Don't worry. It's a sure thing."

Things didn't really start to pick up at The Madeleine until mid-night. By three a.m., the party would be going full tilt. Since this was the legal closing time, owner Onazime Coulture, a good-natured former butcher, would lock the doors to keep out new arrivals, especially ones in dark blue uniforms, and continue to serve until, as Narwin put it, "the last rat was hung."

Long before that, in the quiet early hours of the evening, Narwin gave himself over to poetry. He would sit facing the door at his customary corner table with a yellow notepad, three or four clear-barreled black ink extra-fine ballpoint pens and a glass of beer and sip and scribble. This activity ceased around eleven, when he would be joined by people from, as the poet put it, "all walks of life." They would sit down, have a beer or two, tell a joke or a story or discuss a personal problem and drift away to be replaced by others. Narwin was glad to see them, whoever they happened to be, and was always willing to hear whatever was on their minds. He introduced them around, ordered beer, laughed with them and listened and listened — and listened again — and they loved him for it.

On one such night, a Tuesday in February, with a sleety rain falling on the city, he was engrossed in conversation with Irwin Liam, a lion of a man and a masterful poet. Liam had a Lotharian reputation, one he was careful to nurture in the not unmistaken belief it helped sell his books. The two were immersed in their favourite topics, money and poetry, and why, in this backasswards world, the two seemed to be mutually exclusive, when they were joined, uninvited, by a middle-aged man wearing an expensive suit.

"I couldn't help overhearing you," he said, "You guys write poetry, eh? Are you any good?"

Liam gave the guy the once-over and said, "You kidding? This is Narwin Cochise, the greatest living love poet of the post-war period."

The stranger was obviously impressed. "I don't know anything about making poetry," he said, "but I do know how to make money. And I'll tell you this, I'd pay a lot right now for a few of the right words." He then launched into a long rambling tale about his sorry love-life and how he'd never had any success with women, which hadn't bothered him much until recently, since up until then he'd been busy making himself rich but, as he finally wound down, now he saw that without someone to love, money was nothing and his life was ashes.

"Your life is ashes and I'm leaving," broke in Liam who had none of Narwin's tolerance for this sort of whining and who loathed businessmen generally and rich self-absorbed businessmen most of all. He made for the door, calling back over his shoulder, "Narwin needs a patron and you need a poet. I know you two will have a lovely evening."

Grant Donnelley introduced himself and ordered double brandies. When the two half-filled tumblers arrived, he began, "Your friend's right. This is an auspicious evening, me meeting you like this. A crazy idea just popped into my head. I've got a proposition for you. You write something that will get this girl in the sack with me and I'll pay you big bucks."

He raised his glass.

Narwin leaned forward, uncharacteristically leaving his glass firmly on the table. "You call that a crazy idea? You listen to this one: I write love poems, poems which reflect the transcendent glory of the infinite manifestations of love, that universal power which quickens the soul and lifts the emotions from the mud into that glorious purity of paradise that lives in every heart." He paused for a moment and straightened his back, forming a steeple with his fingers. "What I'm saying, Mr. Donnelley, is there's more to poetry than you seem to think. I'm not saying it won't get you laid, but it may get you a lot of other things you didn't bargain on as well."

"Oh, yes, yes. Of course, I understand that. More to poetry than that, eh? Why yes, Mr. Cochise. Of course there is. I don't pretend to... yes."

They drank.

By the time he left, several hours later, Mr. "Call-me-Grant" Donnelley had made a down payment of fifty dollars, agreeing to pay Mr. Cochise five hundred dollars more, not when the lady, Bernice, actually slept with him but when she professed her love. Narwin estimated it would take four to six poems to win her and he asked a few questions about a dinner party the couple were to attend together that Saturday. They arranged to meet at The Madeleine the following Monday when Narwin would have the first poem ready as a follow-up to the weekend date.

"So how did it go?" asked Narwin from his chair at The Madeleine the following Monday evening, as soon as a flushed Mr. Donnelley had seated himself.

"OK."

"Only OK?"

"She talked to the man on her other side half the time."

"And you?"

"I love just sitting next to her. I don't care whether she talks to me or not."

"Not good, Mr. Donnelley, not good. Did you tell me the name of the people where you went to dinner?"

"The Marshalls, Bert and his wife Ellen. He's a business associate." Mr. Donnelley was a little impatient.

The poet added something to the yellow pad in front of him, tore it off the sheet and passed it to his patron.

The work was simply titled "Bernice." It read:

'How did the party go in Westmount Square?
I cannot tell you; Bernice was not there.
And how did the Marshalls' party go?
Bernice was next to me and I do not know.'

An uncomfortable silence ensued.

"It's so, ah, simple, eh."

Narwin read it again.

"It's good, eh? Don't you think? Look who I'm asking! You wrote this and I'm asking you if it's good." He pounded himself on the forehead.

"I had some help from a *Monsieur* Belloc."

"Belloc, Schmelloc. Who cares, if it works."

And it did work. He sent it the next day with a dozen long stemmed roses in a crystal vase. Bernice phoned him at the office to thank him for the wonderful note. "You have a flair, Mr. Donnelley," she said, "I never imagined. When will I see you again?"

They went to a movie Friday evening, *Pillow Talk,* starring Rock Hudson and Doris Day. When Narwin woke on Saturday, around one, there was a note on the kitchen table asking him to call Mr. Donnelley. Urgent was underlined.

"I need another poem, fast," he said as soon as he heard Narwin's voice.

"You saw her again?

"Last night. We went to a movie and then had dinner. She went on and on about the poem. Wanted me to write something for her then and there. I promised her something today. You gotta do something. I'll give you an extra fifty bucks."

"One hundred."

"Alright, one hundred," he agreed without a pause, "I need it by four. No later than four."

Narwin didn't like this. It was inconvenient. The Muse couldn't be summoned with a flick of the fingers. Still, a hundred smackers was a hundred smackers.

After a few questons about their date, he arranged to meet Donnelley at the diner across the street at three forty-five. Ginette served them coffee.

"Don't you think she's got a lovely ass?" Narwin asked as she put down two heavy white ceramic cups with green lines around the rim.

Mr. Donnelley smiled at Ginette in a goofy way.

"Take it from me: the only women who offer any competition in the ass department are Jocelyne and Solange. And they both work here."

His patron was too impatient to do anything but nod foolishly.

"You've got something for me?"

"Yes."

"Can I see it?"

"Better than that, I'll read it to you. It goes like this:

'How you watched Rock Hudson
with his burnished hair,

Narwin in the greasy spoon where he habitually
had lunch. He was a great admirer of the three
waitresses who worked there and who are widely
believed to have provided the inspiration for his
rhymed masterpiece, "Nylon Tomatoes."

and listened to the silver in his voice,
I could see gold rivers in your eyes,
How he took you to places swept with stars,
    this dancing with desire,
The way you sighed when it was done.
Rock Hudson could take you from me.
    Is it time?'

"Gimme that," Mr. Donnelley said, snatching the paper. "I don't get it. Of course Rock Hudson could take her from me. That's obvious. We both know that. Rock Hudson could have any woman he wants."

"But she wants you."

"You think so?"

"You've got to believe it if you want it to happen."

"What's this: 'Is it time?' Time for what?"

"What do you think it's time for, Mr. Donnelley?

He blushed and slurred, "So... so I'll try it on her."

"She liked it," he told Narwin on the phone early Monday afternoon.

"How much did she like it?"

"We went for a walk in the park. I took her to dinner at the Ritz."

"What did she order?"

"*Filet mignon.*"

"That is liking it a lot, to have steak for supper."

"Yes."

"And..."

"And she kissed me goodnight."

"Really! Good for you and good for her, Mr. Donnelley."

"On the cheek."

"You have to start somewhere. The cheek is a nice place to start, wouldn't you say? Love, Mr. Donnelley. Love, not lust. No. No."

"Oh."

In the third poem, for which an entirely smitten Mr. Donnelley

Bernice about the time Grant Donnelley
solicited Cochise's help in his attempts
to seduce her.

paid him one hundred and fifty dollars up front as an installment on the five hundred, he tried something a little different. More delicate. Time to move the relationship to a higher plane. That evening at his table at The Madeleine, for almost two hours, he was lost in the misty valleys, amid the soaring rocks, the quiet ponds and twisted pines of ancient China.

He wrote:

> 'A white lotus and a new moon
> Float on the still river,
> We started at dawn from the green city
> And rested in the afternoon as the boat drifted.
> The way the moonlight mingles in the oak leaves
> Reminds me of our other lives together.'

The presentation was important, he told Mr. Donnelley when he came to pick it up. Narwin suggested he arrange for a sumptuous meal at The White Orchid, the city's finest Chinese restaurant. After the sweet and sour pork, the almond chicken, the Buddha crepe, the lotus steamed rice, the iced lichee nuts, Bernice was to find the poem hidden in a fortune cookie.

Mr. Donnelley thought it perhaps the best idea he'd ever heard. Ever since Bernice had started to respond to him, he was a changed man. He was no longer the brusque businessman with an attractive patina of shyness. Always outspoken where money was concerned, he now seemed to fancy himself a bit of an expert on poetry and love as well. He was not above suggesting a word change here and there "just to polish it up." Did Narwin think the reference to oak leaves was appropriate? Should it perhaps be something "more Chinese?" And what about this word "mingle?" Was it precisely the right one? Would mixed, perhaps, be better? You had to think of how these things would be interpreted, you know.

Narwin knew. He said, "A man who acts as his own lawyer has a fool for a client," and left it at that.

Mr. Donnelley backed off but when the time came to pay, he

The building where Grant and Bernice spent their final evening. The mock-Tudor structure was built as a secret love nest by the park's designer in the 1930s and later fell into disrepair. It was converted to restrooms in 1967 and is still in use for that purpose today.

made a show of peeling three fifties off his wad.

Narwin didn't hear from him for a week; then, a little after ten one morning, he was awakened by a nervous roomer and his dog, Rex.

"I'm sorry to wake ya, Boss. Ya know I'd never do that unless I had to. There's a guy on the phone. He's been calling for three hours. Says he'd got to talk to you. Life or death. I been telling him to take a flying leap. Sounds like he's going to jump off a bridge or somethin'. Says his name's Donnelley. Ya want to talk to him or should I just rip the phone out?"

"I hope this is good, Mr. Donnelley," Narwin said as he picked up the receiver.

"Thank God it's you. I've got to see you."

"I'm still asleep. Come by the club around eight."

"No. I have to see you now. I'll buy you lunch."

"I don't eat lunch."

"Please, Narwin. Mr. Cochise. I'm suffering. Can't you hear that? I've got to see you. I desperately need your help."

"What happened? The fortune cookie didn't work out?"

"Oh it worked, it worked perfectly. Maybe too well. But look — I can't do this on the phone. I have to see you."

He wasn't one to break his routine: "OK. Come round to my place about twelve-thirty. We'll talk then." And he promptly went back to bed.

When Mr. Donnelley arrived, Narwin was in his bedroom with Rex, a part Husky, part Alsatian, teaching him never, never to jump up on the bed the way he had that morning.

"What you've got to do," he was explaining to Rex's owner, "is praise the dog for doing good. You can't train an animal by mistreating it. All you end up with is a dog that's so pissed off with being hit, it's just waiting for a chance to bite you or take it out on something smaller — like the kid downstairs."

Rex took all this in while standing in the middle of the unmade bed, looking as though he was about to urinate on Narwin's pillow.

"Down, Rex. Down," said Narwin in a voice that sounded as though it came from the seventh ring of Hell.

Rex looked at him out of his pale yellow eyes and growled.

Narwin fixed him with an iron stare and for a moment you could feel the balance shifting back and forth. Just when it looked as though Rex was going to mark the bed as his territory, the dog lost his nerve and gently got down.

"Good boy," said Narwin. "What a good sexy Rexy," and tossed him a dried marrow bone from a cache in a dresser drawer.

Throughout this demonstration, Mr. Donnelley stood impatiently in the bedroom doorway. Now Narwin suggested he take a seat at the kitchen table and got him a quart of beer.

Mr. Donnelley sat carefully, pulling up his trouser legs so he wouldn't crease them.

"You have to help me," he began, ignoring the beer. But he couldn't go on. There were three men in their pyjamas sitting at the table playing Hearts as their dogs sprawled on the lino at their feet. One of the dogs twitched and yelped, chasing rabbits in its dreams. Mazie, a fat, overfed, beige hound who looked as though she had some hog in her, sighed and farted.

"I can't do this here. Can't we go somewhere else?" said a wild-eyed Mr. Donnelley.

"Hey, guys, do me a favour. Take the beasts for a walk, would you?" asked Narwin, adding a calming second spoon of sugar to his coffee. "So?" he said to Donnelley.

"I need another poem. If I don't get it right away," blurted Mr. Donnelley, "I'll... I'll lose her forever."

"Wait. Wait. Wait. What happened at the Chinese restaurant? She found the poem. Then what?"

"It was wonderful," he smiled despite himself, remembering.

"How wonderful?"

"She just thought it was the most beautiful thing. She got up and gave me a hug and a kiss right in front of everyone."

"And?"

"And we went to Vermont together for the weekend. She thinks Vermont is very Chinese. We drove down Friday in the Buick."

"What's Chinese about Vermont in March?"

"She says it's the way the trees look or the melting snow or something. How should I know?"

"Not important. Go on."

"So we get there. Topnotch. The best. I had reservations for a suite but she needs her own room. She's got class. I understand that. I get her an adjoining single. We have dinner by candlelight in front of the fireplace in the dining room. Had to tip the head waiter twenty dollars to get it. She smiles and flirts and says nice things to me, but all through the meal I can tell she's expecting something. I know what it is, a poem, see. And I know I can't deliver. She doesn't say anything but by the time we say goodnight she's pretty frosty."

"My kind of girl."

"Saturday she gets up late. I have breakfast alone. I give her two hundred bucks to get her hair done and buy something nice. She takes the car."

"And they say poetry is dead."

"Dinner Saturday, same deal. She's waiting and I can't deliver. Worse than that, I'm so worried about not having a poem for her that I can't think of anything else to say. She's wearing this new dress, has her hair all done up and I'm a dope. I try to tell her about this business deal I'm working on — just to make conversation, you understand, for something to say — I've got the demolition on the plumbing from this apartment building they're taking down. Solid lead. I'll make a killing on it."

"She wasn't interested?"

"She said perhaps we could enjoy the silence together."

"Such wisdom. And Sunday?"

"That's when it got bad. I tried to call you Saturday night but I couldn't get you so I decided to write up something myself. I had to. She needed poetry. She was counting on me. Anyway, I thought I was kind of getting the hang of it. It didn't look so hard."

"You wrote a poem for her?"

"Yes. Well, maybe not a poem." He paused, "It rhymed though. She has such a lovely name. I thought I would rhyme it with her name."

"Bernice? What was the theme?"

"Well, in the end, it was, about, you know..."

"No, I don't know. What was it about?"

"Cheese."

"Cheese. What does that rhyme with? Her name's Bernice."

"I thought I could pronounce it, you know, Berneese. It's what you poets call..."

"Poetic license?"

"Yes. And there's this kind of French cheese — Camembert, they call it — that she's very fond of, eh? Do you know it? It's smooth and creamy and rich. Delicious. It's just a choice thing. Like her. She introduced me to it and I thought... well, once I got into writing the poem, I guess I lost sight of things. I got so excited by what I'd written, you know, working out the words and all. I didn't think about the theme, eh."

"You compared her to Camembert?"

"I lost track. I wasn't thinking. She needed a poem. I had the kitchen tuck it in with the crackers when they brought the cheese plate at Sunday brunch. It was, you know, like the fortune cookie idea, eh? You see..."

"I see..."

"She read the poem and then she sat very quiet for a long time, looking kind of funny, and then she got up and picked up the whole cheese plate and dumped it in my lap and walked out."

"Poetry is a powerful force."

"She took the Buick and left. I got back this morning on the bus. Had to spend most of the night trying to sleep on a bench at the terminal in Burlington, waiting for a connection."

"I see."

"What should I do?"

"You know, Mr. Donnelley, Bernice did not treat you well."

"It was me, I didn't treat her right."

"No. You did your best by her and she treated you like shit. She took your money and your car and she didn't have the grace to take your poem the way it was intended. She's seen your other work. She knows what a talent you are. You played a little trick on her, a little test of her humanity, Mr. Donnelley, and she failed miserably."

"You think so?" he said, looking at Narwin as though he came from Mars.

"I do."

"You're kidding, eh?"

"I've never been more serious. Bernice done you wrong, sir."

"Yeah, eh?" he said slowly, chewing on it.

"Yes. And we're going to do something about it. When are you seeing her again?"

"I don't think she'll ever see me again."

"You have to get the Buick back."

"I thought I might just let her keep it as a way of saying I'm sorry."

"That's nuts. So far the only thing the woman's got going for her is that she likes poetry. How the rest of her is so out of whack, I don't understand, but we're going to fix it."

"I'd like that but I don't think it's possible. She's gone."

Narwin said nothing for the next ten minutes. He drank a little beer, scribbled a few notes on a pad. "Call her and make a date for Friday," he said at last.

"She'll never see me again."

"Oh, I think she will. You'll soften her up with five dozen roses and a little verse I'm going to write for you. Come to the club at eight thirty." Narwin got up, went into the bathroom and turned on the shower.

Mr. Donnelley was waiting when he arrived at The Madeleine.

Narwin asked, "What happened? You sent the roses. Did she sent them back or something?"

"No, nothing. I haven't heard from her. What did you expect?"

"Tomorrow's Tuesday. Don't do anything. Don't try to get in touch. Then Wednesday, late in the afternoon, let her stew a bit, send her ten dozen roses and this"— he slid a yellow sheet from his pad across the table.

The page was headed "A heartfelt apology" and it read:

'I hoped my verse would make you smile
I missed the target by a mile,
It wasn't poetry, wasn't fun,
I've lost you now, what have I done?
Oh dear, Bernice, what can you think?
Shall I return the painted mink?'

"Mink? What's a painted mink? Like the coat?" said Mr. Donnelley putting the page down and looking puzzled.

"Yes," said Narvwin. "A very expensive kind of mink coat."

"I'm giving her one?"

"That's up to you. Even poetry has its limits. Send her the note and the flowers. When she calls, fall all over yourself with gratitude that she's consented to see you again after your shocking insult. And make a date — a very special date — for Friday night."

Whether it was the poem or the extravagant roses or the promise of the mink, Bernice consented to see him. Following Narwin's instructions, he picked her up Friday evening in a horse-drawn *calèche*. It was the first week in April and, though chilly, not cool enough to affect the bank of spring flowers and pink and white roses which overflowed the double seat opposite them. Also, the cool air gave Bernice a chance to snuggle in her new fur coat. Mr. Donnelley later told Narwin that they had actually held hands like teenagers as the carriage took a turn around the park.

The *calèche*, driven by one of Narwin's many fans, came to a stop outside what appeared to be a small stone house partially hidden in a copse of trees. It had been built by the park's original designer as a retreat which could accommodate small wedding parties and other intimate gatherings. The idea was, it could be rented out and so would eventually pay for itself. That, at least, was how he presented it to City Hall. In fact, it never hosted a single paying event. During his lifetime, the man used it exclusively as a private grotto where he entertained the young women of which he was famously fond.

It was a beautifully constructed cottage consisting of a single marble-floored room which rose to an elegant ceiling of carved beams. An enormous fireplace dominated one wall. The silk divans and oriental carpets had long gone but the room retained a mysterious otherworldly air. Especially tonight.

Narwin, with the help of the roomers — Rex's owner, who had worked for the Parks Department and had neglected to turn in the key when he was sacked — had worked all day cleaning out the cobwebs, washing down the walls and polishing the floor. They had also set up more than two hundred candles which flickered and flared, bathing the room in supernal light. The air was perfumed with incense. Maple logs glowed in the fireplace. Mr. Donnelley invited an entranced Bernice to sit down on the elegant divan — borrowed for the occasion from the antique store that shared the ground floor of the rooming house — and offered her a glass of ruby port poured from a cut-glass decanter which caught the light in an enchanting way. Flute music wafted softy from hidden speakers. They were almost alone. Narwin, curious to see how the drama he had concocted would turn out, was seated with a beer behind a Chinese screen in the shadowy far recesses of the room.

When she was comfortable, Mr. Donnelley, following his script, proposed a toast: "To Beauty."

And another: "To Joy."

And another: "To Peace."

And another: "To Happiness."

They sat for a few minutes in silence, she in a kind of dream, and then he repeated, from memory,

> 'I go now to live in the rose garden of my heart,
> Sweet fragrance fills me with delight,
> Beyond thought and will
> I am my finest, purest self,
> Light falling from a higher place
> Fills me with peace and love.'

While he spoke she did not move but gazed across the candles into the fire as though she saw angels dancing in the flames. They sat for a long time in silence then she said softly, "Please say your poem again." He spoke each line, one by one, and she repeated them, apparently transfixed by some sweet inner vision. After a long time, the mink slipped from her shoulders and she stood, drawing Mr. Donnelley up beside her. She took both his hands in hers and looked at him intently for a long time. Gone were the hard lines around her mouth, a pale, beatific smile transformed her face; her "prove-it-to-me" eyes now gazed out at the world as innocently as a babe's. "I love you," she said, "And I love myself and every creature in this magnificent world. Thank you. Thank you for showing me who I really am." She lifted a finger to her lips, kissed it and pressed it to his. "Stay here. I must be alone for a few moments, dear one."

She stepped out into the night. For a moment he could see her looking up at the moon and the city lights which glowed through the trees at the edge of the park. Then the dark swallowed her up.

He reached down and picked up the mink and held it to him as though she were still inside it. He was filled with a greater sense of peace and happiness than he could remember. Peeping out through a crack in the screen, even Narwin could smell her perfume.

She was gone maybe ten minutes. When she came back in she appeared to have returned to something of her old self.

"It's chilly out there, hon," she said, "Help me on with my coat, would you? I'd forgotten we'd come in that carriage thingee. Pity we can't call a cab. That horse'll take forever to get back to civilization and I feel like champagne. Some good champagne would be nice, don't you think?"

Narwin thought Donnelley looked so light and happy, he could've gotten high on a glass of tap water. As soon as they left, Narwin took a shortcut across the park to the front of the Ritz where the carriages lined up and pulled himself up into a *calèche* owned by his friend, a prime seat to watch the next act.

Halfway back, in the carriage, the flowers now luminous in the moonlight, Donnelley asked Bernice if she had felt anything "special" back there.

"You mean the poem, hon? I just loved it. Love it to pieces."

"I...I feel so, ah, calm, you know? Kind of peaceful inside," he began.

"Yeah, I know what you're saying. I felt floaty-like for a minute. Scared me to death. I just didn't feel like myself. I mean going out like that without my new coat and all. You put a spell on me, you wizard. A girl's got to protect herself against spells. You never know what she might do." She snuggled into him and then in her normal voice said, "Say, hon, why don't you give the driver ten bucks if he can get this nag to gallop to the bar at the Ritz."

As they passed under each park light her face seemed to grow harder. He saw things there he'd never noticed before. A selfishness. At the grotto her face had glowed with kindness and humanity. Now she had ordered these dangerous qualities back to their rooms and locked the door. A girl can't be too careful.

At the hotel, he paid the driver. "Keep the flowers. Give them to your wife or girlfriend," he said.

She'd already started up the stairs toward the entrance to the Ritz Cafe. In the glare of the lights under the marquis she looked cheap and tawdry, even in the twenty-five hundred dollar coat.

"Come back here, Bernice," he said with such force that she

Mr. and Mrs. Grant Donnelley,
charter members of "The Immortals,"
on a Sunday stroll, 1961.

turned and descended to the wide sidewalk without a word.

"Give me the keys to the Buick."

"You were so mean to me I thought I'd keep..."

He held out his hand. There was something about him that couldn't be denied. She opened her slim purse, took out the keys, dangled them for an instant in front of his face and dropped them at his feet. "Pick them up yourself, Mr. Wizard."

"That wasn't polite, Bernice. Impolite people don't deserve beautiful things."

She crossed her arms and clung to the coat as if it were one of her young. Her narrow face shone with rage and greed.

"If you hand me the keys like the nice girl I know you are," he continued, "You can keep the mink. Maybe it will help melt your cold, cold heart."

She looked as if she were about to spit but she bent and picked up them up and handed them to him, did a sarcastic little curtsy and flew up the stairs into the bar.

The next evening at The Madeleine, when Mr. Donnelley finished his story, Narwin burst, "I loved that line. Melt your cold, cold heart! Brilliant. Just what she deserved. Poetry."

"Well, you know, it's sort of from a song."

"It's how you use it that counts," said Narwin, and he ordered beer for everyone in the place. Someone played *Green, Green Grass of Home* on the jukebox.

Not long afterward, Mr. Donnelley married Marie Lebeau, his secretary of twenty-five years. The following summer Narwin bought a farm up the river about seventy miles from the city. It had always been a dream of his and he never said where he got the down payment. He moved the roomers and the dogs up there and they worked at putting in vegetable gardens and building greenhouses. For a couple of summers in the mid-sixties, individually tissue-wrapped Sunny Farms Slo-Gro tomatoes and cucumbers were available in the city's better food shops. The label was an oval with the silhouette of a man and a dog.

I went away to school but I heard that the place became a commune in the late sixties, with Narwin as the resident guru. In 1972 I was in Cincinnati selling men's Viyella socks and shirts for a start-up company out of Winnipeg, when my mother called me with the news, "Your cousin Narwin died three days ago," she said. "The funeral was today. You can't imagine the number of people who came. He must have known half the city."

"What killed him? Was it an accident?" I said in a state of shock.

"No, dear, he suddenly got very sick. Some strange liver infection, I think. There were four of them out at the farm who got it. Your cousin and three women. They were in isolation at St. Justine's. The doctors couldn't figure out what it was. Two of them pulled through but Narwin and the other one died. Nice girls, the ones who got better; I met them at the funeral. I think the one who died was called Solange. Something like that. She and your cousin were buried up at the farm side by side. Don't you think that's sweet, dear?"

Yes, I did think it was sweet.

Mr. Donnelley is still alive. He and his wife spend most of their time taking cruises and going to resorts that offer self-help courses as part of the package. He and the missus are members of a group based in Phoenix called The Immortals. They contend that if you can get yourself into the right state of mind, you can generate changes at the cellular level that will allow you to live forever. So far it's working for the Donnelleys.

I saw Bernice on late night television a week or so ago. She's got her own show called "Bee-Bee's Psychic Love Line." They say she's making a bundle.

DE

Plonk

◆ At the turn of the century the town of Haute Clamart-sur-Drôme, nestled snugly in the foothills of the Midi-Alpes of the Luberon region, was known locally for two things: its sturdy if undistinguished red wine and the inaccessibility of the region to the outside world. For centuries wine had been the single economic backbone of this provincial backwater, and for just as long a single mule track had sufficed to bring the wine barrels to markets in the towns of Orange and Avignon. Most of the population of the region were in one way or the other employed in the wine trade, from growing and tending the sturdy Cinsault grapes to the making, transporting and selling of the wine. The product itself was a rough-spirited *vin de pays*, high in alcohol content and most often sold by the litre straight from the barrel; in other words, the kind a contemporary wine reviewer might charitably refer to as "plonk." Plonk or not, the good people of Haute Clamart-sur-Drôme were very fond of their grape concoction, and despite its rough edges consumed impressive quantities before, during, and after, as well as any time in between.

It was here in the town of Haute Clamart-sur-Drôme that my grandfather Aristide Gervais was born and grew up. By the time he was sixteen he had long left school behind and was working in the vineyards, expertly pruning, transplanting and cross-breeding

Aristide and Pauline's home on rue Quicampoix. Today the room is used for the storage of taxidermy supplies.

the wine stock. Over time he developed considerable skills at grafting the stubborn Carignan grape stock onto the admirable Cinsault root, so well suited to the rocky soil and unrelenting sun of the region. The robust red which resulted from this hybrid was a markedly improved wine, far less insulting to the palate than the regular Cinsault red. The locals, however, would have none of this new-fangled monkey business. They liked their wine the way their fathers and grandfathers had liked it, good and sour, and that was that. So all in all it could be said that the good people of Haute Clamart-sur-Drôme were governed more by tradition and convention than by plain reasoning.

When Aristide reached the age of majority, he went to the house of Henri Montfort and asked for the hand of his only daughter, Pauline, in marriage. The old man, a dour conservative, and a true *pisse-vinaigre* of the old school, as tart as the local wine, threw Aristide off the front steps. For a solid three minutes the old man held forth and hurled every sort of un-Christian malediction at Aristide, who stood his ground and insisted on receiving Pauline's hand. This whole performance, of course, was nothing more than an elaborate smoke screen. As everyone in Haute Clamart-sur-Drôme knew, Henri was as impoverished as a fifth grape pressing. For a proud man of tradition and honour, anything short of an extravagant wedding celebration would tarnish his good family name. There was just no other way. In the end Henri's adamant refusal protected the Montfort's threadbare reputation, protocol was observed, and the lovers, as custom demanded, eloped. To keep up appearances, six heavily armed Montfort boys spent the next five days going through the motions of scouring the hills around Haute Clamart-sur-Drôme looking for the pair, who of course had long ago departed for Paris on the overnight third-class coach from Avignon.

At the tender ages of twenty-one and twenty, a couple of fresh-faced provincials, Aristide and Pauline found themselves in Paris where they set out to conquer the great metropolis, not an easy task for those with few connections and even fewer francs in their pockets. With their distinct Luberon accent favouring the rounded "e" at the ends of words and their quaint Provençal manners, Aristide and Pauline frequently found themselves objects of derision on the part of their Parisian compatriots, who even at the early part of the century were renowned for their haughtiness.

Aristide's and Pauline's limited financial resources forced them to take a tiny room on the third floor of a run-down building on Rue Quicampoix, a narrow street which runs adjacent to the thriving Marché Centrale Les Halles. This market, located in the heart of the right bank, was nicknamed "The belly of Paris" and it was here that most of the produce from the provinces was traded: oysters from Bretagne, champignons from Perigord, lemons from Arles, artichokes from Alsace, plump pungent sausages from Toulouse, confit de canard from the Massif Central region and the sweet fruit of Normandy orchards as well as wine from every region of France. On days when Pauline and Aristide could not afford even the most frugal of meals, they would hungrily wend their way through the myriad of stalls, ogling this abundance of riches. Here and there they would pick up scraps of discarded vegetables, which Pauline would use, along with the occasional pieces of bone donated by a kindhearted butcher, to cook up a splendid ragôut, redolent with the herbs and spices of Provence. So all in all the two of them managed to eke out a living, but it was a living marked by hardships and disappointments. As time went by their once-confident dreams of a bright future started to fade, and as their hopes soured, so did their love. The rude realities of daily life, as so often happens, were beginning to extract a toll. Their meagre savings, which amounted to a mere pittance, were fast running out, and in the end Aristide was forced to take a job as a menial labourer with the Paris Metroplitan Railway Authority. At that time the PMRA was engaged in the great undertaking of excavating a network of new tunnels under the city in order to extend the Paris Métro system. The work was exhausting; besides an eleven-hour shift starting at nine at night, it required a strong back and a powerful pair of hands. Aristide's responsibility consisted of shovelling dirt and boulders onto a trolley, which he would push along a set of tracks leading to the unloading area, a temporary dock set up on the bank of the Seine, from where the dirt was carried away by river barge.

One night Aristide was taking his lunch break in a small recess along the tunnel, well away from the noise and dust of the digging. He unwrapped his baguette and a casserole of cold vegetable fricasée which Pauline had prepared, as well as a demi-litre of the most wretched *vin ordinaire*. As he began eating he leaned his tired back against the dirt wall, and as he did so, a rock loosened and fell onto the dirt floor, revealing a small opening in the wall behind him. This was not at all unusual, since the digging crews had regularly trespassed into the ancient caves and tunnels which honeycombed the old city. At one time Aristide and the digging crew had surprised a couple of well-stewed clochards soundly sleeping off a world-class bender in an unused catacomb below the church of St-Julien-le-Pauvre.

As Aristide probed the cavity with his hand and felt about, all he could make out was a cold stone floor. He loosened another rock, enlarging the hole a bit, and manoeuvred his miner's lamp through the opening. Peering into the cavity he could only make out an orderly arrangement of what appeared to be rows of black disks. By moving the lamp back and forth he soon recognized that he was looking at rows of wine bottles stacked in every direction as far as the glow of his lamp could reach. There were hundreds of bottles, maybe thousands. Clearly this was a large wine cellar. For a man of Aristide's Provençal sensibility the scene was very tempting indeed. In the end he overcame whatever scruples he might have had and grabbed the first bottle his outstretched hand could reach. He furtively wrapped it in his scarf and manoeuvred the rocks back into position to close up the hole.

When Aristide arrived home at ten the next morning, he had a

Les Trois Étoiles in its heyday.

Paris flood of 1910.

quick wash in the basin and, dead on his feet, fell into bed. It was not until five that afternoon, when he awoke to find Pauline cooking supper on the small stove, that he unwrapped the bottle: a Chateauneuf-du-Pape 1886 from Domaine Beaucastel. Aristide didn't know at the time that 1886 was not only an outstanding year for Côte du Rhone wines but at more than two hundred francs a bottle this vintage represented at least two weeks of backbreaking labour in the tunnels. As Pauline and Aristide silently began their supper, the addition of this extraordinary *grand cru* to their frugal meal began to play tricks on the palate and the mind. At first Aristide was dumbfounded. This was *terra incognito* to his unschooled taste buds. Never had he encountered anything like it. As the two of them drank, their mean little chamber gradually took on a new guise. It began to warm, and then it began to glow. Their heavy hearts lightened, the burdens of their miserable existence eased, and as they eagerly drank from their cups the sun of Provence seemed to burst through the tiny window. Soon they were back in their beloved Luberon, with its sweet smell of rosemary and lavender. That night their dormant love was rekindled.

The following night Alphonse went back to the same spot in the tunnel and once again loosened the rocks and put his miner's lamp through the opening. He looked around a bit before reaching for another bottle from a different part of the wine rack.

That evening Ariside's and Pauline's little room radiated in the soft warm glow of candlelight reflecting off a bottle of red Chapelle-Chambertin. The meal Pauline had prepared, a simple Fricassée Madeleine, a hearty speciality of the Luberon region spiced delicately with basil and laurel, was an even match for the wine. Since it was Sunday, they stayed up until late in the night recollecting in the most tender terms the early days of their courtship. When they fell asleep in each other's arms, it was almost two in the morning.

On Monday night during his lunch break, Aristide decided to explore the wine cellar. He loosened a few more stones around the hole, making the opening large enough to let him slip through. He emerged behind a succession of wine racks which seemed to extend in every direction. As Aristide moved down the aisle he noticed small tunnels branching off from the main cave, each lined with still more wine racks. Near the front was a set of stone steps leading upstairs, and adjacent to the steps a small wooden cabinet with glass doors. Inside the cabinet, cradled on the shelves, were eighteen identical bottles bearing the following label: Hermitage Rouge, Côtes du Rhone, Domaine Paul Jaboulet, 1881. This without doubt had to be an exceptional treasure. But time was running out. His lunch break was almost over. On his way back Aristide studied the layout of the cave. Each section of shelf appeared to hold a particular vintage, and each rack was neatly labelled and arranged according to region. Large red paper labels indicated the great wine areas of France: Savoie, Chablis, Beaujolais, Anjou, Buzet, Haut Poitou, Languedoc, Tursan. After careful reflection Aristide selected a Cabernet Sauvignon from the estate of Château Sebastian Charpontier. He crawled back out of the cave, carefully replaced the stones in the wall, and with the wine wrapped in his scarf, returned to work.

In the morning on his way home from an exhausing night in the tunnel, Aristide decided to find out what might be in the street above the cave. They were digging in the area of Boulevard St. Michel, some blocks north of Boulevard St. Germain, so it was fairly easy to determine. When he located the address on Boulevard St. Michel, he found himself facing *Restaurant Les Trois Etoiles*, Paris's most famous eatery, and certainly one of the most expensive. Rumour had it that Poincaré himself, the President of the Republic, ate lunch and supper daily at the restaurant. Its wine cellar was reputed to be the best in all of France, with over 20,000 bottles of the finest vintages. In some circles *Les Trois Etoiles* was considered not only a national treasure but an institution as hallowed and revered as l'Academie Française or the Bibliothéque Nationale. Aristide scanned the façade, then moved along the side street, observing the scullery maids at work as they scrubbed large baking pans and copper cauldrons in the courtyard behind the restaurant. Next to the wrought-iron gate sat several crates of empty bottles, the grand remains of the previous night's consumption. Aristide slowly sauntered by the crates while he scanned the labels of the bottles. Only the best. Not a single *vin ordinaire* in the lot. He quickly swiped two empties as he passed and slipped them under his coat.

Later, as he passed a wine-merchant's store, he purchased two bottles of *vin ordinaire* in the standard dark-green bordeaux-style bottle commonly used in France. At home, Aristide immersed the two empty bottles he had swiped from the restaurant in a bucket of water and soaked the elegant labels off. Next he removed the labels from the two full bottles of *vin ordinaire*. Then, with great care, Aristide took the two labels from the empties and affixed these onto the bottles of cheap *vin ordinaire*, using a thin mixture of *caoutchouc* spirits as an adhesive. When he was done and the glue had dried, the two bottles of vin ordinaire, now sporting the labels of fine wines, were in every respect indistinguishable from the real thing. In this manner, Aristide, over time, conscientiously substituted the pilfered vintages with the most common kind of plonk. And no one seemed to be the wiser. When on a rare occasion one of Aristide's forgeries turned up on the table of some restaurant patron, few if any among the clientele of *Les Trois Etoiles* were disturbed in the least. After all, with something as impetuous as a *grand cru*, one should expect a bit of spoilage now and again. Those among the clientele who came from humble beginnings recognized the wine for what it was: an impoverished and pissy little forgery, the kind they had had to endure as conscripts in the army. But they kept their knowledge to themselves. After all, who but the bravest dared to take on Monsieur Bernard Lalique, the sommellier, whose temper, arrogance and inflexible authority were matched only by that of the president of the republic? Those who in their privileged upbringing never had to endure a wretched

Aristide in
the uniform of
an army
trench digger.

Aristide in his
vintner's guild
attire. Taken on
the morning of
his departure for
"Le Grand
Concours des Vin"
which took place
in Paris in 1948.
His Cabernet
Sauvignon picked
up two gold
medals and
a silver.

wine could not have guessed its origins, and most found it to be an unusually vigorous and intense vintage.

Life improved for Aristide and Pauline. As Aristide's back strengthened and hard callouses grew on his hands, the once gruelling work became less tiring. And as Pauline's skill at haggling with the tradespeople at Les Halles got better, so the quality of their meals improved. Aristide had taken to making a short detour on his way home from work, passing by the restaurant in order to scan the menu posted on the window. Each night he would recite the list to Pauline, who would attempt to cook up some economical version of the table d'hote for the following night. During the ensuing two years Aristide and Pauline consumed nearly 700 bottles of the finest vintages France had to offer. They went about this endeavour with admirable method. Aristide bought a large map of France which he hung on the wall of their little room. Using coloured pins, he would mark off each village, domaine and château as it was tasted. Except for the white wines of Alsace, they managed in time to work their way through all the great wine regions of France. Only one bottle from each estate was ever selected, and hoping to avoid or at least delay detection, he always picked the last bottle from each section of the rack. That held true for all the vintages except for one: the eighteen bottles of Hermitage rouge 1881 stored away in the wood cabinet. Those were found to be so exceptional that over time, marking special occasions such as birthdays, saint's days and other religious holidays, Aristide and Pauline polished off the lot, substituting as usual the pilfered bottles with handsomely labelled *vin ordinaire*. During this period, Aristide's once woefully untutoured palate improved, and in time he acquired an extraordinary ability. The bouquet of each vintage he tasted was engraved on his palate, so much so that at the mere mention of a château and a year he could invoke every little hint, subtlety and nuance of that vintage. In this manner the two of them eased the drudgery and tedium of daily existence. And as for moral scruples, Aristide had few, if any. Not that he was by any stretch of the imagination an immoral man, but the way he saw it, God had bestowed this gift as a small compensation for the brutal labour he had to perform daily in the tunnels.

Things might have gone on in this manner forever had it not been for one thing. When the autumn of 1910 arrived it began to rain. It poured continually for months on end and by December the sewers started to back up while the Seine breached over its banks, inundating the lower parts of the city. Soon some streets were only navigable by rowboat. These events brought Aristide's work to a standstill for almost three weeks as the crews could only wait out the disaster. When the water finally receded the extent of the devastation became clear. In some places the tunnels had collapsed entirely, while in others massive obstructions of sediment and rubble clogged the excavations.

At *Les Trois Etoiles*, this cruel trick of nature played havoc with the finest wine cave in all of France. As the brackish waters quietly seeped through the walls, the neatly arranged bottles remained firmly cradled in their places on the racks, and there they sat as the rising waters submerged the entire cave. The noble vintages suffered not at all from this soaking, except for one thing: the labels. Back then, these were routinely affixed using a water-soluble flour paste.

When the flood receded, the labels were swiftly carried away by the rushing water. By the time Monsieur Bernard Lalique, wearing a pair of waders, finally made his way down into the cave, the enormity of the disaster became clear. For once in his life Monsieur Lalique was seen sobbing uncontrollably as he flailed about in the murky pools of water. This was not only a catastrophe — it was a national disaster. There seemed to be no way of determining what sort of vintages the thousands of unmarked bottles contained. Except, of course, for the seven hundred bottles Aristide had so assiduously substituted over the years. By a mere stroke of luck he had employed a water-resistant rubber adhesive for his little fraud, with the result that his labels remained firmly affixed to their bottles. And because Aristide had sampled his way methodically through each and every vintage, his diligence saved *Les Trois Etoiles* from total ruin. Few stopped to wonder why, by and large, just a single bottle of each vintage should have survived the ordeal with the label intact. However, when it was found that all eighteen bottles of Hermitage Rouge 1881, the pride of the cellar, had retained their labels, there was a great deal of wonder. The conservative newspaper *France Soir* got wind of the story and ran the front-page headline "Miracle chez *Les Trois Etoiles*." This caused a few religious zealots to make a pilgrimage to the restaurant where they held a candlelight vigil outside the kitchen door for three nights running. Monsieur Lalique, by no means a religious man, recognized the phenomenon as a sign of divine intervention. That night he went to Notre Dame Cathedral where he lit eighteen candles to St. Vincent of Zaragossa, the patron saint of viticulturers. Using the surviving labels as a guide, it was possible for Monsieur Lalique to restore order to his chaotic wine cellar once again. In time new labels were ordered from the various vineyards, and soon *Les Trois Etoiles* was back in business, with its sterling reputation and extraordinary wine cellar intact. The priceless bottles of Hermitage Rouge 1881 were put away under lock and key in the cellar, to be kept for some day in the future when events of majestic proportions would demand a *grand cru* of this magnitude.

Early that spring, as the Métro tunnel neared completion, the dirt walls were enclosed in a thick layer of steel and concrete. Pauline and Aristide, now deprived of their daily allotment of fine wine, packed up their few meagre possessions and left Paris. Over the next year they made their way across France and worked in vineyards, for a short time even managing a modest wine shop in Auvergne. By the summer of 1911 they were hired to help out in a small vineyard in the Beaujolais district near the town of Villefrance-sur-Saône where Aristide, with his expertise in the wine field, soon found himself managing the vineyard. Over the years this wine, a muscular red Beaujolais, improved markedly and with time carved out a nice little reputation for itself. And as the vineyard prospered, so did Pauline and Aristide. They bought a fine little cottage in the countryside and had three children in quick succession, one of them my father.

The growing family's pastoral bliss came to an end when Kaiser Wilhelm's Huns swarmed across northern France in the summer of 1914. Within a matter of weeks Aristide found himself conscripted into the French army. After a few weeks of rudimentary training he was sent to the front to endure the daily punishment of trench warfare. One of his letters to his wife reads as follows:

"My dearest Pauline,

I find myself back in the tunnels again, for my unit has been assigned to a detachment of trench diggers. As a matter of routine we have to put up with German snipers who seem to delight in aiming their bullets at us as we attempt to shore up and repair the broken walls of the trenches. There is no relief from the daily onslaught. In some ways, this miserable toil reminds me of our early days in Paris. But unlike the tunnels of the Métro, which at least provided us with the noblest of wines to alleviate the pain, here we are doled out a daily allotment of *pinard*, the worst kind of wretched wine one can imagine. It has become clear to me that a wine of this nature imbues one with only the basest of temperaments and causes a most sour and disagreeable disposition, one perhaps appropriate to the task at hand. A great wine is great because it makes the human spirit soar, while an impoverished wine cripples that spirit."

During a minor skirmish on the Marne in the fall of 1917 Aristide received a shrapnel wound in his left buttock, and as a result spent the next four months recuperating in a military hospital near Tours. When he returned to his family, with a slight limp in his left leg, he quickly resumed his work in the vineyard and set about the task of rearing his children.

The moment of glory finally came to France on November 11,

1918, when the Germans capitulated. The gala opening of the peace conference, held in the gilded halls of the Quai d'Orsay in Paris, took place the following January. It promised to be a glorious affair. The American president Woodrow Wilson, British prime minister Lloyd George and French president Clemenceau warmly shook hands to a long-lasting peace. The conference, as it turned out, was to be a prolonged and bitter affair, while the ensuing Treaty of Versailles left nothing but acrimony and rancor in its wake. But on that first day of the conference, as the assembled dignitaries raised their glasses in a toast to peace and brotherhood, Monseur Lalique, the sommelier of Les Trois Etoiles, was there to oversee that protocol was observed. In his capacity as the most revered sommelier in all of France, he had been entrusted with the responsibility of selecting a majestic vintage appropriate for this momentous occasion. As the heads of state toasted each other and emptied their glasses down to the last bitter drop, they could hardly have cared that they were drinking the last eighteen bottles of Hermitage Rouge 1881 left in the world.

TS

Bull on a Bike

Uncle Henry's Olympic challenge

◆ Uncle Henry was an s.o.b.. But he was the sort of tough bastard people secretly admire, the kind you want to impress. I didn't meet him until he was a very old man, ninety-four or some god-awful age. I was eight or nine. I thought he was the greatest human being ever to walk the earth, like a National Monument or something. I was proud to belong to the same species. He always wore a black suit, a white shirt, a black tie, black boots, a black fedora, and he ate cigars, literally. As many as five fat ones a day. When I asked him why, he said his doctor wouldn't let him smoke them.

He drove a 1937 Packard Landau that was so big he could load two heifers in the back seat and still leave room for a bale of hay, and he did. "Better built than any damn pick-up," he used to say. Once he got the cows in, he'd slide the chauffeur's window closed so they couldn't stick their heads into the front seat, and off we'd go. He'd take me around with him to the farms he owned in northern Vermont, picking up payments from the hard-scrabble farmers whose mortgages he held. Money was always in short supply and he often accepted payment in kind — chickens, sacks of carrots, potatoes, beets, turnips and game — mostly racoons and rabbits but sometimes a haunch of deer or moose. He didn't do it out of compassion. "Everybody pays" was a motto he lived by. He took whatever he was offered "because it's the only damn thing they have that's worth anything." In the seventy-odd years he was in business, he owned maybe a hundred farms — some of them as many as twenty times. They were small spreads, seldom more than forty acres and mostly scraggly third-growth bush and stony pastures with only eight or twelve acres good for corn or hay. He sold them to people who couldn't afford much of anything and when, after a year or two, they couldn't afford the mortgage either, even in cabbages, he'd foreclose and sell the place to someone who could.

North Mountain was that kind of town in the 1940s. You pumped gas, worked at the saw mill, fixed up old cars, dug graves, cut grass, signed on as a hired hand on one of the bigger dairy farms, were just plain out of work, or you bought a farm from Uncle Henry. Since he sold property to the same families, sometimes even the same spread, over and over again, he got to know his clients well and in his way he took care of them. If they were out of food, a side of venison had a strange way of finding its way to a hook in the barn on a dark evening. Shoes materialized the day before the kids went back to school; clothes, newly washed and mended, mysteriously migrated from one family to a poorer one. A sickly kid who'd come down with rheumatic fever, everybody called Ratty, once spent over a year in a Burlington hospital with Uncle Henry picking up the tab. I once asked him why he gave stuff to people, and he tipped his hat back and said, "Keepin' 'em healthy, keeps me wealthy." Topic closed.

Uncle Henry was a schemer, that's for sure. Once he got an idea, he gnawed on it and worried it until it almost killed him. In 1934, at the age of seventy-four, he decided to compete in the 1936 Olympics in Berlin. The way he saw it, he'd be a cyclist on the U.S. team. I didn't get the whole story until 1958, two years after my uncle died. His friend Carter Foss let me pry it out of him. Dr. Foss was in his eighties by then and I spent a summer working for him while his nurse Elva went down to Rutland to look after her mother in her final illness. I had medical ambitions

Henry Luddhearst, 88, twelve years after
he competed in the 1936 Berlin Olympics,
seen here near North Mountain, Vermont,
inspecting corn with a hired hand.

myself at the time but three months of working at that alternately boring and exhausting rural practice cured me of the notion forever. Getting the details of my uncle's life out of the worthy physician wasn't easy. Dr. Foss wasn't one to discuss his "unusual" cases, even with a relative. Here's the story I managed to piece together from what the doctor told me and what I could fill in from the diaries my Great Aunt Willy left behind when she went to her reward in 1962.

The weather in Vermont in May 1934 was unusually pleasant. This was in sharp contrast to what was going on in other parts of the country. The doctor remembered a dust storm that same month that swept three hundred million tons of topsoil out of Texas and Oklahoma into the Gulf of Mexico. In fact, the storm had been the chief topic of conversation when my uncle and his cronies got together to shoot pool and play poker in the secret room on the third floor of my uncle's commodious white house on Maple Street. It was a room I visited only twice. He took me up there one night by the secret staircase that started in the shed attached to the house and ended in what seemed to me an excellent substitute for heaven.

You stepped into the room through a narrow mahogany door onto the plushest, most intricate Persian carpet I'd ever seen. Near the entrance was a magnificent oak pool table with ornately carved legs and deep braided red leather pockets. Over it hung an enormous rectangular orange-fringed stained glass shade with well-endowed, diaphanously-clothed women in alluring positions, which shone an unearthly light onto the vast deep green universe of the table. On one wall, cues made of exotic polished woods stood in their brass rack like a corps of thin soldiers. Another wall held a huge gold-framed picture of a hunting scene from mythology, the huntress Diana with stags and dogs and a jealous Zeus staring down from an illumined cloud-tossed sky. The far end of the room was a dark stained-glass window. My uncle asked how old I was. When I said, "Thirteen, Uncle," he switched on a light behind it.. Shimmering at the end of the room was the most beautiful woman I'd ever seen, pale as starlight. Her red kimono hung open from her long delicate neck to the blushing tips of her perfect toes. "I call her Simone," was all my uncle said. He took a seat on one of the red leather chairs at the mahogany card table which slumbered in Simone's shadow and said, "Sit down, boy. You and me are going to play poker."

After one of the regular card games early in the summer of 1934, Uncle pushed back his chair, poured everyone an extra shot of Canadian rye and raised his glass: "To my success in Berlin."

Before he drank, Bob Forrester, who owned the bank in Newport, said, "What in hell are you up to now, Henry?"

"I'm ridin' a bicycle for my state and my country in the '36 Olympics."

"No fool like an old fool," said Bob as he tossed back the whiskey. The others didn't say a damn thing. You didn't want to cross Henry.

Uncle started training the next week on a brand new Schwinn with three forward gears, that he'd ordered from Boston. It cost him twenty-seven dollars and a dollar seventy-seven for shipping and it was a beauty. Uncle adopted his usual attire to accommodate his new venture by shedding his suit coat and tie and rolling up his shirt sleeves and pant legs. To force himself to train, he vowed to leave his car of the time, a 1929 Desoto, in the barn, and made the rounds of the farms on the Schwinn. The first day he did ten miles over dirt roads and he was so exhausted that he went to bed at 8:30 without his customary bowl of milk and stale corn bread. The next day he did six miles, nine the day after that, eleven the next. He kept a record of his mileage day by day in his black account book, which came down to me through Aunt Willy; it's written in sepia ink in a flowing nineteenth-century hand. That Sunday, for the first time anyone could remember, he fell asleep in the family's front pew in church. His wife, Violet, had to wake him when the collection plate came by.

After the first two weeks of training, Uncle felt done in. His legs were killing him and he was so stiff he could hardly get out of bed in the morning. He went to see the doctor.

"I said I was going to ride in the Olympics, Carter," he began as soon as he hobbled into the office. "And I am going to ride in the Olympics. And you're going to help me do it. My knees feel like they've got boulders in 'em. Gimme some fancy liniment or something out of your cabinet, will ya?"

"Henry," said Dr. Foss, "I can give you anything you can swallow but it's not going to make a bike racer out of you. You're seventy-four years old, Luddhearst. You should have been dead nine years ago."

"But I ain't, am I, Carter? You ever seen legs like this on a rooster like me?" He dropped his trousers and pulled his long johns down to his ankles. "You ain't, have ya, Carter? I've only been training but two weeks and they're hurtin', but look at that muscle on 'em. It's really gonna happen, Carter. Now gimme somethin' strong to take the pain away."

Dr. Foss filled a syringe with distilled water, gave him a shot in his knotted thigh and told him it was the strongest stuff he had and that he'd probably feel like vomiting for the next twenty-four hours and might keel over any time at all. The next week Uncle was back for another shot. And he had another idea.

"I been out at the Washburn place," he said while rolling down his pant leg. "Been looking at that bull of Harv's, Big Brutus. You know, he's fifteen years old and still the best damn fornicator in the northeast. You see the build on him? If I could get him on a bicycle, he could pedal all the way to New York City and back in a day. Carter, I want you to tell me what he's got that I haven't got."

"To start with, Henry, he's a bull. He's got four legs and a pecker that's two feet long. You want any more?"

"What makes him so damn strong? You're a doctor. You're supposed to know these things."

Dr. Foss put on his most learned tone, "As a member of the cat-

The manager of the 1936 US
Cycling team on a country
road near his home in Raleigh,
South Carolina. The man who
clocked Henry's record lap.

tleus grandus genus, Big Brutus shares certain genetic characteristics with other members of the species. These characteristics are chemical in nature and are produced in the testes and transferred from generation to generation through the ejaculate."

"Don't fool with me, Carter. Give it to me straight."

"It's his balls, Henry. He got his power from his Daddy and he gives that power to every heifer he freshes."

Henry put on his fedora and walked out without a word. Next week he was back with a quart bottle of semen from Big Brutus. "You told me it's in here, Carter. What do I have to do? Drink it?"

Dr. Foss held the bottle up to the light. It was filled with a bluish liquid lined with creamy strains.

"Oh, I wouldn't drink it, Henry. I'd inject it," he said without really thinking about it.

"Start injecting," said Uncle, unbuckling his belt.

Dr. Foss was an intelligent and curious man. He had considered a career in research when he first graduated from the Harvard Medical School and was proud of the two articles he had co-authored in *The New England Journal of Medicine*. The trace of an idea had crossed his mind. "Come back in ten days," he said.

Henry came back every week for the next ten but all his friend would say was that he was working on it. Dr. Foss wasn't seen around town much that summer. He even missed several Tuesday-night poker games. He spent many evenings in his small lab behind the office, hunched over a microscope, surrounded with books he'd ordered from his alma mater. Finally, in late October, he lingered after one of the card games and suggested he and Uncle Henry go for a stroll. At close to midnight, the pair entered the doctor's office. Dr. Foss had his friend sit opposite him at his consulting desk like any other patient.

"Henry," he began, "I've got something for you. Something that I think might help build you up a little quicker than normal. Now here's the thing. I've always been one to play by the rules. You know that. It's in my nature to dot the i's and cross the t's. I like to

General store in northern Vermont. Henry relied on outlets like this one to sell tickets in his illegal but highly successful "10 fer 10" lottery.

know where the line is and I have respect for it. I don't cross it unless all my papers are in order. Now don't take offense, Henry, but I know you see the world a little differently or we wouldn't be having this talk at all. You've played it pretty wide and handsome all these years and the style fits well on you. The way you see life, borders are for crossing and not for getting caught." Uncle nodded. "All right then. We've always been straight with each other. This stuff I've developed should be tested first on animals under very careful conditions comparing a group of, say, rats who are taking it, with a group that isn't. That way you can tell if it works or not, and get an idea of what else it may do to you, what the side effects are. I haven't got the facilities for that and you haven't got the time. I don't think this stuff can do any real harm, but who knows? Before I give it to you, I want you to promise two things: one, that you'll stop taking it if I say so and you won't sulk or pressure me for more; and two, that you'll never, ever tell a soul about it. Not Violet. Not anybody. If I ever hear a whisper about this, Henry, I will consider our friendship dead and buried."

Uncle looked at his friend for a moment and remained silent, his face framed in the greenish light from the desk lamp, and then he said: "What might it do?"

"It may make you as tough as you were forty years ago or your hair may grow or your balls may fall off or both. Or it may do something else entirely. Or it may do nothing at all."

"I fancy myself with a thick head of hair and those other parts ain't nearly as useful to me as they once were. You got a deal, Carter."

So uncle began the injections. He needed three a week. Because he didn't want it to show, he took the shots in his posterior. Before long he was suggesting that if he ever needed work he could hire his ass out to the Ladies' Aid for a pincushion.

And Henry trained. He'd tried to keep riding after the snow came but most of the roads around North Mountain were impassable to anything other than a horse and sled. The ruts and rocks and ice were hell on the Schwinn so he rigged up a contraption in the barn using an old water-fed axe grinder. He took the back wheel off the bike and attached the high gear to the grind wheel by whittling down the wooden axle and hammering the gear into place with a sledge. Next he linked the pedal chain over the gears and propped up the front wheel with six eighty-pound sacks of oats, three on each side. December, January, February and most of March, Henry was down in the barn three or four hours a day, pedalling like a mad man. He wasn't shy about what he was doing, "trainin' for the Olympics," he'd tell anyone who asked. He invited the whole town to come and watch him and sharpen their tools at the same time. Half the farmers and most of the lumberjacks in the valley took him up on it. Some nights there'd be a dozen people in the barn behind the big house drinking and cracking jokes and honing blades and watching Henry sweat.

What they didn't see under Uncle's black trousers and long johns were his legs. What had been ugly, knobbed and stringy things grew into saplings, then young maples and finally thick oaks. Once a week Carter Foss measured his thighs and calves. By the end of March, when he went back on the road again, his calves had grown from eighteen inches to twenty-two and the tape stretched to almost twenty-eight inches on each thigh. Even the doctor was impressed. As for side effects, there were some. His hair did thicken, as the doctor had joked it might. As for his testicles, Henry found more use for them than he had in many years. Violet told her friend Leela that all this training was doing Henry some good. There were other effects. He was more apt to fly off the handle and his ambition knew no bounds.

He was also subject to black moods. He hadn't come by for an injection for two weeks in the fall of 1935, when he ran into at Dr. Foss in the street late one afternoon. "I'm an old fart," he told his friend. "A crazy old fart."

But the very next day he was on top of the world. He stormed right into the examination room and slapped a *New York Times* on the table beside a startled Mrs. Tremblay, who had her blouse open while Dr. Foss listened to her heart. "See that," Uncle stabbed at the print, "See that!" There was a picture of a sleek-looking man on a racer, pedalling like the wind. "Read, Carter. Read." Uncle stabbed again, this time at the caption. "Rider at cycle time trials covers the mile in a swift 2.04 minutes."

"Two ought four minutes," bellowed Uncle. "I can do that standing on the handle bars taking a piss," Then he noticed Mrs. Tremblay, snatched off his hat and backed out of the room saying, "I thought you might be interested in that, ma'am."

Now there was no stopping him. He sent a telegram to the United States Cycling Federation: "Vermonter mile under two minutes STOP Put on team STOP Reply now." The wire had the advantage of being under ten words and so qualified for the minimum rate. When no reply was forthcoming, Uncle sent a letter. When there was still no word, he drove down to Burlington and telephoned from the Wentworth Hotel.

The manager of the U.S. Cycling Team had to be called to the phone from the garage where he worked as a mechanic in Raleigh, North Carolina. In a broad accent that Uncle had trouble making out, the voice explained that he got the wire and the letter but that he just wasn't much of a writing man and anyhow he had to save every penny to help get the team to Germany. This was a revelation to Uncle.

"You mean you're paying your own damn way?"

"Yes, sir, I most certainly am — that is, if I can get the money together."

"Can't the damn federation or whatever the hell it's called pay? What's wrong with those boys? No gumption or somethin'?"

"Thing is, sir," replied the manager, "when it comes to the United States Cycling Federation, sir, we are it."

"You are it?"

"Yes, sir. Me and the boys on the team constitute the entire organization and that's the truth. Nobody much cares about bike racing. The track teams and the swimmers got all the support."

"But what about the Olympic trials? I read about it in the paper; sounded like a big deal. I saw the picture of that fellow Byrd. What are you telling me?"

"Well, sir, we did have a trial, sure enough. I rode up from Raleigh for it. About twenty-five racers showed up, including a *New York Times* reporter fellow who's just crazy about bike racing, We had a time of it, I can tell you. When it was over, though, it turned out only four of us could get time off and could hustle the savings together to make the trip to Germany."

"You mean to tell me," Uncle sputtered, fell silent and began again. "You mean to tell me any damn person who can pay gets on the team? Because if that's what you're telling me, I am on the team as of right now." He paused. "So now I'm on the team," he continued, "What do we need? Bikes? Uniforms? Those sissy little hats I saw in the paper, we got any of those?"

The manager allowed as how they did not.

"Well, put your mind at ease. With Henry Z. Luddhearst on board, this team is going first class. You'll be hearing from me."

And so it was that, less than a month later, the governor of the great State of Vermont, quietly initiated the 1936 Olympic Cycle Fund with a grant of $500, an amount matched by an anonymous private citizen. In the late fall of 1935 you couldn't walk a block in Burlington or St. Albans or Rutland or Bennington or Brattleboro or Manchester without being accosted by a kid who wanted to sell you a special Hershey bar for a nickel to "help our national bicycle team." Three nights out of seven all over the state, there would be a knock on the door and a child would be begging for old bottles or old clothes or old toys or a few pennies "to help our biker boys."

In North Mountain, Uncle presided over the fund drive as National Campaign Manager of the United States Cyclist Federation. There were bake sales and rummage sales and bridge tournaments and whists and bingos. Uncle, in transgression of state and federal laws, quietly launched a weekly draw where you paid a dime and you could win ten dollars. He called it the "10 fer 10." By the fall of 1935 you could buy a ticket at most any general store in northeastern Vermont.

"It's for a good cause, ain't it, Carter?" he said when his friend called at the house and questioned the morality of the scheme.

"So's Roosevelt's New Deal," his friend chided him, "and haven't I heard you call him that-damned-diddling-of-a-devil-with-a-walking-stick?"

Uncle grinned like Mephisto himself and went back to his ledger.

The doctor was tougher when it came to Uncle's demands for "more stuff." Since putting himself on the team, he'd doubled his training schedule. Three days a week he'd pedal forty miles and seventy miles on Saturdays, including sprints on a track he'd had built in the pasture behind the house. The rest of the time he spent running the campaign and looking after his own business. He trained even while he was doing paperwork. He'd had Violet sew pieces of lead into canvas pouches with loops through the top for a belt. He strapped them to his calves and did leg raises under the desk while he wrote letters demanding money for the team from anyone he could think of. His legs were like a twenty-year-old's. He felt, he said, like "one million dollars" and he wanted five injections a week instead of three. Dr. Foss said no.

"Look at me, Carter, not a blamed one of your fearful side effects. Hell all of 'em are great. What are you so damned worried about? I haven't felt this strong since the first year I married Violet and that was in 1879. I need more. I've got a race to win."

The doctor listened to his heart. Fifty-three beats a minute. Even when he checked it right after Uncle did a hundred-yard sprint on the Schwinn down Main Street, it was only one hundred and thirty-three. His blood pressure was low too, very low. "What about your urine, Henry? Is it a nice healthy colour?

"What's a healthy colour, Carter? Yellow as an egg yolk? Clear as a trout stream? Dark as a stallion's? What do ya want to see?"

"Pale. It should be pale."

"Then pale it is."

"And do you get up often at night?"

"Get it up as often as I can, doctor."

"Don't joke, Henry. This is serious now."

"I'm not peeing down my leg like my old Daddy was at my age, if that's what you mean."

On Henry's medical record, Dr. Foss wrote, "Frequent night urination" and told his patient to get out of his office, that he couldn't tolerate the sight of him another minute and he'd get five shots a week "over my dead body and probably yours too."

A week later, it almost was over Uncle's dead body. Two farmers brought him down in the back of a horse and buggy. He'd regained consciousness by the time they carried him upstairs to Dr. Foss's office, but he had a nasty gash on his head and his eyes were dilated.

"What happened, Henry?" said the concerned doctor when they laid him out flat on the examination table.

"Ask those fellas," muttered Uncle.

While the doctor sat him up and examined his pupils, the farmers explained that Mr. Luddhearst had come out their way to pick up a young heifer but that while Mr. Luddhearst was loading the calf into the back of the Desoto, their bull got loose and took a run at the animal while she was half in and half out of the car. Mr. Luddhearst tried to stop it, they said, but he couldn't and he got knocked down and hit his head.

"I ain't that bad," protested Uncle, trying to stand, "But the damn horny fool destroyed my automobile."

The good news was Uncle was right as rain in less than a week. The bull and the heifer were better for the experience. The Desoto had to be sold for scrap.

If it hadn't been for the Olympics themselves, the send-off would have been the highlight of the trip. North Mountain's tiny station was decked out in red, white and blue bunting and the crowd was said to rival the one which came out to meet favourite-son Calvin Coolidge's whistle-stop campaign for President ten years before. The high school band played their rendition of the Star Spangled Banner, underscored by a tuba purchased second-hand with funds earned by student commissions on the Hershey Olympic Chocolate Bar campaign. In his steam-cleaned black suit and freshly blocked fedora and sporting a full, dazzlingly white beard he'd grown over the winter, Uncle looked more like the rabbi of some orthodox sect than a bike racer.

That was not, however, the image he presented to the other members of the cycling team when he met them for the first time on the deck of the German ocean liner, *Wasser Schwann*, three hours before she set sail for Bremerhaven.

Before boarding, Uncle spent the two days in New York at the Plaza Hotel, much of it in a private room off the barber shop in the basement. He felt thirty years younger and he was damn well going to look it, he told Edward, the chief barber and a man of many talents. Edward said he would see what he could do, that uncle must put himself in his hands.

"Anything but make-up," said uncle, "none of that namby-pamby stuff."

After half an hour of combing and study accompanied by much standing back to consider the overall effect, to Uncle's great discomfort Edward washed his hair, cut the sides very short and left the top long. He then dyed it a becoming dark brown, almost black, and wove in some extra pieces of the same colour which he said came from the head of a famous French prostitute, a fact which delighted Uncle. He next fashioned the beard into a neat goatee, which he dyed as well. After a facial to "tone up tired muscles" and two hours spent with hot towels wrapped around his face, Uncle was pronounced by Edward to look not thirty but forty years younger. The effect was perfect — well, almost perfect. As Edward turned the barber's chair and they gazed at his handiwork in the

Berlin Stadium, site of the 1936 Olympics.

A 1934 Packard similar to the one Henry used to transport heifers and which he claimed was "better built than any damn pickup (truck)."

brightly lit three-way mirrors, both men realized something was lacking.

"The eyes," said Edward under his breath.

Yes, the eyes. Despite the facial, they still looked like pale blue stones floating in a troubled sea of foam and blood, surrounded by the crumpled canyons of seventy-four summers. Edward excused himself and went upstairs.

When he returned a few minutes later he stood behind his client and carefully lowered his prize onto the patrician ridge of Uncle's nose, a pair of very large, very dark sunglasses. Edward stood back, clapped, and did a little jig. Uncle beamed.

"I look like a damn fool," he said, "but a younger damn fool."

"You must never, ever take them off except when you're sleeping alone," Edward scolded as Uncle settled the bill, adding an extra twenty dollars for the miracle worker.

The man whom the team had so much wanted to meet, their benefactor, the reason they were sailing on this fine ship with money in their pockets and new Schwinn bicycles in the hold, the individual to whom they owed their flashy red, white and blue uniforms and elegant blazers with the 1936 U.S. Olympic Cycling Team crests, was not quite what the manager and riders Messrs. Byrd, Logan, Morton, Simbaldi and Sellinger had envisioned. The man who shook hands with them on that bright windy day in New York harbour, was garbed entirely in black. With the snap brim of his fedora pulled down low on his forehead over eyes shielded by Edward's black lenses, he looked more like a drummer or piano man in a quartet from some gin joint in Harlem than an Olympic athlete.

"Pleased to meet ya," and "Welcome," and "Thanks for everything" and "Good to see you" were about all the team could manage by way of greeting.

Uncle said, "It's an honour, men." And for the next several minutes, the six of them stood in an awkward little bunch, clearing their throats, adjusting their clothes and staring at the skyline until, to everyone's relief, Uncle signalled a steward and asked to be shown to his cabin. "We'll eat together," he said by way of farewell. When the steward left Uncle's cabin he had a small locked leather case which he was to see was kept in the ship's refrigerator — and he was fifty dollars richer.

All of them, including Henry, did eat together once, on the third day at sea, not at the captain's table as Uncle might have wished. The captain was aware of where his nation's leader's sympathies lay and did not think it wise to fraternize with athletes of another country, especially one which, after the Nuremberg Laws of the previous September, included Jews and other racially suspect groups. Instead they dined in the bar on "B" Deck. Henry pronounced his steak not up to Vermont standards but he enjoyed the German draft beer, a taste for which never left him. After dining, he smoked a Cuban cigar — training or no training.

Uncle spent much of the crossing in his cabin, often in his underwear, doing leg raises with twenty pounds of lead strapped to each calf. He also read *She* by H. Rider Haggard, the first and only novel he ever completed. He'd been given it as a going-away present by Carter Foss, who was a voracious reader and who thought it might help pass the time on the long voyage. When Carter asked him on his return what he thought of it, all Uncle said was, "Hogwash." Be that as it may, Dr. Foss was never far from Henry's thoughts. Three times a week the steward knocked timidly on the door, handed in the leather case and waited in the narrow hallway for it to be returned.

The opening ceremonies in August at the new Berlin stadium were spectacular. With almost four thousand athletes, these were by far the largest games held since the modern Olympics began in 1896 — and a major event for the Third Reich, stage-managed by the leader of the nation with the single object of impressing the world. Over eighty thousand jammed in to witness the spectacle which went off with the precision of a military exercise and enough patriotic schmaltz in the form of stirring music to bring tears to the eyes of the many uniformed Nazis in the reviewing stand. The U.S. Cycling Team, if Adolf Hitler noticed them at all, must have been a disappointment to him. They sauntered along in a straggly group, dressed entirely in black from the tips of their shoes to the crowns of their fedoras, between their country's swimmers and wrestlers. The only colour was supplied by the red, white, blue and gold crests on the pockets of their dark blazers. Those back home who saw the *Movietone News* of the event in theaters must have wondered what Albert Sellinger was doing as he passed by the camera. Did he spit? Henry was indistinguishable from the others and, politics or not, he wrote to Carter that he'd felt "proud as hell to be an American" and that "the music was too damn loud."

The first cycling event took place four days later. It was the one-kilometre speed test, a race in which it was hoped Henry Luddhearst would perform well. After all, he said he could do the mile in under a minute and a half. These expectations made Uncle nervous and this, in turn, caused him to drink three very large steins of beer on the evening before at the Beer Hall next to the Hotel Excelsior, where the team was billeted. He later said he lost his judgement because of the "infernal racket" created by four jolly fat men in lederhosen blowing on brass instruments. He could have handled the alcohol even if the steins had been filled to the brim with rye whiskey but he couldn't take the volume of liquid. He was up and down eight times during the night and had trouble getting back to sleep each time. The morning dawned grey and overcast. It was all he could do to get himself into the blue tights and red jersey with white stripes, slip on his dark glasses, tug on his racing cap and grab a taxi down to the Albert Speer Velodrome.

Of the Americans, only he and Sellinger were scheduled for the event. The red, single-gear, brakeless track bikes were primed and ready. The idea, the manager explained to Uncle, as though he'd never done it before, was you straddled your bike and when the starter pistol fired, you pedalled like hell, did five laps of the two-hundred-metre track and coasted to a stop. Despite the two days of practice he'd put in on this very track, the instructions sounded vague and complicated. When the manager asked him how he felt, Uncle confessed that he felt "a little more poorly than a pinch of coon shit."

Each rider went off alone. By the time Henry's number was called about half way through the thirty-man field, the German, Rudolf Karsch, had posted the time to beat at 1.13.72. Arie van Vilet, the favourite from Holland, had yet to ride.

The gunshot seemed to startle Uncle and he got off to a shaky start. He clocked a disastrous 17.31 seconds on the first two-hundred metres. At that pace, he'd finish at almost his mile time for little more than half the distance. He came by at 16.85.9 seconds for lap two and cut that by less than a second in a third lap time of 15.93. Way too slow. This was humiliating. "Get the lead out, Henry," the manager screamed as he went by. Whether Uncle heard the words or not or whether it was his pride or the pressure on his bladder or the cumulative effect of the injections or some combination of all these things, something had an electric effect on Henry. His head dropped down almost to the handlebars and his legs became a blur. Bike and rider suddenly appeared to be shot from a cannon. He covered the fourth lap in a heart-stopping 14.23 seconds. By the time he hit the back stretch on the final lap, the manager was going out of his mind screaming, the stop watch held inches from his face. As he rounded the final bend, the whole Dutch team, who had been lounging against the stands chatting, expecting nothing from the Americans, were on their feet. Henry flashed across the finish line at a stunning 13.27 for the final lap. In his excitement, the manager threw his watch to the ground and stomped on it. Henry coasted around the track slumped over the handle bars, dragging his feet against the wooden surface. The bike tottered and he fell into his teammates' arms. He had to be helped into the locker room where he declined a hot shower, insisting instead that a cab be summoned to take him back to the hotel "right after I take a piss."

At the end of the day, Arie von Vilet took the Gold in 1.12.0 minutes. Pierre Georget of France slipped by the German for a Silver with a time of 1.12.8. Albert Sellinger had a satisfying ride at 1.15.2 minutes, earning tenth place for the U.S., better than the *New York Times* reporter had expected. Henry came dead last at 1.26.43, but of all the riders, he was the happiest. The note from Arie von Vilet, delivered to his room that evening congratulating him on the fastest single lap, was the icing on the cake.

The next day Sellinger was eliminated early in the match sprint, which went to German Toni Merkens with von Vilet in second spot. Two days after that, the four-man team — everyone except Henry and Sellinger — were eliminated in their second heat in the four-thousand-metre team pursuit. The manager felt they should take a pass on the team time trials to concentrate on the road race, the final event. Henry practiced with the team for three days, then dropped out to plan strategy. Byrd was the strongest racer: the others were to echelon in front of him till the last two kilometres when he and Simbaldi, the designated "*domestique,*" would sprint out at top speed with Simbaldi in front, taking the wind for as long as he could to allow Byrd to preserve his energy for the final rush to the finish line. On race day, an ideal cool sunny morning with little wind, the U.S. team carried off the strategy without a hitch. The field was too strong, however, and Byrd had to settle for 44th.

And, except for the closing ceremonies, that was that. Again there were fireworks, marching bands, loud stirring music and speeches full of platitudes about honest competition, the non-political nature of the games and the fostering of world peace. Hitler didn't speak; he was in a blue funk over American Jesse Owens's four Gold medals in track and field, an honor *der Führer* felt history had reserved for Germany, not someone even the German papers referred to as "The Buckeye Bullet."

His displeasure with the Americans' performance had been plain and was reported in the next edition of the Paris-based *Herald*

Tribune. The leader of the Third Reich had second thoughts about his behaviour. Irritating the United States this early on was not part of the master plan. A hasty "goodwill and congratulations" reception was arranged and invitations went out to selected athletes on the German and American teams.

There were no representatives from the track and field teams of either country, but the cyclists were invited. Late on an August afternoon, Mr. Henry Z. Luddhearst of North Mountain, Vermont, dressed in his black Olympic jacket with his hair slicked back, his beard glistening jet black with an unguent supplied by Edward of the Plaza Hotel of New York, his eyes protected by the ubiquitous dark glasses, was presented to a reception line that included much of the German high command.

He must have shaken hands with Joseph Goebbels, who three years before had presided over the burning of twenty thousand books the Nazis judged to be decadent. S.S. Chief Hermann Himmler may have been in attendance and Deputy Leader of the party Rudolf Hess almost certainly was, but Henry recalled none of them. He did, however, vividly remember his meeting with Mr. Hitler, as he called him. "Maybe he was into the schnapps," he told Carter on his return. "He asked me how the weather was in Vermont. I told him it was cold in the winter but in July and August it got warm enough to make damn poor sledding. It took the interpreter fellow about three minutes before Mr. Hitler understood, then he giggled like a schoolgirl. He told me a joke to return the favour. He asked me how a wet dog smells. I said with its nose. I got it wrong. The answer was 'awful.' As he turned to join the party, the leader of the nation asked Uncle if he could explain "Buckeye" to him.

"Bullet, I understand," he said, "but what is this Buckeye?" Uncle said that he thought it had something to do with peas. The only other meeting of note was with a young woman called Leni Reichenstahl.

"Hell of a looker," Uncle said. "Some kind of movie lady. She said I must have wonderful legs and she'd like to photograph them. Can you beat that, Carter?"

Immediately following the reception, he took the overnight train to Paris. He wasn't impressed with the City of Light and told Carter that he'd seen Paris and nobody would have trouble keeping him down on the farm. By the end of the week he'd sailed on the Normandie out of Le Hague and arrived in New York on Labour Day 1936, an entirely satisfied man.

Uncle felt more mellow than he had since the notion of cycling in the Olympics had come to him. He'd taken the last of the injections two weeks before and on his first night at the Plaza, he only got up once to pee. He visited Edward right after breakfast the next day without the sunglasses. After he'd settled himself in the chair and told the barber what a success his make-over had been, he said, "Shave all the hair off my face and head. Every last damn bit of it." Edward began to protest, saw there was no use and picked up his razor. When the last hot towel had been removed and Uncle examined his image in the triple mirrors he was not displeased. "I look," he said to Edward, "like a damn baby who has seen and done it all and that ain't far from the truth." He gave Edward another twenty dollars, then he went upstairs, stopped at the front desk to pick up a fat envelope with Morgan Trust discreetly written in the corner and crossed the street to the Packard car dealership.

What with the sudden loss of hair, his fedora sat a little low around the ears. In his unfashionable black suit and boots, the salesman took him for a rube or some out-of-work depression desperado. Uncle walked around the two shiny luxury vehicles in the showroom and kicked tires while the salesman tagged along after him asking, in an increasingly irritated voice, if he could be of assistance. Uncle slid into the driver's seat of both cars and pulled the seat forward as far as it would go, than he got in the back seat and stretched out.

"Sir," protested the salesman. "You can't just walk in off the street and mishandle these vehicles. These are the finest cars in America."

"Got anything bigger?" said Uncle.

"The 1936 Packard does come in a convertible chauffeur's model but there are fewer than one hundred built each year and they go to a preferred list of our most discriminating customers," replied the salesman in a snotty voice while attempting to manoeuver Henry out the front door.

"Show me one."

"It's customary for these automobiles to be ordered several months in advance."

"Show me one now," said Uncle in a tone even the salesman could not ignore.

"I'll check to see if we have one in stock," he said and scuttled into a back office.

It was the manager, a Mr. Thomas Rowan, according to his card, who returned. "I understand, Mr...."

"Luddhearst."

"...Mr. Luddhearst, that you're interested in viewing the limousine model. By a rare coincidence we happen to have one in at the moment. It was ordered by Mr...., well, shall we say, the owner of a very large department store who finds that, for the moment, he no longer requires a vehicle of this dimension. It's a large car, Mr. Luddhearst," he added, "in every sense of the word."

With that, he ushered Uncle into a small elevator and together they descended to the garage. Mr. Rowan instructed a man in coveralls to "bring up the big Packard."

"It's being washed, sir. Sammy just picked it up from the railway yesterday."

"Bring it wet," said Uncle. Mr. Rowan shrugged and a few minutes later Henry was down on his hands and knees in the back seat.

"It's very roomy back there, Mr. Luddhearst, as you can see," said Mr. Rowan, ignoring his client's behaviour. "The broadloom used in these vehicles is the finest carpeting in America. It would be right at home in a Park Avenue penthouse."

" 'Bout enough room for two heifers and a bale of hay, wouldn't you say?" replied Uncle. Before he could fully consider his answer, Uncle said, "I'll take it."

Mr. Rowan raised an eyebrow and put his hands together, finger to finger. "I see....And how much, Mr. Luddhearst, will you be putting down on the vehicle."

"How much does the damn vehicle cost?"

"Three thousand nine hundred and ninety dollars."

"Then that's how much I'm putting down," said Uncle, pulling the Morgan Trust envelope out of his breast pocket and counting out forty one-hundred dollar bills into the stunned dealer's outstretched palm.

"Keep the change, my friend," he said. "Gas up the car and send that stuffed shirt upstairs over to the Bell Captain at the Plaza Hotel to pick up my bags. I'm driving home to North Mountain."

DE

Philippe's Labyrinth

◆ Philippe-Joachim Beauregard was not really family in the conventional sense. That is, he was not a blood relation of my family, but over the years a strong bond had formed between him and my father, and I always called him Uncle Philippe and his wife Aunt Mathilde. Their five rambunctious children were my favourite cousins. Back then — this was in the '30s — the Beauregards lived in the picturesque Normandy village of St. Malouse, where Uncle Philippe taught mathematics at the local *lycée*.

In order to fully appreciate what follows, you have to understand that Philippe didn't just teach mathematics. The man lived and breathed the subject through every pore of his body, in every aspect of his daily life, and it is clear that he had a rare talent and a most profound understanding of the subject matter. It would be too tedious to enumerate the myriad of ways in which he found connections between daily life and mathematics; suffice it to say that he could discern Fibonicci number sequences from such prosaic events as the final outcome of the annual Tour de France bicycle race, an event he followed with almost religious devotion. Each year he would devote considerable time analyzing the starting line-up before placing a sizeable bet with a Paris bookmaker. Not once in eighteen years had Philippe failed to correctly predict the outcome of the bicycle race.

Over the years he had developed an almost mystical interest in the architecture and construction of medieval cathedrals as well as the hidden mathematics underlying those magnificent edifices. In 1936 he published a volume on the subject in which he investigated, from a mathematical viewpoint and at some length, not only the floor plans and flying buttresses but also the tile labyrinth embedded in the floor of the cathedral at Chartres. The book, now long out of print, is called *Les enigmes mathematiques dans les structures sacrées*. Most scholars considered Philippe a crackpot and viewed the simple tile maze in the Chartres cathedral as a representation of the twelve stations of the cross, where the pilgrims would tread a narrow path to Golgatha and ultimately achieve salvation. Philippe saw it otherwise. Using an impressive array of mathematical formulas, he set out to prove that "for the early Christians, this labyrinth represents a profound understanding of the metaphysical forces shaping and directing our human destiny, turning it, like a mirror image, in on itself." I have tried on a number of occasions to read the weighty tome but I invariably give up halfway through the first page. The stuff is nothing short of incomprehensible. The above quote I lifted intact from the back of the dust cover.

As a result of writing the book Philippe undertook the construction of an exact full-scale replica of the Chartres labyrinth in an unused field adjacent to his large garden. The maze, which measured fifteen by twenty metres, consisted of an intricate pattern of variously coloured and shaped clay tiles embedded in the rich Normandy soil. When it was completed several months later, he would devote endless time contemplating his handiwork, treading and retreading the narrow paths of the labyrinth while speculating on its profound mathematical and metaphysical implications. He was at this time already showing the unmistakable signs of the dementia that was to haunt him for years. His increasingly unbalanced mind would turn the most trivial occurences into bizarre puzzles. Once, for instance, when my family was invited for din-

On the beach at Deauville, 1937. Mathilde and Philipe are the partly obscured couple in the background.

Mathilde and Philipe in front of their St. Malouse house, with an assortment of local children.

ner, we found that Philippe had rearranged the plates, glasses and cutlery in a maze-like web on the checkered tablecloth, insisting we trace our fingers along the labyrinth of forks, spoons and knives to reach the *boeuf bourguignon* in the centre of the tangle. Aunt Mathilde laughed and pretended it was all an amusing dinnertime game, but there was something to her hearty laughter which seemed a bit forced.

About this time Uncle Philippe had conceived of a fantastic maze so large and convoluted that once inside it, the web of twists and turns would render any hope of escape almost futile. The secret of its intricacy lay in repeating an identical circular pattern over and over again, one part being an exact mirror image of the next, thus turning each path in on itself. As mazes go it was nothing short of brilliant. All through the following winter Philippe worked on the blueprint whenever time allowed, refining the concept to the point where he was satisfied it incorporated not only the mathematical abstractions but also the metaphysical profundities of the Chartres labyrinth. When the weather turned mild in March, he began laying out the guide strings for his labyrinth in the unused field behind the tile maze. At the completion of that initial stage a month later, his tangle of guide wires covered an area of almost six hectares.

When summer vacation arrived, Philippe started planting. He was singlemindedin this pursuit. By early August he had covered most of the six hectares with clippings from a fast-growing, dense and extremely hardy Thionville deciduous bush, which he had obtained at a substantial quantity discount from a gardener in St. Lo who specialized in unusual hybrids.

Late that August my family and I spent a week with the Beauregards at a modest bathing hotel on the Deauville seashore. Over the years this annual beach vacation had become a tradition for both of our families, and something we all looked forward to. As this was well before the introduction of leisurewear to our part of the world, it was most educational to observe my father turn his

Philipe
and
Mathilde
in 1946.

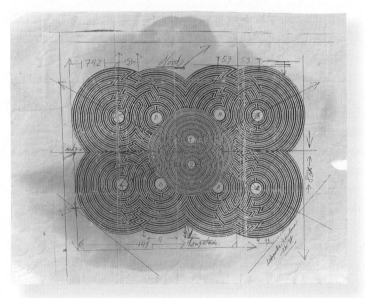

After his illness Philipe systematically destroyed
all references to his labyrinth. Only this early
schematic survives.

single black business suit and a few simple accessories into an impressive array of natty ensembles, from beach wear to dinner wear. Watching him with his farmer's tan wading in the ocean with his pants rolled up, bare-chested except for his suspenders, was an awesome sight. For afternoon drinks he would put on a shirt and an orange foulard.

From the outset of the vacation it was clear to us that Philippe was fast losing his marbles. His obsession with mazes had him spending almost the entire time scratching enormous diagrams in the sand. Twice a day the tide would wash away his drawings and he was forced to start anew. Now and again he would round up the children and set us down in various parts of the diagrams, urging us to find a way out. Aunt Mathilde was clearly concerned by events, and confided to my mother her fears for Philippe's state of mind. During the last night of our stay at the hotel, Philippe was secretly at work in the dark, dragging every single deck chair from the veranda onto the beach. At dawn we caught just a brief glimpse of his maze-like arrangement of chairs before the first tide bore a goodly portion of them off to sea. The hotel management was not amused. It was strongly suggested that should we wish to vacation at Deauville in the future, we would be well advised to seek accommodation elsewhere.

In the spring of 1940 German forces overran France, executing the right flank of their notorious pincer movement through the St. Malouse region. For a short while there was some hectic activity in the area but things soon reverted to normal in the village and life went on much as before. During this time, Philippe slipped deeper into dementia, and the hedges thrived. As he retreated more and more from the real world, he took deep satisfaction in the upkeep of the fast-growing bushes, trimming and pruning them for hours each day. It was during this time that his employment at the *lycée* was terminated, giving Philippe even more freedom to work on his maze. And as the hedges grew, so did the amount of labour he devoted to maintaining them. Soon they were as thick and impenetrable as cement walls, reaching well over two-and-a-half metres in height. Negotiating the narrow green pathways induced a sense of disorientation, followed by claustophobia and panic in the few hapless individuals who tried it.

One curious thing about a well-constructed hedge maze is that, viewed from the outside at ground level, it seems to be no more than a bushy enclosure. There is little to suggest that behind this verdant facade lies a web of paths that can drive an unwary intruder mad. And once inside, it matters little whether the visitor is half a metre from the edge — and freedom — or in the very centre of the maze; either way, he's trapped. In order to navigate his way around, Uncle Philippe planted thousands of numbered wooden stakes along the paths; these markers corresponded to numbers on a map he carried in his shirt pocket. Without both the numbered stakes and the map, an intruder would invariably be lost in the tangle. This point was proven beyond a doubt when a couple of local love birds made the mistake of sneaking into the maze one evening. It was only when their panicked screams were heard by a goatherd some hours later that Philippe, searching for well over three hours, managed to extricate the terrified couple. Aunt Mathilde, at her wits' end and fearing for her brood, ordered them never to go near the maze, and in the end had the village blacksmith install a locked iron gate at the entrance which also served as the exit.

Since Philippe's dismissal from the *lycée*, life was becoming harder for the Beauregards. To make ends meet Mathilde was forced to take in washing from the village, while the children raised rabbits and chickens behind the house. The locals, a hardy breed of practical Normandy peasants, had little time for Philippe's handiwork what with cows to milk, sheep to shear, cheese to be made, fields to be tilled, swine to be fattened and Sunday church to attend. Nevertheless, every few days one or the other of their neighbours would stop by with something for the dinner table: a sack of flour, a side of pork, a jug of milk or a slab of cheese. These offerings were always hurried affairs, with the benefactor long gone before Mathilde could express her gratitude. On one occasion the *curé* paid a visit and that was merely to ensure that Philippe was not involved in some sort of satanic hanky-panky that might corrupt his flock. There was, after all, that episode of the love birds lost in the maze, and he had to make sure everything was above board. When the *curé* left after a guided tour, he was satisfied Philippe was doing important work on behalf of the Lord. To all outward appearances, then, Philippe could, if the situation required it, muster up enough presence to be deemed as sane and sober as a Lyon magistrate. But Aunt Mathilde was not fooled. Despite her ignorance of either clinical, abnormal or behavioral psychology she nevertheless understood that Philippe's twisted labyrinth represented an echo of his disordered mind, and that the two were intractably meshed. When she attempted to share this insight with the medical doctor at the hospital in Rouen, Philippe was prescribed a mild sedative and instructed to perform biweekly colonic irrigations. There is now some evidence to suggest that as the labyrinth grew, Philippe's febrile intellect was spiralling into an identical psychological maze in a sort of mind/matter transference where his inner landscape was being mirrored and articulated in the outer world.

As the Allied forces landed on the beachheads of the Normandy coast in the summer of 1944, the retreating German forces started clogging the roads around the village of St. Malouse. One late afternoon as aunt Mathilde was scouring the back field for pisse-en-lit, she came across a unit of Wehrmacht soldiers bivouacked near the north end of Philippe's maze. The soldiers had already erected four field-tents covered in camouflage netting and were cooking dinner over a portable stove. To her relief, she managed to remain unobserved, hidden behind a bush. From there she could spy on the little encampment, and clearly saw two soldiers trying to break the lock on the gate to the labyrinth. They finally succeeded, using the butt-end of a rifle, and stood there for a while, seemingly perplexed, peering into the green jungle. After a short

A quiet day in the country, July 1944.

conference, they went in and Mathilde could hear their yells and laughter echoing from behind the hedges. It didn't take long for the laughter to take on a tentative edge though, and in a short time the once lusty yells turned to appeals for help. Three soldiers rushed laughingly to their aid and in short order disappeared in their turn into the green tangle. By the time the Normandy sunset was setting the evening sky ablaze with soft red light, all sixteen Wehrmacht soldiers were immured deep within the confines of the thicket.

Through the night, as the Beauregards lay in their beds, they could hear the anguished yells of the trapped soldiers. Downstairs in the kitchen a distraught Philippe paced the floor, muttering and gesticulating as if engaged in a conversation which at times grew quite heated. As each yell issued forth from the maze he would freeze, listening intently, then resume his pacing and imaginary conversation. At dawn the cries stopped.

Just as his family was getting up, Philippe slipped out of the house and made his way down the garden to his labyrinth. Along the way he was seen tearing up the one thing that could guide him safely through: the map. As the sun appeared over the horizon, Mathilde watched silently from the bedroom window as her husband entered the maze.

All that day as Philippe and the errant Germans remained in the labyrinth, the tide of war was turning. The roads around St. Malouse, so recently clogged with Wehrmacht soldiers, were now choked with advancing Allied troops streaming towards the Orne River bridge, the only bridge the German forces had somehow failed to blow up in their retreat. As the main road leading to that bridge passed right in front of Philippe's house, there was a constant stream of armoured vehicles on the two-lane country road. But Aunt Mathilde and her five children were oblivious to the activity. As the day wore on their eyes remained riveted to the entrance of the maze.

It was not until the late afternoon that the first of the sixteen captives staggered out of the gate with his hands in the characteristic gesture of surrender. He appeared dazed as if in shock, and deep lines of exhaustion etched his face. He was followed a short while later by another, and soon after that another. During the following hour at various intervals, the remaining thirteen captives emerged from the maze, sometimes singly, sometimes in groups of two or three. Everything about their bearing suggested utter defeat; the way they were slouched over with their hands in the air, as if a waiting further orders. Philippe followed close behind, and in an unusually firm voice commanded the captives to kneel in the grass. Meanwhile Mathilde, up at the road, flagged down a passing Canadian military unit, who herded the bewildered Germans off for interrogation at the St. Malouse town hall.

As it turned out, this Wehrmact unit had been detailed with the responsibility of blowing up the last bridge in order to stall the Allied advance over the Orne River. Later that same day Philippe and Mathilde were called on by an American intelligence officer who expressed his gratitude and suggested some sort of medal might be in order. Mathilde took the officer aside and had a long talk with him.

One early morning about two weeks later when things had quieted down on the war front, a detachment of six heavily armoured Sherman B-11 tanks came rumbling down the road from Falaise and stopped in the field adjacent to Philippe's house. The commander, a twenty-three-year-old Vermont high school graduate whose French was slightly better than rudimentary, had a short talk with Mathilde, after which the tank crews set to work. Equipped with grappling hooks, the Sherman tanks started at the outer perimeter. By noon they had made some headway into the maze, and as the dense bushes and roots were dislodged they were piled up, doused with gasoline, and set ablaze. All through that day and the following two, smoke drifted over the village of St Malouse as the six Sherman tanks ripped the labyrinth apart. Philippe and Mathilde had planted themselves on chairs in the field and watched the proceedings with unswerving attention. It appeared that as the walls of the maze came down, the walls muddling Philippe's mind crumbled as well. The layers of pain and confusion that had marked his handsome face for so long were gradually being stripped away.

As all this was taking place, a crowd gathered along the road to watch the spectacle. Over the day as the tanks lit into the hedges, the crowd grew in size, and by evening there were well over two hundred spectators from the village and surrounding farms. Nobody remembers how it all started, but by nightfall the gathering had taken on all the appearances of a celebration. It was entirely spontaneous, what with the war being over, and with a fine harvest to look forward to. In no time at all the accordion player from Falaise and his horse-faced sister with the voice of an angel had the festivities ripping along. Philippe, for the first time in memory, danced with Mathilde, and very well at that. All through the night the villagers kept coming, bringing food and wine. The party went on uninterrupted for three days and nights, the liberators mixing freely with the locals while the Sherman tanks tore the labyrinth to shreds. It was unforgettable. When on the third day the last bush was finally uprooted and the back field was as level as a *boule* court, the mayor of St. Malouse in his tri-cornered hat, the *curé*, just a bit unsteady on his feet, the tank commander, the accordion player from Falaise and his horse-faced sister, the gardener from St. Lo and the rest of the assembled guests raised their glasses in a toast to liberty, equality and fraternity. As the hearty cheers rose up and drifted across the landscape they could be heard as far away as Bellechasse-sur-Orne, for a moment drowning out the aerial bombardment of the retreating German forces.

From that time on, Philippe reverted in every way to his former self. As with the labyrinth, all traces of his illness disappeared, and if anyone raised the subject of mazes he would just laugh and ignore it. By the fall of 1945 he was back at the *lycée* teaching mathematics, and had found a new pastime in the game of chess. With its endless mathematical possibilities, this game offered ample stimulation for his inquisitive mind. He got so engrossed in the game that for a while he toyed with the idea of constructing a vast chessboard in the back field now that it was nice and level. For once Mathilde put her foot down, and for once Philippe was forced to see reason. Nevertheless, over the years he detected a number of odd correlations between certain chess gambits and the starting line-up of the annual Tour de France bicycle race. Each and every year he would succumb to racing fever and place a hefty sum with his Paris bookmaker. Not once in the ensuing nineteen years did he predict the outcome correctly. But he didn't seem to mind.

TS

Billy "The Kid" Darling

The father who loved him

◆ Billy the Kid wasn't exactly a relative of mine, though he did father a couple of kids (excuse me for that) by my great grandmother's second cousin, Cynthia Prissim. The remarkable thing about my distant cousins was that they were born in Montreal, Canada, fourteen and sixteen years respectively, *after* Pat Garrett gunned Billy down in Pete Maxwell's bedroom at Fort Sumner, the night of July 14, 1881.

Later, describing the events, Garrett said Billy had been making love to Maxwell's daughter in the peach orchard not half an hour before he shot him. Others say Garrett knew Billy would call on Pauline that night and arrived first, tied the girl to a chair, gagged her, and hid behind a sofa, waiting for Billy. When the Kid showed up Garrett said he blew him away like a dog. Some friend, that Garrett. Some liar too, they said. At the funeral, Deluvina Maxwell called him a "piss-pot" and a "sonofabitch." Who could blame her? Half the town hated Garrett, wanted to lynch him.

Six days later he was up in Santa Fe trying to collect the five hundred dollar reward which the former governor, Lew Wallace, had promised for Billy's hide. Acting Governor Ritch said it was a personal thing between Garrett and Wallace and he wouldn't pay, although he finally did cough up the following March. The Santa Fe townspeople raised six hundred dollars on the spot and the

The only existing likeness of
Catherine Antrim, Billy's mother.
She died of TB when he was only
15. Would things have been
different if she'd lived?
(Lincoln County Museum)

folks up in Las Vegas, New Mexico, gave Garrett thirteen hundred dollars. And that's not all the money he got. Not by a long shot. There was the business of the photographs.

On September 30, 1881, the *Santa Fe New Mexican* reported, "It is said there is only one photograph of Billy the Kid extant, and Pat Garrett has that. Most people in this section has (sic) seen as much of the Kid as they want to, and will be able to get along without a picture." Pat had the photo, all right, and he prayed it was the only one extant. That being the case, it would be worth two thousand dollars to him.

A little refresher on how the Kid got his reputation would help throw some light on why that ferrotype was so valuable to Garrett – and how Billy came to parent my cousins in Canada when he was suposed to be in his grave in New Mexico. It all happened pretty quick; less than four years passed between the time Billy first killed a man at seventeen and that bit of business between him and Garrett at Fort Sumner in 1881.

Billy's early life was no *cadeau*, as they say in Quebec. By the time he turned thirteen, his mother, a fine-looking woman with deep lake-blue eyes and luxuriant golden hair, whom he worshipped, was dead of TB. He'd never known his real father and his stepfather had taken off prospecting in Arizona by then. His big brother Joe was addicted to opium. Billy could read and write and, like his Momma, was ambidextrous. His teachers liked him and he could charm the skin off an apple — a talent he parlayed, at age twelve, into a short early career as a song and dance man at a local minstrel show. Like most kids he loved the circus, especially the trapeze artists and tightrope walkers, which didn't stop him from leading the cheering section when they screwed up. What kind of kid was Billy? As one of his friends might have put it: "He was a good kid and all that, but uh-uh."

With his mother in the grave, he bunked in with Sarah Brown, a Canadian who ran the only boarding house in town. To pay for his keep, he took a job washing dishes at the Star Hotel. The owner,

An Oldham tintype, the only
photograph of Billy The Kid to be
generally accepted as genuine.
(Lincoln County Heritage Trust).

Del Truesdell, said, "Henry was the only boy who ever worked there who never stole anything." That didn't stop him from being falsely accused of stealing some clothes and he was arrested for it. He immediately escaped by climbing up the inside of the jail's chimney and lit out for Arizona, possibly in search of his Pa. In the middle of August 1877 he got into a scrape outside a Fort Grant saloon with "Windy" Cahill, a former butcher who'd been razzing him for weeks. Windy got him down and sat on him and in the tussle Henry shot him in the stomach and killed him. The deed done, Billy thought it prudent to head back to New Mexico where he started hanging out at Frank Coe's ranch on the high plain in the south of the territory near Lincoln.

There'd been some trouble in Lincoln County, cattle rustling, shootings and so on. The king of the county was an ex-army quartermaster called L.G. Murphy. Jimmy Dolan, a slight Irish lad about the same age as Billy, was a close personal friend of Mr. Murphy, and about the time Billy arrived, Murphy turned the business over to young Jim. J.J. Dolan & Co. soon had a finger in every pie in Lincoln and was on excellent terms with the commander of the nearby army post at Fort Stanton, a good friend to have.

Also new in town was John Tunstall, an ambitious and naive Englishman in his mid-twenties, lately arrived on the suggestion of a Lincoln lawyer, Alex McSween, whom he met in Santa Fe while looking for a good "investment" in America. John bought some ranch land and started building a general store across the street from the Dolan place. He had steel plate sandwiched between the store's adobe bricks as though he was expecting trouble; perhaps he wasn't so naive after all. Mr. Tunstall planned to get rich. Mr. Dolan planned to kill him. In November the Kid signed on at the Tunstall ranch as a cow hand.

Meanwhile, back in Lincoln, Dolan and McSween were suing each other over this and that. Dolan had the law in his pocket and early in February 1878, Sheriff William Brady attached all

McSween's property and sent a posse to Tunstall's ranch to seize some of McSween's cattle, which he claimed were mixed in with Tunstall's herd. The Brit had his own lawman in tow in the form of his close personal friend, Rob Widenmann, a deputy U.S. Marshall, and the cattle grab was foiled. Still, everyone thought it might be safer in town, so the next day, February 18, Tunstall, Widenmann, Billy and two other hired hands left for Lincoln taking nine horses with them for safekeeping. They didn't know it but Dolan had a new posse on their tail.

Late that afternoon, Billy and a buddy, John Middleton, were riding a quarter of a mile behind the others. Widenmann saw a flock of wild turkeys rise over the brow of a hill and he and a hired hand took off after them, leaving Tunstall alone. At the same time, the Kid and Middleton heard shots and saw the posse coming at them full tilt. They rode up hell for leather to Tunstall, Middleton shouting, "Follow me, for God's sake." Apparently confused, Tunstall stayed where he was and seconds later, one of the posse, Buck Morton, put a bullet through his heart and another shot him in the head for good measure. The Kid and the rest of them took cover behind some boulders but didn't get off a single shot. With Tunstall dead the posse left them alone. Mission accomplished.

So how's Billy making out so far? He was a cocky kid, no doubt about it, maybe even a bit of a smartass, but people liked him. Sure he shot that windbag Cahill, but folks said Cahill was asking for it. We do know that he was short, five-foot-seven, and that he was a fresh-faced, buck-toothed lad who looked even younger than he was. He had good hand-eye coordination with either hand, thanks to his momma's ambidextrous genes. He loved to gamble and could palm cards left- or right-handed. I went to high school with a kid named Robbie Hines with a similar knack. Robbie put himself through college playing mostly hearts, poker and sometimes bridge. He was a little guy too, and a hell of a bowler, a great golfer, a scrapper, sure, but charming. He was the first one in our crowd to get laid. In the 1950s, when nice girls wouldn't even let you touch their breasts without squawking, that was some doing. He did it in the back of his father's Oldsmobile, which also impressed us — our fathers wouldn't even let us drive. Riding around with him the next night in the same car, Ronnie said it was ten thousand times better than whacking off. "Holy shit," sighed my buddy Pete Dram. He spoke for all of us. Ever wonder about reincarnation? I do quite often. If Billy the Kid came back I bet he'd be somebody like Robbie Hines. Come to think of it, maybe Robbie was closer to Billy than that. He was born in 1940 – Billy would have been 81 at the time. Old, but perhaps not too old...

Back in Lincoln on the night of February 18, 1878, forty or fifty men gathered at the Tunstall store — farmers and Mexicans armed to the *dentes*, enraged that Tunstall, the man they hoped would liberate them from Dolan's grasping ways, had been so brazenly murdered. At first light, John Newcomb, who had a farm close to where the killing took place, rode out to bring the corpse in. He found Tunstall in some trees with his head resting on a folded blanket. Beside him lay his horse with a bullet hole in the forehead and Tunstall's hat under his head like a pillow. Ha, ha, very funny. But nobody was laughing.

The same day, McSween, who knew just what a flexible thing the law could be, had the Justice of the Peace issue affidavits against the Dolan posse. The town constable was ordered, under threat of death, to serve the warrant. Billy Bonney — time for the Kid to try a new name — and another of Tunstall's cowboys, Fred Waite, were sworn in as deputies and the three of them presented themselves at Dolan's store to serve the warrant. Jimmy's friend, Sheriff Brady, in the company of a platoon of soldiers sent over from the fort to keep the peace, said the warrants were no good because the killers were members of a legal posse and promptly arrested all three and marched them off to jail. The Kid had just had a lesson in the law of the land and he didn't like what he'd learned. He didn't like the sheriff much either.

Rob Widenmann, using his clout as a Deputy Marshall, managed to get them released. Immediately Billy and Dick Brewer, together with Fred Waite and other Tunstall-McSween supporters, formed The Regulators, whose plan was, roughly speaking, to kill everyone who had been in the posse that murdered Tunstall. A couple of weeks later they chased down three posse members and each of them ended up with nine bullets in them. On April 1, Sheriff Brady and one of his deputies were gunned down in the middle of Lincoln's only street in a rain of bullets from behind a wall. The Kid happened to be behind the wall at the time. A few days later the Regulators came across "Buckshot" Roberts, yet another posse member, and let him have it in a fracas at Blazer's Mill. Roberts was no softie and before it was over he had taken out Dick Brewer with a bullet through the eye from one hundred and twenty-five yards, a bit of shooting that's still talked about. The war was well and truly underway.

News that things were a bit dicey in Lincoln County began to spread to the outside world — indictments and arrests were flying like cow flap in a gulf hurricane. The U.S. Justice Department sent out a man called Frank Angel to check it out. After a brief investigation it was clear he favoured the McSween side and for a while, in the late Spring of 1879, things appeared to be going the Regulators' way. It didn't last. With the renewed backing of the army, Dolan put together a new gang and by July 15, Billy and the rest of the boys were holed up in the McSween house in Lincoln with the Dolan gang outside taking pot shots at them. For the next couple of days a lot of firing went on back and forth. On July 19, the army rolled into town with thirty-five men, a Gatling gun, two thousand rounds of ammunition and a twelve-pound howitzer.

Around nine o'clock that night the soldiers torched the house and picked the men off as they dashed for cover. Five were killed, including Alex McSween. Billy and four of his buddies managed to sneak out along the garden wall in their stocking feet and escaped in the dark. The next day the Tunstall store was looted and the remnants of the Regulators were being hunted down like rats.

What did Billy think? That the world was unfair; that the war was over and the bad guys won. Run for your life, Billy.

Late summer and early fall, there were several gangs around the New Mexican Territory stealing cattle and horses and harassing the citizens and Billy's name kept cropping up. Billy considered himself a gambler by profession. Lady Luck could be fickle, he admitted, and sometimes it was necessary to "borrow" a few horses or steers to get your stake back.

Lincoln Country was getting lots of national press by this time, all of it bad. Even President Hayes got into the act and ordered the new Governor, Civil War general Lew Wallace, who was immersed in writing his epic *Ben-Hur: A tale of Christ,* to do something about it. Wallace, looking for a quick fix so he could get back to his novel, declared an amnesty for all parties in the conflict and Billy and his buddies returned to Lincoln. Sue McSween, the gutsy — and some say wanton — wife of dead Alex, had taken control of her husband's affairs and was suing all and sundry through her new lawyer, Huston Chapmann. He was so successful at relieving the pressure that a year to the day after Tunstall's death, The Regulators felt comfortable enough to make up with Dolan's crew in drunken celebration, which ended abruptly only two hours later when Chapmann was gunned down by one of Dolan's men. All hell broke out and a week later Governor Wallace himself was obliged to set aside his pen and come down to Lincoln from Santa Fe to try to keep the lid on.

He was in Lincoln for a couple of weeks and actually met with Billy and offered him a pardon in exchange for testifying at lawyer Chapmann's murder trial. To make it appear legit, Billy was to be arrested for his other crimes and pardoned after he testified. Accordingly, he was placed under house arrest at the home of Juan Patron, one of Lincoln's leading citizens. Garrett said later they had a high old time there, eating and drinking and playing cards with anyone who would drop by for a game. But after three months with no sign that the Chapmann trial would ever take place, he

John Henry Tunstall beleived
Lincoln County would make him
very rich, not very dead.
(Fred Nolan)

got tired of waiting and simply walked out of Patron's house, climbed on a horse and headed out of town. He was soon back in Sumner with his old friends, gambling, rustling and sleeping with Mexican girls.

Most of the cattle the boys were rustling belonged to John Chisum, a big rancher who was tolerant of the activity — to a degree. Chisum had been playing both sides against the middle in the whole Lincoln County mess. Early in January, 1880, after some discussion between Billy and Chisum's cousin Jim about altered cattle brands, the two men repaired to Bob Hargrove's saloon in Sumner for a drink. When a Texan threatened to kill Chisum, mistaking him for John, the Kid put three bullets under his chin in a space you could cover with a half dollar. It was a love-hate thing with the Chisum family. Earlier in the year our Billy had stuck the same pistol in John's mouth and trotted him around another Sumner bar. Billy thought John should pay him three hundred dollars for the work he did on behalf of Tunstall and McSween. John thought not.

Time went by slowly for Billy in 1880. That hot and lazy summer he hung out with Jim's daughter Sallie. Writing about an evening that July in *The Collected Works of Billy The Kid,* Michael Ondaatje put the couple together on the porch at the Chisum ranch on a dusty, starlit evening — and they weren't alone. John Chisum was there and so was a woman called Angela — and who should be sleeping on the sofa but Billy's old pal, Pat Garrett. Around four in the morning, too drunk to pee straight, an amorous Angela climbed on Billy while he was sitting on the can. Billy tried to be quiet while they made love so as not to wake Sallie, whose room was next to the outhouse.

By the time November rolled around, circumstances had changed. Billy was still looking for his pardon from the governor, whose mind was now decidedly elsewhere. *Ben-Hur* had been published to good reviews in the *New York Times* and he was busy lobbying Washington for a more salubrious posting. By that time,

Pat Garrett, taken in Roswell,
New Mexico, 1887. The only
thing that's absolutely certain
about his relationship with Billy
is that he was six feet four
inches tall, eight inches taller
than The Kid — that's the long
and short of it.
(University of New Mexico)

John Chisum had Pat Garrett installed as the Lincoln sheriff with instructions to "clean out that squad east of Sumner," meaning mostly Billy.

At the end of the month, a posse organized by Garrett cornered the gang at a ranch owned by "Whiskey Jim" Greathouse. During the melee, blacksmith Jimmy Carlyle was killed. The credit for the killing went unfairly to the Kid, who ended up again escaping after dark on foot. On December 12, Billy wrote another letter to the governor, this one giving his version of the latest goings-on — including that of the Carlyle killing — and laying his troubles at the feet of John Chisum who, he wrote, "was benefitted Thousands by it [the Lincoln County War] and is now doing all he can against me." He concluded that if an impartial examination of the events were made, the result would be "far different from the impression put out by Chisum and his Tools." For Billy, the biggest tool of all was Pat Garrett, the new sheriff.

About the time he penned the letter, Garrett got wind that the band would come to Fort Sumner so gang member Charles Bowdre could visit his wife, Manuela. Garrett arrived at the Bowdre residence first and gagged Mrs. B. and tied her to a chair and the posse waited in the shadows for the boys to show. It was snowing hard and difficult to see. Five riders loomed out of the storm and the whole posse started firing. Four of the riders reined up and disappeared back into the driven snow. Tom O'Folliard was hit in the stomach and dragged into the house to die, which he did soon enough, bad talking a card-playing Garrett to the end.

Four days later, on December 23, the posse tracked Billy and the rest of them to an old adobe at Stinking Springs and surrounded it at three in the morning. They shot and killed Charley Bowdre the following morning when he came out wearing Billy's hat to feed the horses and, after an all-day stand-off, the Kid and two other members of the gang gave themselves up. They were taken, under heavy guard, to Las Vegas, New Mexico and put on a train for Sante Fe. Billy was a celebrity by then. At every stop along the

Jimmy Dolan (seated), the eventual victor in the Lincoln Country War. With him is Bob Olinger, one of the men Billy killed during his famous escape from the Lincoln Courthouse. (Robert McCubbin)

way the town folk came down to the station to get a look.

Billy wrote to Wallace four times over the next three months, still looking for the promised pardon, but Wallace, who lived just down the street from the jail in the Governor's Palace, never replied. On April 13, Billy was convicted of killing Sheriff William Brady and sentenced to be hanged in Lincoln a month later. He was taken to Lincoln and turned over to Garrett, where he was held on the second floor of the old Dolan headquarters which now housed the jail and courthouse. The irony was not lost on Billy.

A week after that, on April 28, Garrett put Bob Olinger in charge of the prisoner and went to White Oakes, rumour had it to buy wood for the gallows. Around noon Billy, still in leg irons but affable as always, was playing cards with deputy Jim Bell while Olinger took the other inmates across the street to the Wortley Hotel for lunch. Billy said he had to take a leak so Bell walked him out to the outhouse. After doing his business, Billy hustled back ahead of Bell, leg irons and all, and by the time Bell reached the foot of the stairs Billy was at the top and he had a gun. Bell panicked and turned to run back outside and Billy shot him, with some regret — he had nothing against him; he was just in the wrong place at the wrong time. Bell staggered outside and died in the arms of Geoffrey Gauss, who lived next door and had come running when he heard the shots. Bob Olinger also heard firing and came running from the hotel across the street. Unlike Bell, there was no love lost between the two men and Billy dropped him with a single shot from an upstairs window. With both his guards dead and half the town sympathetic to his cause, Billy could afford to take his time. He sent Gauss for a horse and set to work on his shackles with a prospecting pick. It was slow going and about an hour later with one ankle still locked up, he rode out of Lincoln on a borrowed horse, promising to return the steed. Three days later the horse returned to Lincoln on its own.

Though few knew what he looked like, Billy was as famous in

sallie Chisum, John Chisum's neice,
numbered Billy among her many
admirers. He gave her two candy
hearts in 1878.
(Chaves County Historical society)

his way as Elvis would be a hundred years later. He was regularly reported to be hiding out everywhere from Mescalero Station to Memphis. Then, late in the day on July 14, 1881 he rode into Sumner to call on Pauline Maxwell. Garrett was waiting for him. We've come full circle.

In retrospect, however, July 14, 1881 was perhaps not the most significant day in Billy's life. A case could be made to give December 10, 1880, that honour. That was the blustery day in New York City when Clarence Darling, riding down Broadway in his carriage, read a short item in the *Times* with a Las Vegas, New Mexico Territory by-line which described a desperate cuss called Billy Bonney (aka Henry Antrim, aka Billy The Kid). What caught Mr. Darling's eye was the rough sketch captioned "A lawless murderer." The cocky face that stared back at him was the spitting image of himself. As the elegant carriage jerked and bumped over the frozen streets, a chill surged up Mr. Darling's spine and grabbed him by the throat. He knew in an instant, beyond all doubt, that this boy whom the paper described as a thief, a gambler, a rustler and a remorseless killer of as many as seventeen men, was his son, the fruit of his union with Catherine McCaty, the Irish chambermaid with whom he had fallen deeply in love at age nineteen and whom his father had forced into the streets when their affair — and her pregnancy — was discovered. He still hated his father for it. He hadn't thought of another woman for five years afterwards and another five had passed before he married Jennifer Watts, an entirely suitable young lady, if conventional, whose parents owned a palatial brownstone on the corner of Fifth Avenue and 17th.

By the time Clarence Darling arrived at his Wall Street office, he had relived the most passionate moments of his life — that gorgeous spring of 1860. Her smell, the pale softness of her breasts, the first time they lay together on the linen sheets in his parents' bedroom, the way she held him, her silver laugh, the poetry of her voice. He ached for her still. And he knew their son could ruin him.

The Darlings of County Cork were among the first Irish to come to New York, not ten years after the Revolution. They'd prospered first in furs and then in timber. By the time Clarence came along, the family had moved into textiles and was said to own "half of Manchester and most of Lowell, Massachusetts." It delighted his father to boast that his mills had ruined the British woollen industry. An exaggeration, but not much of one, and an Irishman in New York had to take what pleasure he could in his own accomplishments. Money alone was nearly enough for an Irish Catholic to gain entry into Manhattan's best circles — but not quite. His father entertained lavishly and contributed to all the charities, but when he died of heart failure in 1861, largely from the pleasures of food and drink, he rated only a tenth of a column in the *Times*. Clarence, who did not attend the funeral, had inherited his father's urge for social acceptance at the very highest levels and was intent on achieving the respectability that had eluded his old man.

Grieving for Catherine had focused his mind on business. At the tender age of twenty-three he was one of just twelve New York financiers who met with President Lincoln to map out a plan for financing the Civil War. He celebrated the North's victory by becoming an Episcopalian, and moved into manufacturing and railways. He was, at this very moment, the principal backer of the rail line which was pushing west through New Mexico. It was an enormously costly and risky venture. He was a gambler by nature and had staked everything on the success of the Western Railway, including the mortgage on his new Park Avenue mansion where he lived with his bride of less than a year, now four months pregnant, and which he had financed out of the twenty-seven million stake, much of which had been put up by the banks and investors in the railway. It would not be a good time for it to come out that his bastard son was the most wanted killer in the very territory the rail lines were traversing.

More dangerous, he immediately recognized, was the skein of

topsy-turvy emotions the face in the paper had released in his own heart. He loved Catherine still. He imagined finding her, making love to her again, even bringing her to New York and installing her in one of those new apartments that were going up around the new park.

By the time he rode the new elevator — built in Brooklyn by the Darling Electric Lifting Device Company — to his eighth-floor office, he had the beginnings of a plan. Newspaper reporters were notorious liars, he knew from bitter experience. Billy was still practically a child. The editors would say anything to sell papers and the idea of a villainous boy running amok and shooting people was like money in the bank. "I'm going to find out the truth about my boy," he whispered as he settled in behind the big carved mahogany desk, raised the black porcelain cup with the gold Darling crest and took his first sip of morning coffee.

He began by scribbling a wire to a friend in the Justice Department in Washington, asking for any information he might have on the recent events in Lincoln County, particularly with reference to the individuals involved as might have pertinence to the progress of the rail lines. That afternoon he had a reply referring him to Frank Warner Angel, who was assistant District Attorney for the Eastern District of New York but whose former job had been special investigator for the department in Lincoln County. Darling immediately sent him a message inviting him to dinner at his club.

After an excellent meal of lobster bisque, perch amandine, roast partridge and T-bone steaks of pampered western beef, the two men retired to the appropriately named Lincoln Room for brandy and cigars. Angel told him how Tunstall had been murdered; the McSween house torched; and of the gang warfare that had ravaged the county two years before and still continued in fits and starts.

"Where do your sympathies lie?" asked Darling as the waiter brought a third round of snifters.

"I don't have to tell you, Mr. Darling, that matters like these always come down to politics. A group of men in Santa Fe called

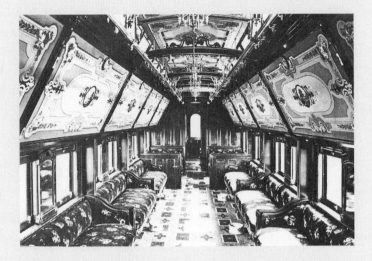

A private railcar similar to the one in which Richard Darling met with cowboy detective Charles Siringo and Pat Garrett at Lamy, New Mexico, in the spring of 1881.

The Ring control pretty much everything that happens in the territory. You probably know them." Darling nodded. Know them! It had cost him almost a hundred thousand dollars in quiet money to get the rail rights-of-way in the territory.

"Tunstall and McSween were both foreigners," Angel continued. "The lawyer came from Toronto, Canada, and Tunstall was a Brit. Tunstall was dead when I got there but I found McSween a decent guy. Way out of his depth, though."

"Did you ever run into anyone called Henry McCarty?"

"Don't recall the name," said Angel.

"He also called himself Henry or William Antrim. I believe he would have been about seventeen at the time."

"Oh, you mean Billy," laughed Angel. "The one they're about to hang. No, never met him. Tough little bugger by all accounts. But he must have had something going for himself; everyone liked him — even the other side. 'Course in one way there weren't any sides. One day they'd be shooting at each other and the next day they'd be playing cards or stealing cows together. He was one of Tunstall's cowboys who escaped from the McSween house the night the army burned it down. The whole operation stank to high heaven. Between you and me, Justice didn't want to touch it. They buried my report and gave me a promotion. You've gotta learn to roll with the punches, right, Mr. Darling? Billy, yes, they say he got away in his stocking feet. Gutsy thing to do with thirty-five soldiers shooting at you."

Clarence Darling walked home from the club that night. He needed fresh air and time to think. Images of the McSween house flamed in his head.

"Poor, poor lad," he muttered as he climbed into the four-poster beside his sleeping wife.

"What, dear?" asked a sleepy Jennifer.

"I've got to go out to Santa Fe," he said.

"Promise to tell me all about it at breakfast," she whispered, fastening her small hands around his neck.

"I promise," he sighed, but they did not breakfast together. He was at the office before seven. He spent the first hour trying to locate a Charlie Siringo, a detective of sorts, recommended by Angel as someone on the ground who might help. As it turned out, he didn't locate him until the day after Christmas in Las Vegas and by then Billy was in custody after the shoot-out with Garrett at Stinking Springs. His wire to Siringo read: "Will pay for information Henry Antrim and company." Siringo's return read: "Garrett jailed Antrim Santa Fe. Trial March. Send $10." The ten dollars went out via Western Union with this message: "Meet me Lamy station, Feb 28 9:00 pm. Bring Garrett." And the reply: "Meeting OK: Siringo $100. Garrett $50." And Darling's: "Done."

Business — and social events, since it was the height of the 1881 season in New York— required his presence in Manhattan until after Valentine's Day. His secretary located a freight train that could accommodate his private car, leaving New York on February 17. He arranged to meet some backers in Chicago on February 20 and 21. If he left Chicago on the evening of the twenty-second he should be at Lamy, fourteen miles south of Sante Fe, by the twenty-eighth, even allowing for the unexpected. Anything from an early spring thaw to a late winter storm, to buffalo on the tracks, to coal shortages, floods, fire and holdups were expected. Nearly anything else could happen to add days to the twenty-five hundred mile trip. He recalled the time he was stuck in Dodge City for eight days because a hundred miles of track west of the city, laid by another line, were a smaller gauge and the line's single train was busy hauling coal. It had taken him most of the following year lobbying other owners — and his friends in D.C. — to establish national track standards.

The trip arranged, he wired Governor Lew Wallace, whom he'd met during the trial of the traitors who murdered Abe Lincoln. Wallace, a major general of volunteers during the war, had served on the military tribunal reviewing the assassination. Wallace wrote back, filling him in on the general lawlessness that plagued the counties south of the capital. He said he had met young Henry Antrim, now more commonly known as Billy Bonney, in Lincoln a couple of years before, and that now he was in jail awaiting trial on several murder charges. He did not mention Billy's pardon or the letters he'd received. He continued: "I thought for a few months when I was first sent out here that I could solve the Lincoln County War in imitation of Solomon. Alas, the task of determining on which side justice smiled was beyond my powers and I ended by being more of a Pontius Pilate, I fear. I met many of the people involved. Some were undoubtedly scoundrels, and a few were possibly saints. I know the lad feels he's been wronged. In that, he is undoubtedly correct. I may have had a hand in it myself, but who is there among us who has not, at one time or another, been dealt with unfairly? History rolls on making victims or heroes of us all." He concluded: "Please understand, Mr. Darling, it is a serpent's nest here in this modest capital and the Governor's Palace is so placed to be at the centre of that writhing mass of vipers. Most of my time is spent ensuring that I am not bitten. When not so employed, I am occupied writing a novel about a freed slave which takes place at the time of Christ. It takes me away, for a few hours at a time, from this hell hole, and gives me peace."

In a short note, Darling thanked the governor for his consideration and reminded him of the significance of the railway to the territory's economic well-being. He continued: "The matter of this Henry Antrim is receiving an untoward amount of publicity in the east. The press seems all agog about the misadventures of the boy they call Billy the Kid. Accounts in the press which highlight lawlessness in the territory have an unsettling effect on investors." In closing, he mused on the importance of timing in all things and suggested that as a student of history, the governor must have read Cicero's account of the killing of Julius Caesar, "in which he writes that there were many powerful men in Rome who would have preferred it if Caesar had been killed several weeks after the Ides of March, once the spring plantings were in, in early May." He closed by wishing Wallace every success with his book and even lied about looking forward to reading it — he had never read a novel in his life — the author having played such a determining role in the freeing of America's slaves.

Darling's train pulled into Lamy station at four in the afternoon on the last day of February 1881. It had been an arduous trip, with a blizzard in Pennsylvania and flooding of the Ohio River that was so severe there was concern for the bridge at Cincinnati. Lamy didn't look like much from the train window. The only building of note besides the station was the new hotel across the way. It was a grand affair, built of stone and containing what he had been told was the longest marble bar west of the Mississippi. He would have liked to go over for a drink, but he feared his appearance was so close to Billy's he didn't dare risk it. His last trip had been seven years ago, around the time, he mused, that Catherine had died. Siringo had found out that much, that the light of his life and mother of his son had died of TB in Silver City in September 1874.

On the high ridges of the Sangre de Cristo mountains, the sun was turning the late spring snow a golden pink that gradually thickened and darkened to the colour of blood. He sent Matthew, his steward, over to the bar for ice and the *Santa Fe New Mexican* and any other territorial papers he could find. He then sent two wires, one to his wife in New York telling her he loved her dearly and was counting the days until his return, and another to the money men in Chicago saying he had arrived successfully "with ten cars of merchandise which will sell for six times what it would fetch in Chicago." He was referring to a new scheme in which the railway was setting up a string of general stores across the west. The merchants in Chicago, he hoped, would be prime backers.

Matthew showed Siringo and Garrett into the dining room of the private car a little after nine. Both men had obviously had a few drinks before they arrived. Charley Siringo shook hands, saying: "Pleased to meet you, sir. Had dinner across the street. Thought we might see you there. This here's Pat Garrett." He laughed nervously.

The man who met them in no way resembled the railroad tycoon Clarence Darling. Clarence had spent days planning his disguise and over an hour applying it. The gas lights in the car were purposely turned low. Clarence Darling was fair and clean shaven but the dark moustache of the man drooped over a heavy beard to entirely cover his mouth. He wore pince-nez glasses and had a ruddy complexion. Afterwards, Siringo remarked to Garrett that Darling "looked a hell of a lot like the governor." Clarence, at five feet six inches, was an inch shorter than his son and was taken aback by Garrett's size.

"Mr. Garrett," he said, shaking hands, "I'm sure I'm not the first to be impressed by your height. You have almost a foot on me, I would guess."

"I'm impressed with this car of yours. Never seen anything quite so grand, Mr...."

"Middleton," put in Clarence Darling, repeating the pseudonym he'd been using with Siringo, "Scott Middleton." He motioned them to sit at a round table draped with a heavy red velvet cloth with tassels which hung to the floor. Matthew silently set down a silver tray which held a silver ice bucket, a bottle of rye, a bottle of brandy and three heavy cutglass goblets. Darling poured them each a healthy shot of rye and a couple of fingers of brandy for himself.

"To success," he toasted. "I'll get right to the point. I represent Eastern and European interests who wish to acquire information and likenesses of those involved in the Lincoln County War. The only thing I'm at liberty to say is that it has to do with large investments made in the territory some years ago which are now before the courts." He had thought carefully about how to approach the subject of taking pictures of Billy out of circulation and had decided, in the end, to be direct and to say as little as possible about the reasons in order to avoid suspicions. Perhaps he needn't have worried.

"How much are these here interests willing to pay?" came back Siringo at once.

"One hundred dollars apiece for each picture."

"I know half of 'em and the other half are dead. Diggin' up information and findin' pictures of 'em can't be too tough," said Siringo.

"If your interests are so anxious, maybe they'd pay a little more," said Garrett.

This was something Darling liked to hear. Garrett was on board. Now that all they were talking about was money, he was on familiar ground.

"Takes some men two months to earn a hundred dollars, Mr. Garrett. Takes some four months. Some never have it all in one piece. We're offering a hundred dollars for each photograph and up to five hundred for Spanish land grant documents." He paused. "Another thing, if you can find every last one of the likenesses of the gang leader, Billy Bonney, there's a two thousand dollar bonus in it."

Siringo let out a low whistle. Darling ignored it and looked straight at the sheriff and said, "How much did you get for bringing the Bonney gang in, Mr. Garrett?"

"We'll see when it's done," replied Garrett. Darling knew he'd touched a sore point.

"Mr. Middleton, you've got yourself a deal," said Siringo. He extended his hand across the table but Darling didn't take it. Instead he rose and stepped around to the back of Siringo's chair. "Now I've got a couple of matters to discuss with Mr. Garrett." Siringo made no move to leave. "Privately, sir," said Darling.

The detective shuffled to his feet, looking hurt. "You forgetting something?" he spit out.

"Your fee for tonight," said Darling, handing him an envelope from his inside coat pocket. "I'll see you out." He walked Siringo to the end of the richly decorated rail car, a hushed museum of red and gold with the dark brocaded curtains closely drawn. "I'm grateful to you, Mr. Siringo, for all your help. You understand that it's necessary to deal separately with Mr. Garrett. The law always has to think it has the inside track. I know I can count on your complete discretion. No one is ever to hear of these arrangements. Am I clear?"

A deflated Charlie Siringo nodded and pulled his hat down. Darling continued, "Frank Angel told me you could be trusted. I'm not so sure about Mr. Garrett. Keep an eye on him for me if you would. There's two hundred a month in it for you. I'll expect weekly reports in New York."

Siringo perked up at this. "You can count on me, Mr. Middleton," he said with a half smile and extended his hand again. This time Darling took it and clapped the man on the back as though they'd been friends for years. The cowboy detective stepped down into the clear, cold New Mexican night and picked his way carefully across the tracks toward the lighted bar. Clarence slipped into the toilet and checked his appearance in the gilt mirror before returning to the car where Garrett lounged with his long legs jutting out from under the table.

"I've been following your exploits, Mr. Garrett. You're a famous man. You've made the New York papers. There are a few things I'd like to ask you about this William Bonney." Darling reseated himself at the table and topped up Garrett's glass. "The first one is, why didn't you kill him at Stinking Springs? I'm sure you had the chance."

The sheriff of Lincoln was taken aback but flattered. The liquor and the elegant surroundings were loosening him up. He took a long slow pull on his drink. "You want to know the truth?" he said finally. "Fact is I planned to kill him but I got Charley Bowdre instead. He was wearing Billy's hat when he came out to feed the horses and I mistook him. Then Billy and me got to talking, shouting back and forth, and by the time he gave himself up late in the day, four o'clock, the killing urge had gone right out of me."

"How well did you know him?"

"Oh, I knew him. Billy and me raised hell up in Sumner more than once. When we were on a tear they used to call us the long and short of it, 'count of the difference in our heights."

Darling felt himself relax for the first time and smiled, "What kind of lad is he?"

"He's not a bad kid. Can be a lot of fun. Wild, goes without saying. Loyal though. He's stood by his true friends. You want to have him on your side in a fight."

"But he's not on your side."

"I guess he's not. Not now." He parted the curtains for a moment and gazed out into the silence and the moonlit grasslands dotted with sage bushes. "Out here in the last few years we've all been on every side. Mostly we've been out for ourselves. The Territory isn't like other places yet. You can still do pretty much as you please. It tests a man. What most of us choose is whatever looks best at the time. No different with Billy."

"Is he a killer?"

"We're all killers, Mr. Middleton," he said in a matter-of-fact tone. "What was it you want to say to me you didn't want Charley to hear?" He took another sip from the crystal glass and examined it carefully before he slowly laid it down.

"It's not only about the photographs. I'm sure a man like you knew that," Darling flattered him again. Then he leaned forward and placed both hands flat on the table in front of him and said in a low voice, "I want Billy Bonney out of jail and out of the country." Billy had often said he'd head south given half a chance and Darling knew the sheriff would assume he was talking about Mexico.

Garrett leaned back in his chair and laughed, "You and half the Territory. It ain't going to happen."

"Yes it is, sir. And you're the one who's going to make it happen."

"You think so, huh?"

"Yes."

"I'm listening," he said, looking directly into Darling's eyes for the first time.

"The trial's coming up in April."

"March."

"Don't be surprised if it's April."

"If you say so."

"Billy's escaped often. Let him escape again. Before the trial."

"Couldn't do that, Mr. Middleton. Even if I had jurisdiction, which I don't, I wouldn't. Cost me some trouble to bring him in and he's going to go to trial."

"And if he's convicted?"

"When, not if. He's up on two counts. If they don't get him for Roberts they sure as hell will for Bill Brady. They'll turn him over to me to take back to Lincoln to hang."

"I expect that's when he'll escape, then. Before you get a chance to hang him."

"Don't seem very likely."

"Then fix it so you're not around," said Darling, very serious. "There's five thousand in it for you."

Garrett poured himself another drink. The gas light guttered.

"Deliver him at a time and a place I name and there's another ten thousand."

"My, but you do want that boy, Mr. Middleton."

"We would prefer him not to go to trial. Twenty-five thousand if you can fix it."

"Can't be done."

"In Lincoln then."

"You do make an offer, don't you, Mr. Middleton."

"What did John Chisum pay you to bring him in?"

"Nothing I care to speak of, sir."

"Suppose Bonney didn't escape. Suppose you killed him. And suppose after that he got on a train and went straight to hell. What then, Mr. Garrett?"

"Just suppose..." said Garrett slowly. After a long silence, Darling offered Garrett a cigar. The two men smoked together for another ten minutes before Garrett left to join Siringo in the bar. Darling watched the glow of the cigar as the tall figure turned into shadow.

March 1881 was a dreary one in New York. Clarence arrived back on the Tuesday before the St. Patrick's Day and was glad to have an excuse — work pressure after being away so long — to beg off riding in his carriage in the parade. Jennifer pouted at first, she had looked forward to dressing up and sitting beside him while the crowds on Fifth Avenue admired them, but when it came, the day was so foul and wretched with driving rain and sleet that she forgave him. Toward the end of the month he received a packet from Charlie Siringo. It contained eleven pictures, including shots of Dick Brewer, Tom O'Folliard, Fred Waits and Dirty Dave Rudabaugh and one of Billy which he said he'd "gotten off a Mexican señorita who put up quite a battle for it." There was also a packet of ancient land grants written on parchment. Clarence Darling laid the photographs out on his desk and pondered the lives of the men whose eyes stared back at him. O'Folliard, he knew, had been a close friend of Billy's. Most of them were dead or in prison waiting to be hanged. They looked so young and, to his eyes, surprisingly innocent.

The day he got news that Billy had been acquitted of the first murder charge, April 6, he received a letter from Garrett saying that he had enjoyed their meeting and that he looked favourably on the arrangements they had discussed. He said he expected "the party" to be in town roughly from mid-April until mid-May and that he should plan his visit for that period. He also enclosed a photograph of Billy with his arms around two women. "Couldn't tolerate the thought of Charlie finding this and taking a hundred dollars from you," he wrote. On the back he'd scribbled, "Billy with Pauline Maxwell and her mother, Marie Beaudoin Maxwell. Ft. Sumner, 1880." Darling immediately made arrangements to travel west once again.

He planned another stop in Chicago, this time to sign the deal on the general stores. The train pulling the Darling car left New York on April 15, the same day the *Times* carried a story at the bottom of page eleven recording the conviction of one William "Billy the Kid" Bonney for the murder of Sheriff William Brady. There was no accompanying sketch. An editorial in the same paper prayed that this trial would "close the book on one of the most lawless and shameful chapters in the history of the Republic." It noted that in recent years "settlers in the West have had as much to fear from roving bands of murderers of their own kind as from the terror of blood-thirsty savages whose cruel acts are more easily understood in that they are perpetrated in defense of land and family."

By April 21, Darling's train was west of Chicago, making good time toward Kansas City. On the twenty-second, a hundred miles west of St. Louis, it ran into one of the worst spring storms of the century. When the train finally limped into the Oklahoma capital, it was April 29. A wire was waiting for Darling, forwarded from New York. It was included with the local newspapers and a stack of business dispatches which Matthew brought him on a silver tray as he breakfasted. It read: "Bird flown. Must catch. Please advise. Garrett." The headline on the Kansas City Post-Dispatch blazed: "Kid Kills Two, Escapes."

His first reaction was one of relief. The boy had escaped. But the killings. Blessed Jesus, what could it mean? He had convinced himself of the boy's innocence. He thought of him only as a victim of circumstance. How could Garrett mess up like this? More blood. His first instinct was to continue on to New Mexico. But Billy could be on the loose for months. It had taken Garrett forever to catch him last time. And this time he might really kill him, deal or no deal. Something had to be done now. But what? He pulled an envelope from an inside pocket and spread out the three ferrotypes of Billy he had received and stared at them as though he expected the boy to give him the answer — and, in a way, he did. Darling idly flipped over the group shot of Billy and the two women and read Garrett's caption again. "Billy with Pauline Maxwell and her mother, Marie Beaudoin Maxwell. Ft. Sumner, 1880." Marie Beaudoin Maxwell. Obviously the mother of one of Billy's girlfriends, yet something had been niggling at him since he first saw her. Suddenly it clicked. He knew her! It was Marie Beaudoin, the sister of Jean-Marc Beaudoin, the lawyer who handled his affairs in Canada. He remembered being introduced to her at a partner's meeting Jean-Marc had hosted on a ship in the harbour five or six years earlier. They'd danced together. She was charming. A flurry of wires confirmed that Jean-Marc's sister had married and that she was living in Fort Sumner. Three days later, enroute back to New York, he had a telegram confirming that she was that Marie and that she would do whatever she could to help.

The plan was simple. Clarence would arrange for a private car to pick Billy up in Las Vegas, that being the closest rail line, and bring him to New York. The mother and daughter were sure they could convince him to do it. And that was that. Except for Garrett.

He'd been quick to claim credit for Billy's escape and the five thousand dollars had been duly transferred to him through a couple of phony bank accounts in Santa Fe. Now he wanted the big money for delivering Billy. "My reputation is taking a terrible beating since he got away," he wrote to Darling. "While he was in custody I tried once or twice to tell him how I could help him get out of the jam but he wouldn't listen. He spent most of the time telling me he was innocent. Just bad circumstances, he said. He near had me believing him. But for all I did for him, and our friendship and all, he never opened his heart to me. I wasn't surprised about him killing Olinger. He hated Billy and said so to his face. In his place I might have done the same. He didn't have to kill Bell, though. Bell liked him, they played cards together near every waking hour. Maybe I should count myself lucky to be five thousand ahead and get rid of him for good."

By now it was well into June and as the days went by Darling was increasingly nervous about Billy's chances of surviving. Siringo was as good as his word and kept him up to date on Garrett's whereabouts. "Billy's hiding out around Sumner, mark my word," read his June 15 report. "Garrett's lost his nerve. He's got good contacts all over the county and must know where Billy is. Seems something's holding him back."

Marie Beaudoin had Garrett to dinner the first time he came up to Sumner in the early part of the month and again on June 22, the shortest night of the year. After sweet potatoes and a few slices of the meat pie she was famous for, the two sat out on the veranda. In the long twilight, as the heat slowly died and the first cool night breezes blew in off the river, she told him what he must do to earn his ten thousand dollars.

"Billy's going to be visiting Pauline for Bastille Day," she explained, "That's July 14, a big day for us Frenchies." She laughed and tapped Garrett on the knee. "They'll be right here in the living room and you're going to sneak in here alone and shoot him dead. Except it's not him you're going to shoot, it's Charley Bowdre, who you already killed last December." And she tapped him again on the knee and laughed louder than the first time.

And that's how it happened. Charley's body had been dumped on his wife's doorstep the day they brought the gang in. The ground was frozen and they couldn't bury him. She washed his wounds and dressed him in his best suit and laid him out in the ice house. Every couple of weeks she'd go in and sit with him and in the spring she couldn't bear to give the body up. Nobody pressed her and in June the corpse was still lying peacefully in cold storage, fresh as the day Charley died. Around ten o'clock on the night of July 14, three Mexicans delivered what appeared to be a large sack of grain to the back door of the Maxwell kitchen. Marie and Pauline dragged it into the bedroom, dressed Charley in Billy's clothes and sat him in a chair near the door. Just before midnight, Pat stormed in and shot the face off the corpse. By that time Billy was fifty miles north of there, slipping onto a rail car on a siding

Place Jacques Cartier in Montreal showing the offices of the Darling Electric Lifting Device Company (top) in 1912. The man in the fedora in the foreground is believed to be Billy Darling.

in Las Vegas for the long trip to New York, the town where he was born.

Did Billy and his father have a tearful meeting in Manhattan? I never heard one way or another but my second cousin Penny Gossage, of whom I am very fond, told Aunt Willy that as an old man Billy liked to tell his grandchildren — who called him Grandpa-with-the-sticks because he used two canes — what a wonderful woman his mother was. "Finest ever to walk the earth," he'd say. "She and my Daddy were like a Lord and Lady."

In the late 1940s, the Darling Electric Elevating Device Company of Montreal, which Billy had run for over fifty years, was changing. His kids were running it by then. After a few tough years in the thirties, the firm struggled into the black during the war, manufacturing submarine periscopes; by 1950 they'd switched to deep-sea diving outfits, but the children didn't have Billy's business savvy and the company went into receivership in 1961.

I never did have the pleasure of meeting Uncle Billy or any of the other players in the Lincoln County War, but they seemed to hover around my family like ghosts. This past summer I was contacted by a Lisa Elkins who comes from West Virginia on my father's side. There aren't many Elkinses left and she'd been searching for relatives on the Internet. We got together in Washington recently and while we were piecing together the family history over lattes at a café in Georgetown, the subject of Billy came up. She told me that Susan McSween, Alex's wife, had become quite wealthy and respectable, had been a friend of the family and had danced with Ambassador Lew Wallace at the Elkins's family home in West Virginia in 1907.

"Small world," she said.

DE

Ambient
Polarities

◆ Of all my relatives Uncle Viggo was without doubt my favourite, as well as the one to cut the most glamorous figure. Yet if you were to scan the handful of photographs of him that have survived, the word "glamour" would hardly come readily to mind. Photographs didn't do my good uncle justice at all. In most he appears as a rumpled, short and rather squat man, and with his thick glasses and unkempt clothes he lacked all the usual particulars one associates with the word glamour. Yet in his time he had about him a dashing air. A kind of charisma that made you like him instantly. He would enter a room and people would just naturally gravitate towards him. This was especially true for members of the opposite sex. Women took to Viggo in a big way, with the result that over the years he was married and divorced a total of five times. His second and fifth marriages were to the same woman, Huguette Turbide, a French actress who gained a modicum of fame by appearing scantily clad on stage and screen in a number of mostly forgotten pre-war French musical comedies.

In his youth, thanks to a modest inheritance, Viggo had travelled the world. He'd lived in New York, Paris, Buenos Aires and Rome, and for a short while had played valve-clarinet with a small jazz combo in a nightclub in Berlin. Apart from this brief stint and a period of three weeks in the thirties when financial difficulties forced him to take a manual labourer job in a textile mill, I don't think Viggo ever held down a regular job. This passing acquaintance with the rude realities of the labour market made my uncle a lifelong convert to the teachings of Karl Marx. It also made him despise anything that even remotely smelled of honest labour.

"There is nothing ennobling about enslavement," he used to say.

Yet every year on the first day of May, International Workers' Day, he would proudly don his mill-workers' smock, brandish his communist party membership card and close ranks with the parade of working stiffs who marched through the streets singing the "Internationale." He referred to this show of solidarity as "fighting in the trenches with the proletariat."

In some respects Viggo didn't have a solid grasp of reality. It was not as though he were a lazy man. Far from it. What he had, and in rich abundance, was a fertile imagination and an extraordinarily agile pair of hands. With these few assets he was able to carve out a modest living as a kind of inventor or "gadget-smith," as he preferred to call it. He'd constructed a workshop in the basement of his Rotterdam house, and it was from here that Viggo over the years cobbled together the more than two hundred and eighty patents he registered in his lifetime, one of them being the dual-compartment food can which later proved to be grandfather Alphonse's financial swan song. Viggo possessed the kind of mind that delighted in the opportunity of tackling some complicated mechanical problem. And once his mind was engaged there was no stopping him. He would work obsessively, singlemindedly, day and night, sometimes for months on end. During these periods he would retreat from the real world in order to concentrate exclusively on the problem at hand, searching for solutions which would incorporate not only practicality but also beauty, elegance and simplicity. On five separate occasions, as he emerged from one of his intensely introverted periods of "abstracation," he would find himself alone in the house, bereft of female companionship. All his marriages ended much the same way. In the ensuing divorce

An early version of the Viggophone.

proceedings his behaviour would be referred to as "the willful withdrawal of affection."

"I was busy at the time, and what with one thing and another, I just forgot," he would plead.

Viggo's first patent, which dated back to 1922, was for a musical instrument, a sort of hybrid between a bagpipe and a zither, which he named the Viggophone. Mastering this unwieldy instrument required outstanding hand-eye-arm coordination, phenomenal embouchure as well as the lungs and endurance of a marathon runner. The Weighart Musical Instrument Corp. of Akron, Ohio produced exactly five hundred and twelve handcrafted instruments, of which only four survive to this day. For a while the instrument's haunting and lyrical tone made it popular with Hungarian czardas orchestras and Argentinian tango bands. The Viggophone saw a brief renaissance in 1936 when Karel Kusak premiered his Dada-inspired contrapuntal opus Asthmatic Rhapsody, a sort of surrealist tone poem featuring a rousing atonal rendition of Bach's Cantata in E Major played on flugelhorn, banjo, accordion and Viggophone. But mostly Viggo concentrated his efforts on the fledging motion picture industry. His most successful contraption was a double exposure split-screen mechanism that allowed the camera to record what was seemingly an actor engaged in conversation with himself. The device was employed with great success in the 1927 German film *Der Doppelganger aus ende der Welt*, and the effect was so star-tling it often left moviegoers stunned, shaking their heads in disbelief.

One evening in 1932, during a slack period between his third and fourth marriages, Viggo was holding forth in his favourite Rotterdam bar, to a bevy of zaftig women of a certain age, when they were joined by a young Dutchman, Jaap van Stricken. Jaap was in town for a few days of business as a representative of the Titan Electricitet Kraftwerke A/G of Nuremberg, the world's largest manufacturer of electrical equipment.

Viggo and Jaap hit it off famously right from the start, and as

Viggo, 1962. Between his
fourth and fifth marriages.

they got to talking about insulators, resistors, capacitators and other electrical paraphernalia the subject naturally drifted to women.

"Well," said Jaap as he signalled the waiter for a fresh round of pilsner. "When I came in here, I sat at the end of the bar for almost an hour, and in that time there were eight men and six women in here. Without fail, all the women at one point or another engaged in conversation with you. In fact, they seemed to initiate it. You didn't do a thing, you just sat there while the women practically crawled all over you. Not once did any of them approach me, or the other men for that matter. It's not as if I look like an ogre, and without meaning to offend you, in some circles, I would at least on the surface be considered a better catch. Yet women avoid me at all costs and always have. And just look at you. For you it's all so easy."

Viggo was taken aback by Jaap's heartfelt outburst. In truth he had never given much thought to his success with members of the opposite sex. He had always taken his good fortune for granted and assumed things were much the same for other men.

"I don't know about it being easy," said Viggo, squirming a little. "I have to struggle like everyone else."

"You don't know the first thing about struggling," continued Jaap. "The only struggle you know is the struggle to keep women at bay. Look at me. I'm twenty-six and not once in my life have I had a date with a woman. Believe it or not, I'm a virgin. And it's not out of choice."

"Well, you know," said Viggo. "Sometimes these things are a matter of chemistry."

"I don't think it's chemistry at all. I think it has to do with electricity," said Jaap. "There are electrical charges that attract and there are electrical charges that repel. Just look at the way metal filings behave when they get near an electromagnet. Once the current is turned on, the magnet exudes a kind of aura, and it's not as if the metal filings can help themselves. They have no choice in the matter. They're drawn into the sphere of the magnet. At our laboratories in Nuremberg, some very bizarre things have happened. Just over a week ago for instance, two young women who are employed in the high-voltage testing facility attacked and sexually molested their supervisor, a fifty-six-year-old engineer who is a devoted father of five and a member of the Catholic reading circle. I'll spare you the more sordid details of the event; suffice it to say that the two women were insatiable. The three of them had spent the day running tests on a batch of heavy-duty telegraph cables. When this kind of work is done the test lab is bathed in an intense energy field because high voltages tend to leak into the surrounding environment, air, water, humans, whatever, creating a sphere of electromagnetic radiation that can profoundly affect the ambient polarities. At any rate the engineer was rushed to the hospital in a critical state of exhaustion. The two women were very embarrassed. They are both engaged to be married and, try as they might, they could not come up with a plausible explanation for their behaviour. Of course the company tried to hush up the whole sordid affair. I've heard dozens of stories of this kind."

Naturally, Viggo's interest was intensely piqued. Here was a promising area, ripe for experimentation of all kinds. In his mind he was already tackling the business of ambient polarities and ways of re-aligning random electromagnetic radiation. As Viggo and Jaap parted late that night, they agreed to set up a modest experiment.

The following afternoon, while most of Rotterdam's male inhabitants were toiling in the factories and offices, Viggo and Jaap met at the outdoor café set in a small forested area of the Rembrandt Gardens, a sprawling park laid out along French lines and somewhat resembling the landscape architecture of the Luxembourg Gardens in Paris. It was a sunny spring day and the park was overflowing with mothers taking toddlers for walks and nannies in groups of two or three pushing prams along the well-groomed paths. In order to ensure as unbiased a result as possible, both Jaap and Viggo were dressed in more or less identical black suits, white shirts, dark homburgs and navy-blue bow ties. On the terrace in front of the café were a number of small marble-topped tables, maybe twenty-five in all, with wrought-iron chairs set around them. Armed with notebooks and stop watches, Viggo and Jaap seated themselves at opposite ends of the terrasse. They planned to meticulously record the seating arrangements and the comings and goings of the female clientele. Viggo and Jaap designated eight tables adjacent to their own at each end as "hot zones," with the remaining tables considered neutral territory. In order to ensure scientific accuracy, they switched places after exactly one hour. At this point Viggo discreetly jammed a short metal spike into the soft ground next to his chair. The spike was attached to a metal wire that ran up the inside of his pants leg and was wound firmly around his naked ankle. This simple grounding device was a last-minute addition thought up by Viggo as a way to determine if his magnetic aura could be neutralized by channelling it away from the body and into the ground.

At the end of the pre-set two hours they retreated to a quiet bar in the Niewhafen district where they compared notes. The facts spoke for themselves:

1st hour: Without exception, all of the twenty-two women who had entered the terrasse during this period had placed themselves within the hot zone at Viggo's end. Three of the more brazen women had initiated conversations with Viggo. Not a single woman sat in Jaap's zone.

2nd hour: After switching tables and after Viggo had inserted the metal spike into the ground, only six women had entered the terrasse. All had seated themselves in the neutral area. Not one had attempted to initiate conversation.

Faced with this data Viggo had to concede there was strong evidence that Jaap's theory might, after all, hold water.

Over the next couple of days, the two of them met at Viggo's house in order to explore the subject further. By the time Jaap returned to Nuremberg they had agreed to develop an apparatus

The "cattle blanket." Moments later the
Holstein would be dead.

that could generate some sort of electrical or magnetic aura. Jaap was to fund the project and supply whatever materials were needed, while Viggo would research and develop the hardware in his basement laboratory.

Over the ensuing months Viggo devoted himself exclusively to the project, at times spending up to thirty-five hours at a stretch in the lab. Now and again Jaap would appear for a few days to check his progress and to unload whatever electrical materials he had managed to filch from the home office. But progress was slow. It took Viggo almost four months of intense "abstracation" before he achieved his first breakthrough, a crude working model he referred to as a "cattle blanket." It consisted of a flexible sheet of netting measuring one-point-two by two metres and crisscrossed by an array of insulators and electrical wiring. Attached by cable was an ingenious but somewhat bulky voltage-amplifier which could draw power from any electrical source, an electrified cattle-fence for instance. In their first crude field test, conducted in a rural setting some ten kilometres from the city, it was determined that the equipment, if improperly handled, could generate enough zap to kill a full-grown Holstein cow. This important finding set them back eight hundred guilders when the grief-stricken farmer caught them in the act. On their second field test some weeks later they found that the electrical aura emitted by cattle of the Holstein breed could be regulated by enclosing the specimen in an intense electrical field. What they hoped to achieve, of course, was a sympathetic electrical aura that vibrated at a similar rate to that of a chosen partner, say, that large bull grazing peacefully in the adjacent field. By adjusting and calibrating the voltage, they theorized they would eventually match the "harmonious oscillation" of any member of the opposite sex. When they finally succeeded in this worthwhile endeavour, the once amicable bull in the adjacent field went berserk and they barely managed to escape with their lives and equipment intact. Incidentally, they also determined that the ambient polarities emitted by an electric cattle fence can be

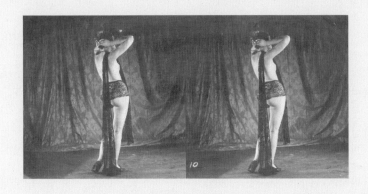

Huguette Turbide in her prime. She always maintained that Viggo was the love of her life.

Jaap and Viggo celebrating their initial success with a river cruise.

very painful, even when applied only briefly to the area around the inner thigh. The cow, on the other hand, having little choice in the matter, was cornered and forced to submit to the bull's amorous advances.

Licking their wounds in a nearby inn, Jaap and Viggo toasted to their success. Despite minor incoveniences, they had achieved important results. So far, of course, these findings held true only for Holstein cattle, but they agreed that with some modifications, the findings could be adapted to humans.

Viggo went back to the laboratory and after a further two months of intense experimentation unveiled "The Harmonious Oscillation Bodice." It was a marvel of cunning and resourceful-ness, employing some of the latest bakelite insulation-capacitators and high-bypass resistance-modifiers from Titan Kraftwerke's ad-vanced laboratory. The outfit consisted of a rubberized full-body suit crisscrossed every two centimetres by electrical wire imbed-ded in the rubber. Superficially it resembled a modern-day scuba diving suit but was somewhat thicker and lacked the headcover and the flippers. The thing weighed well over twenty-five-kilo-grams and was extremely rigid due to the heavy-gauge wiring needed for the high voltages employed. In addition, there was a separate fifteen-kilogram box which held the industrial strength transformer and the all-important control dial.

The first practical field test of the device was planned and arrangements were made with a sympathetic nightclub owner. Work started on a Saturday afternoon several hours before the bar was due to open, since it would take some time to rig the thing up and make the necessary adjustments. First Jaap was stripped naked and his body covered in a light dusting of talcum powder mixed with dried Beulah grass extract. Then he donned a jock strap covered in a thick layer of lead foil, a last-minute addition designed to protect *les bijoux de famille* should the ambient polari-ties decide to go haywire. Finally he was covered in a tight-fitting pure silk tricot. The work of getting him into the "Harmonious

Jaap.
— Nov. 1932

Jaap with the "harmonious oscillation"
suit. (Note the L-shaped mole on his
right cheek.)

Oscillation Bodice" now began with the help of two male volunteers who had been sworn to secrecy. It took over two hours and several rolls of electrical insulation tape to fit the suit properly. Lastly the entire thing was covered in a fashionable tuxedo cut extra large to accommodate the bulky bodysuit.

The rigidity of the outfit prevented Jaap from moving at all. He was carefully manoeuvred onto a sofa in the middle of the night-club. There he sat, in a apparently relaxed pose, one hand casually in his pocket, the other holding an unlit cigarette a few centimetres from his lips. Once he was in position it required enormous effort to move his legs. Bending his arm just a fraction was almost impossible and was accompanied by a loud squeak from the electrical wiring. Connected to the suit was a wire, hidden under the rug, which ran to the transformer unit and the control dial set up on a table in a closet equipped with a peephole into the room.

Around six o'clock the customers started drifting in. By seven o'clock the place was humming, the music loud and the drinking heavy. Jaap was sitting on the sofa, all but ignored by the clientele, while Viggo was crouched in front of the peephole in the closet. As the band lit into a medley of popular Dutch dance tunes, Viggo plugged the cord of the "Harmonious Oscillation Bodice" into the transformer. A high-pitched humming noise arose from the unit. Jaap wriggled nervously in his tuxedo, but otherwise life in the nightclub went on much as before — only more so. Patrons on the dance floor were now doing the hootchey-kootchey, while at the tables the flirting was shameless and expedient. It was hard to tell exactly what kind of business the huddled couples were conducting in the dark corners. Watching this bacchanalian tableau through his peephole, Viggo decided the time had come. The room was ready for a Dutch treat. It was primed for a bit of ambiant polarity. He threw the switch and slowly turned the dial. The humming sound intensified, but was masked by the noise of the band. The needle on the dial lingered briefly in the blue zone. Then it started to climb toward the red zone. For a few seconds it hovered on the line between the two. With a quick twist Viggo turned the dial up. The effect on the crowd was startling and immediate. Within seconds, Jaap found himself surrounded by six adoring females and more were headed in his direction. The powerful aura seemed to reach into the farthest corners of the room. In no time at all, Jaap was surrounded by a large group of women who were pushing and shoving for his attention. At his peephole Viggo caught a fleeting glimpse of Jaap as the mass of bodies pressed around him. Jaap was positively glowing. A huge smile bisected his face as he seemed to be engaged in ten or twelve simultaneous and highly animated conversations. As he was unable to move his arms or hands, one woman had taken it upon herself to refresh him from her glass of beer while another tenderly fed him bits of smoked eel and potato salad. From Viggo's vantage point it was a jolly sight, although it must have been a bit uncomfortable what with all the jostling going on. It also looked as if a cat fight might erupt at any moment. If Viggo wasn't careful, things could easily get out of hand.

Better safe than sorry, he thought. He nudged the dial by a hair and instantly the adoring women lost interest and drifted off, leaving a nonplussed Jaap stranded alone on the sofa. This situation, however, didn't last long. Viggo hardly touched the dial when Jaap found himself surrounded by a boisterous group of men wanting to buy drinks for him. This wouldn't do at all. Viggo quickly turned the dial back down, and as he did so the nightclub owner's thoroughly neutered tom cat leapt in a crazed frenzy from under the piano and onto Jaap's lap. If it hadn't been for Viggo's quick reflexes the consequences might have been serious. He instantly switched the dial back to its original position. The tom cat vanished and once again the adoring women massed around Jaap. At this point, however, Viggo noticed that something seemed terribly wrong. Jaap's once smiling face had turned a sickly crimson and large drops of perspiration covered his forehead. His eyes were panicked.

"Unplug me! Unplug me!" he hollered, which the more adventurous women took to be some sort of sexual encouragement. Viggo quickly grasped the gravity of the situation. Jaap's perspiring body might cause a short circuit in the suit. The plug was pulled, the high-pitched humming ceased, and the assembled women lost interest and drifted off.

It was later determined that the wiring in the suit had acted much like the wiring in an electric blanket, only it was far more intense. All the research didn't go to waste, however. Later that year Viggo and Jaap applied for and obtained a Dutch patent for an "electric comfort blanket," a kind of bed warmer which they claimed had "soothing aphrodisial properties." The blanket was never produced. As for the "harmonious oscillation bodice," they tinkered with it for another year but could never overcome some serious technical problems. These, it turned out, were the result of a minor mathematical miscalculation made in an early phase of the research. It seems that if Jaap had stayed in the suit for another minute or two that night in the bar, he might easily have been fried to a crisp by the force of the ambient polarities. Of course, Viggo didn't know it at the time, but he was in fact skating on the cutting edge of microwave technology. So, although it was successful in some respects, the project was eventually abandoned. Viggo went back to his women and his basement lab while Jaap kept the suit as a souvenir and returned to Amsterdam. Before he left, Jaap confided that despite the discomfort of the suit, the few minutes he'd spent in the nightclub with the women milling around him were without a doubt the headiest moments of his young life.

Some months later Viggo received a note from Jaap, who had been offered a promising position with an electrical manufacturer in Argentina and was leaving for Buenos Aires at the end of the month. He also mentioned that in the months following the experiment all his body hair had fallen out, but he was happy to report that it had started to grow back. Except for two postcards sent by Jaap from Rio de Janeiro, one of which made mention of

The Sun-Mirror

Tuesday June 23, 1951

World's greatest lover marries world's richest gal!

Women everywhere mourn as Cristobal Monteverde weds Sally Arlington.

New York, Monday.
Argentinian playboy and international heartbreaker Cristobal Porfina Monteverde today walked down the aisle for the fifth time. In an electrifying ceremony in train. As the happy couple emerged from the Cathedral, a group of about 200 young women, dressed in black greeted the newlyweds. Prostrate with grief and sobbing uncontrollably they threw themselves in the path of the couple. New York's finest broke up the disturbance. Two of the most vociferous were carried off to the station.

Present at the ceremony were Mr. and Mrs. John Darlington Hurt, of New York city. Mrs. Hurt was wearing a short sable coat over a simple Dior two piece suit. A green hat as well as matching accessories completed the ensemble. Mr. Hurt wore a blue suit the way men have of late taken to 'dressing down'. From Hartford, Conn. came Mr. and Mrs. Donald Sheeland-Winkler. The Insurance tycoon's wife wore a blue sailor's suit with a rhinestone embroidered apron. Her accessories consisted of a chic sailor's cap and two chihuahuas died blue to match her shoes.

Front page of The Sun Mirror, June 23, 1951. The marriage lasted two years and resulted in a nice cash settlement for Cristobal Porfina Monteverde.

a girlfriend, that was the last contact the two had with each other.

After Uncle Viggo's death in 1968, I was appointed executor of his estate. It was a time-consuming task, because in his lifetime Viggo had been a pack rat of the worst kind. His house was crammed with boxes, books, photographs, marriage and divorce decrees, papers relating to his two hundred and eighty patents, blueprints, scale models. It took me every weekend for most of a year to catalog the inventory. Towards the end of this time, I came across a bulky envelope marked "Harmonious Oscillation Bodice." When I opened the envelope, out spilled a sheaf of diagrams bound with rubber bands, an assortment of pencilled schematics, a large annotated blueprint and a small booklet covered in a jumble of scribbles and mathematical calculations. As I leafed through the booklet, I came across a photograph and a newspaper clipping. The photograph, cracked and yellowed, showed a young man. Wearing a bow tie and plus-fours and smiling as he held aloft what looked like a diving suit but must have been the "harmonious oscillation bodice." He was brandishing it in much the same manner that fishermen pose proudly with a lucky catch. The handwritten notation underneath read: Jaap, November 1932. The newspaper clipping, from an English tabloid, *The Sun-Mirror*, dated June 23, 1951, featured this headline: "World's Greatest Lover Weds World's Richest Gal." And underneath, in smaller letters: "Argentinian Playboy Cristobal Porfino Monteverde, in his fifth trip to the altar, marries American multimillionairess Sally Smythe-Arlington, heiress to the Lickety-Good Ketchup fortune." There was also a description of the "electrifying" wedding ceremony in New York and a long list of the socialites attending "this the most glamorous event of the season." The photograph accompanying the story showed a smiling couple embracing as they happily waved to the photographer. I might have been mistaken, but it seemed to me that, save for the slicked-back hair and the Ronald Coleman moustache, Cristobal Porfino Monteverde, international ladies' man and citizen of Argentina, bore more than a passing resemblance to Jaap van Stricken, resident of Buenos Aires and purveyor of electrical equipment.

TS

Aunt Lily's Secret Sex Life

The real story of the Cuban missile crisis

◆ She looked remarkably well. She had always been a large, well-proportioned woman with the kind of robust, shining beauty that was, perhaps, more highly prized in earlier centuries. It served her well. Even in old age, her skin remained firm and rosy. I had last seen her five years before at age seventy-five when she'd looked no more than fifty. Now, just past eighty, she still appeared vigorous and in her prime. A faint smile lingered on her lips. Though I normally loath the practice, in this case I was glad the ceremony included an open casket. Aunt Lily had, in death, once again risen to the occasion.

The funeral service was blessedly short and held, according to her wishes, in the rose garden of the sumptuous Manor Gardenia where she spent her final years. The Manor catered to those who had done well in life and had the bank accounts to prove it. It was July and the roses were splendid. Despite the sombre occasion, I couldn't help but admire the Queen Elizabeths and Lord Mountbattens, such different blooms but each so clearly the apogee of the passion. Surely only the unbridled love of their creators could birth such fragrant magnificence.

While I was sniffing my way to heaven's door, I was joined by Uncle Felix. I didn't know much about him except that he'd been

The family strongly beleives the dancer on
the far left to be Aunt Lily. She was living
in New York at the time and wrote home
fondly of a photographer she called Al. The
Marion Morgan Group was taken by Albert
Genthe, circa 1930.

a childhood sweetheart of my aunt's and they had met again eight years before at the Manor, fallen in love all over and this time had married. I'd attended the wedding, the second for both of them. Felix was a widower and Aunt Lily had marched up the aisle once before too, in Europe sometime during the thirties, a union that bloomed, withered and died in less than a year.

I asked her about it once on my first trip to Paris when I was eighteen and she acted as my chaperone over the strong misgivings of her sister, my mother. Lord, what a time we had. She seemed to know everything and everybody in the enchanted city, from where to gather the best chestnuts in the Bois du Boulogne to the bouncer at a nightclub which was so naughty it never opened before three AM. But I digress. The particular morning the subject of her marriage came up, we were taking a very late morning coffee at La Palette in rue de Seine just around the corner from the hotel where Oscar Wilde, exiled from England after his homosexuality trial, uttered the immortal words, "Either this wallpaper goes or I do" and promptly expired (Auntie was full of such amusing tidbits). The café was a favourite of hers and the waiters fawned over her shamelessly. Perhaps emboldened by the shot of cognac the waiter had dashed in my *café au lait*, I asked her to tell me about her husband.

"Antoine? Oh, Antoine was a terrible prude!" And she burst out with a silvery peal of laughter that had two waiters instantly at our table with another plate of croissants, more gooseberry jam and a fresh pot of hot milk.

I didn't know much more about Uncle Felix, who seemed anxious to talk and steered me to a quiet corner of the garden where a small white wrought iron table and two chairs were set out under a yew tree. On the table was a bottle of Lily's favourite champagne in a silver cooler.

"Sit down, sit down, my boy," Felix said, drawing out a chair. "I'd like to chat with you."

I did as he suggested; it seemed the only appropriate response. It was a hot day and it was exceedingly pleasant under the shady leaves, and though I would miss my aunt, we weren't so close that her death would otherwise have much effect on my life. Uncle Felix had lost much more, it seemed to me, but was apparently taking it well. I surmised that his years with Aunt Lily had caused him to look on the bright side even of death; she had that kind of effect on people.

As soon as we were comfortable and had exchanged the usual pleasantries, he filled the glasses and proposed a toast. "To Lily."

"To Lily," I echoed as we clinked glasses and drank.

He settled back in his chair. "Your aunt was an amazing woman."

I nodded, "Yes, yes, she was. She showed me around Paris when I..." He cut me off.

"Not merely amazing but powerful as well," he continued. "She had friends in high places, as they say. Did you know that?" He had something on his mind and I sensed it would be bad manners to interrupt so I merely shrugged and raised an eyebrow.

"She was a woman who lived many lives," he continued, "and yet she was extremely discreet. As far as I know, she never 'spoke out of school,' as the expression goes. Your aunt wasn't one to kiss and tell." For a moment I thought he winked at me but it could have just been a trick of the light in the leaves. He leaned forward and assumed a more confidential tone. "There's one story that perhaps only three people in the world know and all of us are now in our eighties. Your aunt felt it would be a pity if the tale was forgotten after she had 'left the body,' as she put it."

I recalled a telephone conversation years before in which Lily confided that she had had a recent flirtation with eastern religion inspired by a master she met in California whom she said had "thrilling hands."

Uncle Felix paused and took a thick envelope from the inside pocket of his immaculate blazer. "She asked me to give you this," he said, handing it to me. "She said I was to make sure you read it and that I be available to answer any questions you had. I thought you might read it now."

"Of course," I said readily, my curiosity thoroughly aroused. I started to tear open the pale blue envelope with my name on it in Lily's florid hand.

He stopped me. "Not quite yet," he smiled and continued. "Your aunt asked me to give you a little background first. I have to warn you, it's, well, an unusual story. When she first suggested it, I was opposed. It was too personal, I almost said, too embarrassing, but that's the wrong word. But she insisted — you know how it was impossible not to do what she asked once she'd determined that you must — and she was going to die and this was, after all, a very minor request in the larger scheme of things, so finally I agreed."

I nodded again, more anxious than ever not to interrupt the flow.

"She told me to relax and enjoy it. That's how she put it. She said you were no prude. I think she envisioned us sitting here like this. It would have amused her."

"I'm totally intrigued," I said. "Please go on."

He topped up our glasses and began: "The story starts a long time ago when your aunt and I were kids growing up in Toronto. Lily was the sister of my best friend Eric, your Uncle Eric who died in the car accident. Lily was a couple of years younger and Rose, your mother, was five or six years younger than that. Eric and I had another friend, Chip, and during our teens the three of us were inseparable. We spent practically every waking moment together when we weren't in school. We biked all over town; we went camping; we played scrub football together in the fall; we cut classes and shot pool together in high school; and we double- and triple-dated together. We talked about anything and every-thing that came into our heads, from whether the known universe was actually just so many molecules floating around in some gar-gantuan cosmos to how much money we'd make in our lives, to sports, to sex. In our mid-teens, sex became the topic of choice. For every other subject we discussed, we talked twice about sex because despite the endless talk it was a subject about which we knew practically nothing. Sex education in the schools was non-existent and if the adults knew anything about it, they weren't saying. We knew the mechanics in a rough way; it took my first wife to teach me how rough," he twinkled. Now that the story was underway, I could see he was enjoying himself; the telling was releasing some old pressure in him.

"What we really wanted to know was what it felt like," he went on. "We'd gone through the library looking for anything even faintly related to sex but came away without much for our trouble. We were looking for illustrations, photos, descriptions, comics, anything at all, as long as it was about sex. We were empty slates waiting to be filled. We were three very horny fellows.

"Then one day Eric called me all excited. He'd just been to a bookstore on the far side of town and he'd struck gold. He'd spotted an illustrated sex manual called *For a More Meaningful Marriage* and a rack of magazines which contained back numbers of *The Sunshine Club*, the official organ, as it were, of the Naturalist Society of America. 'Did you get them?' I practically yelled down the phone. Well, he hadn't. He didn't have the money, four dollars for the manual, I think it was, and perhaps seventy-five cents each for the magazines. That was a lot in those days. He was also afraid to buy them. He thought they might report him to the school as a pervert.

"It took three weeks to come up with the money and a way we might get our hands on the material, which is what we'd taken to calling it. By pooling our allowances — and adding two seventy-five I'd saved from my weekly paper route — we managed to come up with six forty-five which would pay for the manual, two magazines and return streetcar fare for the three of us."

He paused for a moment, "Is this OK? Am I boring you? I promise you it gets more interesting once your aunt comes into it."

"Go on, go on," I urged. "Did you get the material?"

"We set out one afternoon at three o'clock, right after school. I remember it was a wet day in early spring with most of the snow already gone. We were at the shop by four. Eric took us in and pointed out the manual on a top shelf at the back and then he showed us where the copies of *The Sunshine Club* were kept in a rack behind the counter. We could see the black and white cover photos from where we stood whispering and making fools of ourselves. On one of them, I recall there was a naked woman playing volleyball. 'God, Felix, do you see the knockers on her?' Chip said in such a loud stage-whisper that a woman a few yards down the aisle turned her head. We were nervous as cats. Just as we'd worked up enough courage to go back and take down the marriage manual, Eric panicked. He'd noticed that the person behind the counter was a woman. He motioned us madly to leave. When we were safely back on the sidewalk he swore it had been a man the last time. We began to walk around the block arguing about how we were going to get our hands on the goods. Eric said he shouldn't do it because he'd found the place. I said I shouldn't do it because I'd put up more of the money; so Chip was the designated buyer, but none of us could imagine how it would be possible for him to buy them from a woman. Finally we decided he should go in and ask when the man would be on duty. Chip didn't think much of the idea but it was better than going home with nothing to show so he finally agreed. Seconds later he was back on the sidewalk, all smiles, the 'gentleman' would be starting at four o'clock — in just ten minutes. At five past four Chip went back into the store and three minutes later was back on the sidewalk with a plain brown paper bag, grinning from ear to ear.

"We caught the next streetcar back to Eric's place, not daring even to sneak a peak at the 'material' in public. Eric's parents both worked and would be away until six. We rushed into his bedroom, slammed the door and each of us grabbed a publication and ooooed and ahhhed and passed them around in virtual silence for the next twenty minutes. Naked women, men and children and

---

163

then more naked women. We were agog. We were shocked. What kind of woman would let her picture be taken like this? Were these sluts or what? Eric said he didn't think they were sluts, he thought they were nature lovers, and we collapsed on the floor in spasms of laughter."

Uncle Felix glanced at me as though to ask, "Are you all right with this?" I urged him to continue.

"Of course we were tremendously aroused, barely able to contain the bulges in our trousers. This was the first time any of us had ever seen women *au naturel*. Then Eric suddenly remembered he had a clarinet lesson and he was out the door, telling us to stay around until he came back and to stuff the mags under the mattress if his parents got home before he did."

Here Felix paused and replenished the champagne. As he did, he peered at me over the rim of his spectacles as if trying to gauge whether he should continue. There was no doubt in my mind that he should.

"What happened then?" I demanded.

"I've caught your interest, have I?" he smiled. "Well then, I'd best get on with it. Chip and I were so engrossed in the material that we hardly noticed Eric had gone and we didn't hear anyone come in until it was too late. When I looked up, Lily was standing in the doorway. I flung the marriage manual I'd been reading under the bed and Chip, who'd been lying on Eric's bed, buried his copy of *The Sunshine Club* under the pillow — but left out in full view at Lily's feet was the other copy, the one with the naked volleyball player on the cover.

"Lilly strolled in, picked up the magazine and began flipping through it. I made a grab for the magazine but she pulled it away so we just let her look at it. There was something tremendously exciting about watching her turn the pages and pause and turn some more and look again. She did it ever so slowly. For Chip and me the room filled up with an electric tension.

"After what seemed like an eternity, she handed the magazine to me and said, 'You poor guys. All you get to look at are boring breasts and hair down there. I get to see penises and they're way more interesting.'

"Chip and I were so stunned we almost stopped breathing. Had she just said penis? I was speechless but Chip, always ready with a quick quip, said, 'I'll show you mine if you'll show me yours.'

"She smiled in that wonderful generous way she had even back then when she was fifteen, and ever so slowly began to lift the hem of her school tunic. She held it up with her left hand and with her right pulled down her bloomers and bent and slipped them off. Then she did a charming little twirl, holding her skirt up for our exclusive benefit. It was the most delicious sight I had ever seen. I thought I would burst.

'Your turn,' she said to Chip. Without a word he stood up, dropped his trousers and tugged down his Fruit of the Looms. It may have been the first erection Lily had ever seen but I'd never seen one either, other than my own. Chip's was a sight to behold. It stood straight out from a mat of golden hair, thick and fresh and rosy as an exotic fruit. Lily and I simply stared at it for a moment, then she pulled her tunic off over her head, unbuttoned her white short sleeved-blouse, deftly unfastened her bra and let it fall to the floor. Her gorgeous breasts were an easy match for Chip's penis, fabulous fruit from a corner of the same Eden. She then moved forward and gave Chip a slight push and he fell back onto the bed. She knelt down beside the bed and played with his standing penis dreamily for a few moments, then lowered her curly blond head and took it in her generous mouth. I watched awestruck as she moved over him. He lay back with his eyes tightly closed, his hands pressed against his ears as though blocking out a loud noise. Later I would tease him about what a great lover he was. In a very short time he twisted and groaned and buried his hands in her hair. She lifted her head, still smiling, and told him to push over. She then lay down beside him, her legs dangling over the edge of the bed, and motioned me to remove my trousers. I did so clumsily, my

165

own penis at excited rigid attention. While Chip lay back recovering, she leaned back on her elbows, opened her legs and indicated that I should kneel on the floor in front of her. I was so excited I was trembling but, good boy that I was, I did what she indicated and in a few seconds my tongue had its first taste of what I have since always considered the sweetest fruit in God's universe. She too soon started to moan and I felt a gentle hand on my head directing my motions. It was all too much for me and I exploded just as she too began to climax.

"The delicious deeds done, we dressed hurriedly like naughty children and spent the next several minutes wiping the side of Eric's bedspread where I had had my accident, wondering, in hushed voices, if it would stain."

Uncle Felix paused. I could scarcely keep from clapping my hands and doing a jig, I was so charmed and excited by something that happened over sixty years before.

My mouth was dry. "That was... a great story," I said, clearing my throat.

He relaxed and leaned back a little in his chair. The trill of cicadas rose through the full heat of the afternoon; under the yew tree it was cool and pleasant.

"Lily said you'd appreciate it. And that was just the beginning, of course. The genie was out of the lamp and we couldn't put it back even if we'd wanted to. For the next couple of years the three of us kept doing it every chance we got. Not that it was very often. We had to have an empty house to do it in when our parents and brothers and sisters were out and we could all get together at the same time. We tried it once at a park in some bushes at night but we were so afraid of being caught that it spoiled it. In all, the three of us probably did it ten, maybe fifteen times, no more than that. We always did the same thing except sometimes she did it with me first and then Chip did it to her. We never told anyone and we never thought of going beyond it. It was great and that was enough.

"Lily went away to college when she was seventeen and Chip

and I had girlfriends by then who weren't half so sympatico as Lily," he winked. "After a while I started to look at the whole episode as being just a part of growing up, something we'd grown out of. The war came along and I lost touch with Chip and Lily. I later learned Chip spent a year working at a munitions plant and then signed up and was posted to England and took part in D-Day. I was in England at the same time in the RCAF but we never crossed paths. After the war I married Eleanor and settled down in Toronto; we had three kids. In my thirties I started my own ad agency and did pretty well. I thought of Lily every now and then, of course, but completely lost track of her. Funny thing was that the older I got, the more I thought about what we'd done and how satisfying it had been. I never told Eleanor about it; we just didn't have that kind of relationship."

My interest in Aunt Lily, always on simmer, was now doing a high-rolling boil. He must have mistaken the silly grin on my face for something else. His face clouded with concern and he leaned forward and said softly, "I'm not embarrassing you, am I?"

"Embarrassing me?" I blurted. "This is one of the most enchanting conversations I've ever had. Is there any more?"

He shrugged and raised his glass, "Your aunt came back into my life eight years ago, as you know. I'd retired, my wife had died a year earlier and I was feeling old and sorry for myself. Then out of the blue, the phone rings and it's Lily. She's back in Toronto, is looking for a place to live and thinks it might be a nice idea if we met for dinner. I agreed at once. We dined together that very evening in the dining room at the old King Edward Hotel downtown; it had just opened after being restored to its former splendour and that night it glittered. We were a little awkward with each other at first. It was odd talking to someone you'd known so well and who knew so much about you and who you hadn't seen in half a century. A bit like being at your fiftieth high school reunion, I suppose. We were nervous at first but then we talked a blue streak while devouring a four course meal — you remember how much she enjoyed beef Wellington — and drinking two bottles of the same champagne we're drinking today." We toasted and he went on. "By midnight, the dining room had emptied and we moved into the bar for a glass of Prince Hubert de Polignac Cognac; she insisted I try her favourite. She'd told me earlier she'd spent twenty years in Europe after the war — you knew that, of course, you visited her in Paris — and that she had studied languages and spoke French, Spanish, Russian and could get by in Japanese. She also told me how she'd worked for an American financier in Geneva, some fellow who started one of the first mutual funds in the late fifties. The funds really took off and she was with him during the high-flying years and made a lot of money herself; then sometime in the sixties, she sensed the party was over. She found a good job at the UN in something she called Special Services. She did well on the diplomatic circuit. I don't have to tell you she was the kind of person you'd trust with your life, even on first meeting."

He paused and folded his hand in his lap.

"Well?" I urged.

"I've come to the end of my part of the bargain. It's time for you to read her letter. I'll come back in half an hour or so in case you have any questions." And with that he sauntered off in his impeccable blazer towards the rose garden. I gazed at the envelope for a moment, then tore it open and began to read.

Dear Nephew, it began. By now my sweet Felix will have told you about our innocent little adventure when we were children. He was so nervous about telling you that I had to make him promise because it was necessary as a prelude to this letter. It's something important that happened to me and I wanted to pass it on. Consider it an old lady's vanity, so let's plunge right in, shall we?

It happened in 1963 when I working with the United Nations in Geneva. I was told, on very short notice, that I was to be sent to Zurich on a special mission. No instructions other than I was to act as a translator in some talks between some high mucky-mucks. The meetings were to take place at the Haus zum Kindli, a discreet little hotel at 1 Pfalzgasse in the old town. I had to sign a formal oath of secrecy, unnecessarily, I thought, since I already had top security clearance as the Deputy Assistant of my department. I was also required, in the interests of security, to make my own travel arrangements. Word was circulated in the department that I had returned to Canada on a month's holiday.

I took the train for the short ride to Zurich, went to the hotel by cab and had to walk the last block because the little street was apparently closed for repairs to the cobblestones. The cabbie refused to carry my bag more than ten metres, against regulations, he said. The Swiss can be so infuriating. As a result, I arrived at the hotel carting my own suitcase, a Vuitton, yes, but heavy. The hotel too seemed to be undergoing repairs. It had the look of a place that had been closed for months and had no immediate plans to reopen — ever. I was ready to go straight back to Geneva but as soon as I touched the bell, the door was opened by an efficient-looking gentleman in a dark suit who took the bag and showed me to an elegant room on the third floor. I had just begun to unpack and settle in when the telephone rang and I was ordered to report immediately to the Café Brun on the ground floor. I had noted the café on my way in, it looked closed and shuttered. I knew the Café Brun; it was the only American jazz bar in Switzerland and I spent many an evening there when I lived in Zurich in the fifties. The highlight had been a performance by Maynard Ferguson. What a wonderful man Maynard was!

The room looked quite different that day. The heavy curtains were drawn and the tables had been rearranged to form a U-shaped conference table. There were about twenty men in the room, some of them obviously government people and the rest security. Everyone was smoking furiously.

Two men came forward though the haze to greet me as soon as I was ushered in. One was a Russian who spoke very little English, the other an American who spoke no Russian whatsoever. They both seemed very glad to see me. It turned out that Nikolai and Bob were the heads of their respective delegations and what I heard over the next twelve hours was enough to make me wonder if I, or anyone else on earth, would survive for another twelve.

It was October 1963 at the time of what the world called the Cuban Missile Crisis.

As I soon discovered, that was just a cover-up for the real crisis. Three days earlier, two days before Kennedy's famous "Get-the-Missiles-Out-of-Cuba" speech, a Russian submarine had "accidently," Nikolai insisted, sunk an American crab boat in the Bering Straits. Seventeen men had died — the Americans called them fishermen, the Soviets called them enemy agents and maintained that the so-called fishing boat was, in fact, a heavily armed spy ship bristling with surveillance equipment. They were reinforced in that position, they felt, when one of the new U.S. nuclear Polaris submarines stationed under the polar ice, torpedoed and sank a Soviet sub with a loss of eighty-seven lives. Bob and Nikolai were charged with patching things up. They were bickering like school boys. After the first hour, I thought to myself that if these fellows were the hope of the world, we were in very serious trouble.

Nikolai kept losing his temper. I'd observed that many Soviet diplomats had developed short fuses since Nikita Khrushchev took off his shoe and shouted and screamed and banged it on the table at the UN in 1960. I put it down to the follow-the-leader syndrome — men can be so childish. When Nikolai had his dander up, which was all the time, he'd threaten to flatten Washington with what he called "the Soviet Union's vastly superior intercontinental ballistic missile arsenal."

Bob was a tense New Englander who didn't like being yelled at. He responded softly but you had the feeling that at any moment he might pick up the phone — each of them had a hotline to their respective leaders at their elbows — and say quietly, "Mr. President,

I recommend in the strongest possible terms that we bomb the living shit out of the Ruskies before they do it to us."

After eighteen straight hours of this, everyone in the room was exhausted and very much on edge. If anything, it felt as though the talks were actually slipping backwards. At one point I noticed that while I was translating, I was idly doodling a series of intense black circles on a pad of UN notepaper. Under several I had unconsciously printed "The Abyss" in ragged block letters. The aides on both sides were pale with tension and lack of sleep. They alternately shuffled papers or suddenly nodded off only to jerk awake an instant later when their head fell forward and begin shuffling again. The tension was almost unbearable. Finally it was suggested we break for four hours, but they couldn't even agree on that. After forty-five minutes of heated discussion, a compromise was reached. We'd adjourn for two hours and forty-five minutes.

The support staff and security people immediately headed upstairs to their bedrooms. I was about to follow them when both Bob and Nick decided to have another go at it. They asked me to stay to translate and each dismissed their single remaining bodyguard. As soon as the three of us were alone, Nikolai went behind the bar and dug out a bottle of Poire William and three shot glasses and we slumped onto one of the old brown leather banquettes which ringed the room with me, little Miss Translator, in the middle.

For the first few minutes, nobody said anything. We were so done in that we simply stared off into space like zombies. Then Nikolai raised his glass with a faint smile and said "Skol." Bob and I joined him and he refilled the glasses. Another five minutes slipped by in silence. Negotiations appeared to be deadlocked when I felt something on my right knee. Could it be Nikolai's hand? I did nothing to discourage him; somehow I found it comforting, a welcome relief from contemplating the end of the world. The silence grew. Now the hand which had been doing lazy circles on my knee was caressing the inside of my leg just above the knee. But what was this? Another hand, this one on the other side, brushing casually against my thigh which was so efficiently sheathed in my best black Chanel skirt? Another few minutes went by in silence with Nick and Bob letting their fingers do the talking. I poured the third drink, just a finger. "Skol," I pronounced and as the soothing pear-flavoured Swiss national drink went down the hatch, I turned first to one negotiator and then the other; each beamed back and the action under the table intensified. A few more minutes of this and east and west would meet in the middle of neutral territory. Who could tell what might happen then? Decisive action was called for. I turned to Nikolai, took his hand in the shadows and said in a casual voice, "*Lyuoobiteh vui lizatye pisyu?*"

"Ya, ya," he replied with the kind of enthusiasm communists in those days reserved for the final victory of the proletariat. I then turned to Bob, squeezing his hand as it gathered for the final assault, and whispered in his ear. He raised an eyebrow and his face filled with the happy vacant look we'd see a few years later on youngsters in San Francisco, high on pot and free love.

A moment or two later, the American and the Soviet delegates were simultaneously struck with the need to get some shut-eye. The three of us rose as one. Nikolai scooped up the bottle and we left the cafe and stepped into the hotel's tiny elevator. I pushed three. Bob reached around me and pressed five and Nikolai asked in a formal way that I touch four for him. When the door glided open at the third, I took both men by the hand, brazen hussy that I am, and led them to my room. There was a tense moment while I searched for my key but once I'd pulled them into my lair, it was like playing a well-rehearsed game.

As soon as we got inside, I threw off my tailored jacket, giggling girlishly, and pushed Nikolai back on the bed while I wriggled out of my skirt and removed the lavender lace panties, leaving the matching garter belt in place. Then, with my arm around Bob's neck, I pushed him gently to his knees, slipped down on the edge of the bed, opened my legs, which still shone in their pale nylons and guided the Bostonian's head to the soft part above the stockings' tops where his head wanted to be. It turned out Bob was a take-charge kind of guy; no sooner was he nestled there than I felt a warm tongue pressing softly against me. Delicious. While Bob luxuriated, I kept Nikolai amused by allowing him to free my breasts from the silken captivity of my Paris bra and then to celebrate their liberation with his clever tongue, properly schooled, he whispered between tastes and tender sucks, under the summer birches and midnight stars of the Ukraine. Bob was obviously in no hurry, so I helped my little babushka slip off his trousers to see what else he might have learned in the Russian moonlight. What a lovely surprise! A fine little commissar, positively brimming with good health and with a magnificent head that looked as tasty and sweet as a freshly picked apple, all surrounded by a magnificent forest of glossy black hair. What a pity that he didn't bring it out to show it off more often, I teased. By now my breasts were flushed and swollen, with the nipples standing up like the little pleasure soldiers they were. Time for the changing of the guard. I pushed the Russian's head gently down and who should pop up but the American! Nikolai and Bob had no difficulty in agreeing to change places. Who said these two weren't prepared to act bilaterally? Bob managed to remove his Brooks Brothers trousers and boxers while he worshipped unconditionally at the Temple of Teat. His tall puritan father was in the middle of a full work-out, fairly bursting with well-intentioned elegance and purpose, standing proudly in a patch of sandy hair that smelled fetchingly of sunny pines. By his strutting and posing I could see he positively doted on the attention I lavished on him. What an egotist the fellow was. He'd do anything if only I'd stroke him. With the jewel of the Ukraine down below seemingly intent on lapping up every drop of water in Lake Balenchin, it was almost more heaven than I could bear. I had just begun to entertain the marvellously muscled Harvard man in earnest when my legs went weak and began to quiver and a flood of joy welled up from below, filling every pore with sheer delight. When I came back a little to myself, I leaned over and drew Nikolai back up so I had one man on either side. No sooner had he joined us on the bed that I felt both men's fingers inside me and this sent me spinning again into one of the strongest climaxes I'd ever had, washed away by wave after wave. It was so wonderful to have two men again! As the torrent peaked, I slipped from their busy fingers to the floor, and knelt on the thick carpet and took a gorgeous penis in each hand. I couldn't wait to taste them. The two men now lay side by side and I moved first to Nikolai's strong smooth organ and buried it in my mouth as though I were drinking in the whole of Russian history. I heard the wind go out of him in pleasure as I gently drew Bob's sturdy pilgrim toward me. This was the first time since Felix and Chip that I'd had two men all to myself and I was as excited as if I'd been fifteen again. I ran my tongue gently over each in turn and thrust gently down. Each mouthful of satiny skin gave me intense pleasure as though I were bringing peace to all mankind. Both men caressed my hair as I moved over them like the Empress of Ice Cream. The tension of the negotiations, the Poire William, the sudden unexpected turn of events, even our exhaustion contributed to the high-wire act. It was almost more than we could bear and soon both men shuddered and rushed forward together to the American-Soviet United Republic of Climax, tumbling me into yet another series of orgasms that swept me off to another planet entirely.

By some miracle our moans and groans didn't wake all of Zurich. When the sea subsided and the stars came out again, all was peace and silence and serenity. I kissed each softening penis tenderly one last time, wriggled up between my new friends, pulled up the quilt and the three of us settled into a deep sleep.

An hour later we were startled awake by a panic call from the desk. It seemed negotiations were about to recommence and both the principals were missing. Had I seen them? How could I possibly have? I'd been in my room since the meeting broke up. I was to report to the Café immediately.

An hour after that, while I was on my second *café au lait*, the Soviet and U.S. delegates arrived looking remarkably refreshed. Rumour had it that they had been in private session hashing things out. The gathering was called to order and after a mere forty-five minutes of what were privately called "cordial talks," each party, with the full support of their respective governments, agreed to let bygones be bygones with regard to the recent regrettable incidents. Twenty minutes later, Mr. Khrushchev was filmed by Moscow television announcing that the missiles were being withdrawn. The crisis was over.

And so, nephew dear, is this letter. By the time you read this, my soul will know just what kind of karma I accumulated during this incarnation. I have a very positive feeling about this blessed time on earth.

Your loving aunt,

Lily"

I slowly folded the pages and slipped them back in the envelope. I felt damp, almost as though I'd gone through the negotiations and their resolution myself.

I must have been gazing off into space when Felix reappeared.

"Food for thought, what?" he said taking his seat again.

I simply exhaled and grinned like an idiot child. I hardly knew where to start. I had a thousand questions on the tip of my tongue, but before I could ask even one of them, we were joined by another man about my uncle's age He had a ruddy complexion, a full head of silver hair and dark and ocean blue eyes that twinkled when he spoke. I stood up to be introduced.

"I'd like you to meet someone who's been living here at the Manor for five or six years. He knew your aunt well. Admired her very much. He's an old friend. In fact, the three of us grew up together. Meet Chip Farley."

If he noticed my jaw drop, he covered it up nicely. The three of us sat down and shared the last of the champagne and chatted amiably about this and that. When it was time to leave, Uncle walked me to the car. I shook hands, said goodbye, and walked around to the driver's side, but I did have one pressing question. "Uncle Felix," I called across the roof of the car. "What was it Aunt Lily said to the Russian?"

He came around to my side, a trim, dapper man, thoroughly at home in the world. He motioned me to bend my ear to his lips and he whispered: "Do you like to eat pussy?"

DE

The Goulash Baron
of America

◆ The black and white photograph on the following page, one of only three known to exist, shows the town of Haute Clamart-sur-Drôme as it looked back in 1918. This town in the district of Luberon, France, is where my granduncle Alphonse Gervais was born in 1888. In fact, he spent a charmed childhood growing up on the second floor of an ochre sandstone building on the town square, Place de la Republique. It was in this building, at the age of eighteen, that Alphonse was discovered *flagrante delicto* with the *zaftig* wife of Haute Clamart-sur-Drôme's only notary. Naturally, as was the custom in Europe at the time, Alphonse was run out of town. Having dishonored the notary, his *zaftig* wife, his entire family and himself, and in the process broken every sacred law of man and God, there was simply no other alternative. At the tender age of eighteen, disowned by his own family, shunned by the townspeople and without any source of income, Alphonse, by now a bitter youth, drifted down towards the great port of Marseilles. In time he signed on as cook aboard a cargo vessel bound for the French possessions in the Pacific. It didn't take long for Alphonse to realize that this line of work was not for him. At the first opportunity, which happened to be Galveston, Texas, he jumped ship.

After drifting across the country doing odd jobs for a while, Alphonse eventually ended up in Tucson, Arizona, where he found

Haute Clamart-sur-Drome in 1918.
The photographer, Albert Gérard, spent four
days in the village documenting daily life.
A mix-up in his darkroom later destroyed all
the plates — except for this one.

work as an assistant cook in a canning factory. Being a quick study, in no time at all he had taken to the local vernacular and had absorbed the fundamentals of the cutthroat business ethics of the day, which briefly stated were: "the business of America is business." It didn't take him long to start up his own modest enterprise, supplying K-rations to the U.S. Cavalry, which was, at the time, engaged in suppressing a rebellion south of the border. Initially his business wasn't much, just a single discarded canning machine purchased for peanuts from his former employer and mended, for the price of a single share, by a Mexican plumber. The unloading of the canning machine would soon cause the former employer no end of grief. Not only did he find himself regretting the transaction but he also found himself undercut by Alphonse's sharp business practices. Beef, the principal ingredient in K-rations, was cheap, especially if you substituted "scruffing," an industry term for the sinewy leftovers discarded by butchers, and Alphonse, with his shipboard experience as a cook, knew a few handy tricks to fool the palate. It also helped that army purchasing officers were not immune to the odd bribe. By the time the Mexican rebellion was over Alphonse had accumulated a nice little nest egg and, hoping for some sort of renewed military action, didn't waste a moment gearing up for the next outbreak of hostilities. When it came, it was huge; by the time The Great War was into its second year Alphonse had twenty-three factories humming twenty-four hour shifts in eleven countries as they turned out canned breakfast, lunch and dinner for troops on all sides. By 1917 he was reputed to be the twenty-fourth wealthiest man in the world and was known throughout the Continent as the "Goulash Baron of all the Americas." The single share earned by the Mexican plumber who had mended Alphonse's first canning machine was now worth in excess of eighty-six thousand dollars. Using a little-known statute in Arizona labour regulations, Alphonse had the Mexican declared an "unauthorized alien entity" and got him deported. His few assets were forfeited and handed over to the state registrar's office where Alphonse, evoking the "felonious casualty remuneration" clause, acquired the share at its face value of six dollars.

With the outbreak of peace, Alphonse deftly switched his world-wide canning operations to civilian production while expanding his business empire into a myriad of more or less shady real-estate holdings.

"War or peace, what do I care, it's all business," he used to boast. "One way or the other the little fuckers need a place to live and something to eat. For a price I'll give them both." This, in a nut-shell, was the essence of Alphonse's business ethic, an oxymoron if there ever was one, as well as the cornerstone of his company's mission statement.

By the middle of the twenties Alphonse, according to rumour, was earning a million dollars a week, and was honing his skills as an unprincipled cad. In no time at all, he had, at least on the surface, acquired the polish of American society and taken to the local cul-ture like "horseradish takes to a medium-rare rumpsteak," as he was fond of saying. In order to give ample scope to his outlandish ten-dencies Alphonse moved his offices to a sumptuous address on Fifth Avenue in New York City. From there he could regularly be seen going out on the town for a bit of "after-hours entertain-ment." As biographer Reichardt Beauchemin put it, his preferred activities involved "assorted scenes of mirth and physiological examinations, often involving several women as well as a curious mélange of exotic victuals." These late nighters also entailed heavy drinking and the occasional boxing-match or bit of burlesque, with stops along the way at private "lunch nooks" in order to sati-ate his untamed appetites. Alphonse liked to keep his supply of women flowing, seducing and drawing them in by sending notes, flowers and canned goods. He would move in on the life of a young woman, often an innocent shop girl, overwhelm her with his wealth and power, and when trust had built up he would "stew her," often repeatedly. After that he would dump her. In almost every respect the workings of his private affairs differed not a whit from the ethics of his business operations.

In the end he was once again caught *flagrante delicto*, this time by a concealed camera. An ambitious showgirl, Esther McGrath, wielding an assortment of unflattering photographs involving the two of them *au naturel* in the company of a glazed Sachertorte, threatened to go to the authorities. It was an elaborate setup, and to avoid scandal Alphonse was forced to marry the showgirl. Though she produced two healthy sons, Jerome and Hector, it was a marriage in name only, particularly since the paternity of the offspring was in some doubt. All in all, though, these matters didn't in the least slow Alphonse down. He soon carried on as before with his after-hours entertainment while ignoring the young family to whom he allowed only a meagre stipend. Over the years he increasingly came to resent his wife, and with the aid of an army of attorneys plus a series of questionable legal loopholes, succeeded in having her and the two boys excluded from his estate. Later, when he received the hefty bills for this costly bit of business, he was so outraged that he fired his large staff of attorneys and in fact sued them. In the end his litigation caused two of the lawyers to be disbarred from the state of New York for life.

Alphonse, then, knew better than most how to maintain and nurture a grudge. Reichardt Beauchemin, in his book *In the House of the Robber Barons*, puts it this way: "When it came to resentment Alphonse had prodigious stamina and ....[it] appears to be the one motivating factor in his shabby business affairs as well as the leitmotif of his lamentable private life."

There was one grudge, though, that Alphonse couldn't dismiss with the same efficiency, the one that had been gnawing at him through the years and wouldn't go away. It was the dishonour and humiliation his native Haute Clamart-sur-Drôme had inflicted when he was run out of town back in 1906. By the late twenties, as Alphonse neared his fortieth year, he decided to deal with the matter once and for all and set out to avenge this bit of early outrage.

Alphonse at the age of seven with his classmates.
At this time he was already being labelled
"headstrong" by his teachers.

In the summer of 1928 he set sail for France aboard SS Normandy, the flagship of the French Line. Not being one to do things by half measures, he booked the entire sweep of first-class cabins on the upper deck, including the art-deco dining room where he would consume his meals in solitude while the other twelve hundred and forty-seven passengers were jammed into second class and steerage. According to his biographer, "At night he would lollygag with the floozies from steerage," often concocting elaborate hide-and-seek games through the deserted staterooms while the blindfolded twelve-man orchestra played fox-trots. When the ship docked in Cherbourg, a private train coach was there to whisk him south, and the following evening he re-entered his childhood home after an absence of almost thirty years. To his chagrin, there was no one to welcome him. His parents had died years before and his only brother, Aristide, had long ago left for Paris. As for the wife of the notary, she was now but a shadow of her former voluptuous self and, in any event, when they briefly crossed paths that afternoon, didn't remember him.

The following morning Alphonse set to work. In the course of the day he summoned most of the local advocates and notaries as well as the mayor and three councillors to his rooms at the hotel.

That afternoon the rumours hit the streets of Haute Clamart-sur-Drôme, then spread like wildfire through the sleepy Mediterranean town and across the rolling hills of Luberon. The news was doubtless the biggest thing to hit those parts since the Roman aqueduct was built almost two thousand years earlier. In a nutshell, this was the deal: Alphonse was prepared to purchase, provided a suitable price could be agreed upon, the land as well as all the buildings bordering the main square of Haute Clamart-sur-Drôme, including the town hall, the hotel and his childhood home.

All hell broke loose. In the first few days alone, fully one quarter of the real estate bordering the square changed hands. Frantic sellers mobbed the notaries' and attorneys' offices, who worked double-time trying to decipher centuries-old deeds and moth-eaten record

Arizona, 1910. Alphonse on his horse Bismarck, with the Mexican plumber holding the reins.

books. The mayor, a staunch champion of the people, in a last-minute change of heart, called an emergency meeting hoping to stall the selling spree. At the end of the meeting, the municipal council voted unanimously to unload the town hall along with the square and for good measure throw in the statue to the unknown soldier, the fountain, the park benches and the two *pissoirs*. Over the ensuing weeks the remaining buildings changed hands at a rapid clip. As Alphonse was quick to point out, it was a perfect lesson in the behaviour of a market economy.

"I want to buy, they want to sell. I have the money, they have the properties. What they do with the money is no business of mine, and it's no business of theirs what I do with the buildings."

This sudden muscular infusion of riches into this once piss-poor town, with its carefully nurtured and cultivated traditions, caused a severe strain in relations between the "haves" and the "have-nots." In quick order centuries-old customs vanished, while gambling, divorce, drunkenness and whore-mongering, once alien to this provincial backwater, rose at an alarming rate. Six *gendarmes* had to be called in from Avignon to keep some semblance of order. The social fabric was strained to the point of rupture as years of friendship turned to hostility at the drop of a hat, while fortunes were won and lost at the cardtables or squandered in the new bordello.

"They should learn to roll with the punches, the way I had to roll with the punches," Alphonse chuckled.

Adding to the state of chaos was the huge invasion of architects, engineers and labourers whose jobs were to dismantle all the buildings bordering the town square. Each brick, stone, beam, rafter, stair, door, window and roof-tile was carefully taken down, numbered, classified and crated in such a manner that it could later be reassembled. By the summer of 1929 convoys of trucks started to haul the entire disassembled town square, consisting of 18,647 numbered wooden crates, to the port of Marseilles for shipment to America. They left Haute Clamart-sur-Drôme in total ruin.

Where once there had been peace, harmony and trust, there was now only animosity, greed and betrayal. Where once there had been a proud town square teeming with *elan vitale*, there was now only rubble. And just to add salt to the wound, in the centre of the ruins Alphonse had his labourers erect an enormous metal billboard advertising his canned merchandise.

Alphonse was elated.

"That ought to teach 'em," he crowed. "Those peasants messed with Alphonse and look what happened. This billboard will always remind them that when you mess with Alphonse, you mess with disaster."

And indeed, at this point disaster struck. The crash of November 1929 wiped out Alphonse along with his maze of interlocking companies. In a twelve-day period he saw his vast fortune disintegrate. In the end the horde of creditors left him nothing. Over the years he had accumulated an impressive and loyal legion of enemies who had been waiting in the wings for just this day. Where they could, they prodded things along as they watched Alphonse's downfall with ill-concealed glee. A bit of newsreel footage of the day bore witness to his final humiliation. When shown in movie theatres across America, it evoked laughter. "The former goulash king once again finds himself in a stew as two federal marshalls are forced to restrain and handcuff the reluctant ex-zillionaire as they evict him from his sumptuous Fifth Avenue offices. Oh, how the mighty have fallen."

His grandiose plan of rebuilding Haute Clamart-sur-Drôme in the desert of Arizona vanished like a *fata morgana*. The wooden crates were left to rot on the docks of Marseilles and it was not until 1961, after three recessions, two depressions and a world war, that the municipality found the funds to clean up the mess.

Alphonse attempted a desperate financial comeback in 1936 with his innovative "Canned Radio Dinner." The product consisted of a single can with two compartments, the main course in one end, the dessert in the other. Despite the fancy label and a five cent rebate program, the recipe was merely a tiresome repetition of the K-ration he had used earlier. It was an instant flop. America had lost its taste for scruffing and Alphonse lost what little money, dignity and self-esteem he had left.

Over the next few years he would drift aimlessly from town to town doing odd jobs. His imperious manner and lack of manual dexterity made him ill-suited for a tight job market and, when he was hired at all, he would usually be fired in short order. With the entry of the U.S. into the Second World War, Alphonse tried to sign up as a merchant-marine cook but was rejected out of hand because of his age. Eventually, near the end of his rope, he stowed away on a freighter out of Pensacola bound for Europe. When the ship docked in the port of Marseilles, he was arrested by the *douaniers* and handed over to the local *gendarmes*. After a short stint in the local *bagne*, he was let out, only to find himself once again wandering about aimlessly. In time he ended up at the docks.

It was there, in the fall of 1947, in the port of Marseilles, wandering among the 18,647 rotting crates, that Alphonse finally gave up. As the crisp fall evening settled over the port, Alphonse sat down on a stone and began to cry. He cried for his miserable life until he could cry no more. Some time later he got up and meandered through the heaps of old crates which contained what had once been his childhood's town square. Here and there the rotting crates had given out and spilled their contents on the ground, mostly large stones, but now and again a door, a roof tile or window-lintel could be seen. As he made his way through the crated remains of Place Republique he could make out the faded lettering on the boxes indicating their contents. One sprawling area held the various parts of the *Mairie*. And over there, parts of the Bolducs' once elegant mansion. In one large crate, as the lettering indicated, was the wrought-iron balcony belonging to that house, the very same balcony from which the Bolducs used to hang a huge *tricolour* on Bastille Day. Farther along he came across three crates containing the statue to the unknown soldier, and just

The Goulash Baron himself at the
height of his power in 1928, mere
months before his downfall.

beyond that, the parts of the once glorious hotel where he and his family had gone on Sundays for dinner. Tucked in an area between the Chevalier house and the Café de la Paix he found the crated remains of his childhood home. As night fell over the port, Alphonse set to work. In turn pushing and pulling, he enlarged a small space between two boxes and, using the front door as well as parts of a banister, cobbled together a tiny shelter among the mass of broken crates.

That night he slept the sleep of his childhood. When dawn broke, he gathered his few belongings in his small bag and left the port. For seven beautiful autumn days he wound his way through the rugged hills and valleys of his childhood, eating from the abundance of ripening fruit and sleeping under the starry skies. On the seventh day Alphonse reached the end of the road, Haute Clamart-sur-Drôme. There was now no more road to be had.

For the remainder of his days he eked out an existence of sorts as a beggar, much reviled by a resentful population. At night he slept in a makeshift lean-to under the huge metal billboard amid the rubble of the town centre. Each morning, afternoon and evening, in a never-changing ritual, he could be seen in his rags, wending his way through the cobblestoned backstreets as the locals hurled their insults, contempt and foodscraps in his direction. Day after day he would silently endure these humiliations, and it seems clear he was searching for a measure of redemption in this elaborate rite. It also seems clear he had found a home as well as a useful place in the life of the community. By his unspoken acceptance of the town's scorn, he was atoning in small measure for the appalling injuries he had caused, while for the locals he served as a useful target for their rage as well as a convenient butt of their often cruel jokes. When Alphonse finally died at the age of seventy-three, still not at peace with himself, few if any in Haute Clamart-sur-Drôme cared.

In the 1980s, as Reganomics gained wide respectability in the business world, a number of prestigious MBA programs intro-

Alphonse in Place de la
République, 1959. The sign
was torn down in 1962.

duced "Alphonomics" as part of their curriculum. Alphonse's business acumen was widely admired and in some cases imitated, while the underlying factors of pure luck and raw intuition dovetailed neatly with the dogma of trickle-down economics.

The tract of Arizona desert originally intended for the reconstruction of Haute Clamart-sur-Drôme changed hands a number of times after the collapse of Alphonse's financial empire. For a short while in the '50's it was used as a two-screen drive-in theatre and later converted to a go-kart track and mini-putt golf course. For a period in the late seventies it was the home of the "Cascade Flats" trailer park and campground. By 1987 the land was purchased by the Gingermeyer Frozen Food Corp, which erected a huge aluminum-sided factory on the site. Today from this location they supply the entire southwest with Gingermeyer's frozen "Hungry Guy" TV dinner, a flip-top double-sided aluminum tray with the main course on one side and the dessert on the other.

TS

Big Morty

◆ When my nephew Mortimer "Big Morty" Gervais graduated from high school at the bottom of his class in 1991, he had long ago decided to become a long-haul truck driver. This career choice was no mere whim but a dream he'd harboured since he first saw the movie *Convoy*, starring Kris Kristofferson, back when he was eight. When it came to cars, trucks, rigs, semis, pick-ups, vans, sedans, convertibles, coupes and any other stripe of automobile, Big Morty was a natural. At ten his vocabulary was littered with words like carburator, camshaft and transmission and by the time he was twelve he had an encyclopedic knowledge of the lore and mechanics of auto-engineering. Not only could he fix a car, any car, he could tell by the sound of the engine what was wrong. From the imprint of a tire on a gravel road he could tell the make, model and year.

On Mort's nineteenth birthday his father, in his infinite wisdom, presented Mort with a certified checque amounting to the tuition fee for an eight-week big-rig driving course at the Kenworth Driving Academy in Bakersfield, California. For Big Mort, this was like being accepted at Harvard. Needless to say, he graduated at the top of his class and passed his road test two days later, hauling a fully loaded Kenworth semi along the interstate from Bakersfield to Reno, Nevada, in the required time with no demerit points.

He was hired in short order by the Ivarcom Corporation of Needles, Arizona, to haul their line of frozen "Frenchie Chef" products all over a territory consisting of New Mexico, Arizona, Nevada and parts of California. Big Mort was a happy man. Sitting high up in his cab, he would rap with other good buddies on the CB as he crisscrossed the four states in his Mack freezer-rig. He was Kris Kristofferson in *Convoy*. He was king of the road.

"Frenchie Chef" was a line of frozen *boulangerie* products sold to choice supermarkets and upscale bakeries, the kind that has sprung up in the last few years, often in conjunction with a cappuccino café. Their product line, prepared at the ultra-modern plant in Needles, consisted of baguettes, croissants, brioches, pain au chocolat, éclairs, pain blé entier, mille feuilles dough used in Napoleon pastries and a mouth-watering assortment of other Gallic delicacies. Iron-ically, when the idea of marketing this gourmet product in the Southwest first came up, Ivarcom Corp VP of marketing Hubert Meadows suggested it would be a waste of money. "Cowboys don't eat French pastry; leave that inky-dinky parlay voo stuff to the Euro-trash. Cowboys eat beans, steak and apple pie." How wrong Mr. Meadows turned out to be. Cowpokes took to these dainty Gallic delicacies in a huge way, almost as a response to President Bush's call for a "kindler, gentler nation." In retail jargon the southwest U.S. is often referred to as "cowboy country," and early consumer demographic studies had shown there might be a small niche market for this kind of product, especially in artsy colonies like Taos and Santa Fe. But when the company ran their clever TV ad showing two leather-faced cattle hands on their trusty steeds blissfully munching éclairs as the cattle around them stampeded, the product took off in a big way. On the Amex Frenchie Chef went from $2.40 a share to $12.36 in six months.

At the time, "Frenchie Chef's" basic recipe for bread and pastry dough varied very little from the time-honoured recipe in effect when Marie Antoinette suggested the plebes eat cake. However, as an American company, they couldn't leave well enough alone.

They just had to tinker and add a few wrinkles of their own. For starters, an exceptionally potent stabilizer was added to reinforce the powerful action of the yeast. "The fluff factor," they called it. The dough was then kneaded in giant steel vats and the malleable mass rolled out and processed into a variety of shapes. In order to arrest the action of the yeast, this phase was completed in a three-degree-Celsius "cool room." At this point the dough was flash-frozen, making what would later become a golden and crusty loaf of French bread appear as rigid and dense as a thin stick of wood. The beauty of this scheme was that the dough would take up very little space, making it easy to transport. When delivered, the baker would just pop a few frozen sticks on the bakery sheet and room temperature, plus the wondrous action of yeast, would cause the dough to rise sixfold in volume in just a few hours. Light, fluffy and airy. Twenty-eight minutes at 325°F in a triple-convex Freitag industrial oven and voila: golden French bread that would be the envy of any Parisian *boulanger*.

One July morning Big Mort set out for a delivery of frozen bread and pastry dough to a wholesaler in Santa Fe, New Mexico, the farthest point in his territory. The interstate is an almost flat straight line through mostly arid desert, whereas the old 114 is a two-lane winding road hugging the natural contours of the land-scape. For a long-hauler like Mort the old 114 offered romance, adventure and the prospect of riding the eight-ton Mack freezer-rig round hairpin turns, over rutted gravel roads and up steep climbs while throwing up huge clouds of dust. The outlaw bandi-to making his getaway with Smokey in hot pursuit. Big Mort had hardly gone more than forty miles before he encountered a detour caused by a washed-away roadbed, the result of a flash flood some days earlier. As he followed a succession of badly marked signs and questionable turns, the road narrowed and became increasingly more rutted. Soon it was down to a single track. And then it ended. Here was big Mort sitting in his Mack freezer-rig at the end of a track in the Mojave desert, and it was getting hot. He got on the CB radio and tried to raise a few good buddies, but the radio was dead. And worse was soon to come. When Mort tried to back out, he found he was stuck. The wheels would only turn in place, digging further into the sand. No amount of forward and reverse, alternating two-wheel and four-wheel drive, would move the rig. He even tried the old rocking motion they use in the snow up in Canada, but to no avail. So he sat there for a while and tried to come up with a solution to his dilemma. This was one thing they hadn't taught at the Kenworth Driving Academy. He decided to take a nap; it would clear his mind and somebody might come along. At least the air conditioner in the cab worked. As Big Mort was snoozing off, the "Koolaero" freezer unit which cooled the merchandise decided to act up. With all the forwarding and reversing the intake valve for the unit had become uncoupled, and as a result it started to suck in the scorching desert air and waft it over the frozen pastry dough.

A few hours later Mort was awakened by a low rumbling noise. The cab was swaying to and fro and from time to time a sharp crackle or pop could be heard. He checked the rear-view mirror, rubbed his eyes and checked again. The aluminum sheeting which covered the outside of the truck was bulging at the seams like a balloon about to pop. It was heaving and throbbing along the riveted seams as if about to give birth. And then with a sudden sharp snap one of the rivets zinged across the desert floor, ricocheting off a series of rocks before coming to a halt. And then another. And another. Mort was suddenly fully awake. He tore out of the air-cooled cab and into the searing desert heat — just in time. It was like a rifle range out there, rivets popping this way and that and caroming off rocks everywhere. All along the seams, rivets were being torn out of their moorings and propelled through the desert air like bullets from an AK-47. The belly of the Mack was splitting open. With a sudden thud the truck ripped apart. Ragged pieces of aluminum panelling flew through the air, decapitating cacti, Jimson weed and other vegetation in their path. Then the yeast-

Mort and his
mother on the day
of his graduation
from the academy.

The fluff factor at work.

enriched dough began oozing like a lava flow from the belly of the ruptured Mack.

When they found Mortimer the following afternoon he was severely dehydrated and suffering from shock and heat stroke. He was heli-vacuated to the emergency unit of the Bakersfield Cummings Memorial Hospital, where he recovered in short order.

As for the Mack freezer-rig, it was neatly baked into what could best be described as a mammoth brioche, measuring twelve feet by twenty-two feet across. Golden and crispy on the outside, it was baked to perfection by the unrelenting Arizona sun. The inside, strewn with debris from the exploded truck, was a bit on the doughy side, though somewhat lighter and airier in the upper parts. Topping the giant brioche was the truck's side panel with the "Frenchie Chef" logo, a well executed caricature of a mustachioed Gallic chef, in his white chef's hat with his fingers forming an "O" as he is about to blow a kiss. Issuing from his mouth, a cartoon balloon with the words, *Ooh-la-la, c'est formidable!*

TS

Long Distance Listeners

To hear and hear not

◆ My great-great maternal grandfather, Carruthers Toggsham, born in Bristol, England, November 13, 1789, fell in love only once in his life, at age fifty-six. The object of his desire was Oleander Gardyne, a beautiful and spirited sixteen year-old whose family owned sugar plantations and a rum distillery in St. Kitts in the British West Indies. Fate smiled on the couple and Captain Toggsham had soon installed his new wife in a large, elegant white clapboard house, overlooking the harbour, in the best section of Portland, Maine.

Four years passed and Oleander was now twenty, her son Hollis, my great-grandfather, almost three. For the last hour the two had been shrieking around the house playing hide and seek, much to the disapproval of the housekeeper, Mrs. Eliza Camden. Hollis hid, Oleander played seeker. First he hid in the front hall clothes cupboard. Very scary in the dark, almost suffocating among the tall ghosts wearing musty winter coats. She found him almost at once. She found him again in the kitchen cupboard under the sink. And under his own bed. And even in the dining room where he lay very still, stretched out on two chairs, invisible, he supposed, behind the heavy green velour table cloth. Next he persuaded Mrs. Camden to hide him in the hope chest in his parent's bedroom. Remarkably, she discovered him there too. She found him every time and tickled and tickled him until he escaped and hid again.

Now he had found the perfect place. He had just managed to push open the heavy door and wriggle out onto the widow's walk, a tiny balcony built into a turret at the house's highest point. He lay on his stomach and looked out through the rails over the grey slate roof of his home across the steep dark roofs of the neighbouring houses and all the way out into the harbour. It was very high up there. He didn't dare stand up. But what was this? The trap door opened a crack, then more than a crack and then he saw his mother's dark cascading curls, then the floaty lavender silk bow at the nape of her neck. She turned and he saw her twinkly brown eyes and, before he could catch his breath, she was tickling him and tickling him and saying, in her soft lilting voice, "I found you, I found you, my beauty boy." And she covered him with kisses, not forgetting his perfectly formed, if somewhat large, ears.

It was a fine July day in Portland with a sky full of fluffy clouds. Mrs. Camden wouldn't have lunch prepared for another hour, so Oleander and Hollis lay on their backs and looked up at the sky and searched the clouds for dragons and elephants and fairies and elves and God smoking a pipe. After a blissful half-hour, Hollis said to his mother, "Daddy's coming home tonight."

"No he's not, pet lamb," she teased giving him a squeeze, "He won't be home for another week. You miss him, don't you."

"Yes, he is so coming home," said Hollis, nodding his blond head vehemently, "I heard him tell Uncle Abe."

"Of course you did, my fine little man." And she laughed and scooped him up in one arm and tugged open the door with the other.

"I did, I did, I did," protested Hollis as she carried him down the steep stairs into the cool quiet house.

She set him down on the polished maple floor, biffed him gently on the nose and said, "Tapioca pudding for dessert. Last one at the table is a dirt rat with a long scaly tail."

Captain
Carruthers
Toggsham
about the
time he
arrived in
America,
1807.

The Captain's packet refitted for steam. Hollis
could hear it twenty-five miles away.

She had just tucked Hollis into bed that night, the boy protesting, as he did every summer bedtime, that it was still light and he should be allowed to stay up, and finally was only persuaded to lie down with his fuzzy rabbit after she told him, for the eighty-second time, the story of how, when she was a little girl, she "did a bad thing." In tonight's episode, to her father's fury, she had let all the chickens out of the hen house and chased them into the sugar cane field so they could be free to go where they liked and not have to live in the smelly hen house.

"Did you get a beating, Mummy?" asked Hollis hopefully. Before she had a chance to answer, there was a banging at the door and, without even waiting for it to open, a boy called, "Come quickly, Mrs. Toggsham, come quickly. Captain Toggsham's schooner's just rounded Parrish Island. He'll be dockin' in the hour."

She sent round for the carriage and scarcely had time to bundle Hollis up in a blanket and reach the harbour before her husband came down the gangplank. Hollis's parents hugged and kissed shamelessly as the boy danced around them, pulling at his father's dark coat. For the moment his father ignored him, lost in Oleander's perfumed embrace. Despite the difference in their ages, she loved him as dearly as he did her. She knew before she married that he would be gone for half the year, trading in the islands and up and down the eastern seaboard, but that didn't make parting any easier or his absences any shorter. At last, he lifted his son up on one arm, kissed him on the cheek, slipped his other around Oleander's willowy waist and helped them both into the carriage. On the way home an excited but sleepy Hollis said, "I knew you were coming home today, Papa."

"Didn't I surprise you just a little? We're a whole week early."

"He did tell me you'd come today, Cary, dear. He said he heard you telling Uncle Abe."

His brother Abraham usually stayed home and looked after business in Portland, but his health had been poor that winter and

Carruthers had persuaded him that a month at sea would set him right.

"Did he now? And when did you hear that, son?"

"Before lunch when I was playing hide and seek with Mummy," the boy said earnestly.

"And what did you hear me say?" asked the Captain, now mildly interested.

"You told Uncle Abe you'd be home early because of the storm."

It was true. That morning, as he stood on the bridge with his brother, he'd commented on their speed. Pushed by unusually strong winds generated by a storm south of Cape Hatteras, they were setting new records everyday.

"You heard me say that?"

Hollis nodded as he drifted off to sleep in his father's arms.

It was wonderful to have the Captain home — the schooner was in dry dock and he wasn't scheduled to sail for twelve weeks — and the family spent the remainder of the summer having a good time. Their favourite activity was to take the carriage and a picnic to the beach at Cape Elizabeth, five miles south of the city. They would go out after breakfast and spend the whole day at the seaside. The Captain would remove his boots and roll up the legs of his black serge trousers. Oleander bundled her skirts and, balancing a frilly white parasol, went barefoot in the surf. Hollis wore his sailor suit with the short pants and frolicked after her.

In the mornings they searched for creatures in the rock pools around the granite and marble breakwater that extended out into the ocean for almost one hundred yards. They'd build sand castles. After lunch they napped in the shade of the pine trees along the beach. Later they read and finally flew the big kite the Captain had made while at sea.

Hollis's prediction of his father's early return was soon put out of mind as a curiosity. So when, in mid-September, the boy looked up from his porridge and said, "Papa, Papa I hear a boy shouting and crying. He's being drownded," Oleander reached gently over and took his small hand in hers and explained, "It's drowned, son, not drownded. And nothing of the sort is happening. No one's being drowned here."

"No, no, not here," exclaimed the child, peeved at his mother's ignorance. "Down at the beach where we go. We have to help him."

"Don't be silly, son. How would you know that?" said a stern Papa.

"I hear him, I hear him, I hear him," replied the little boy, smacking his spoon into his bowl and spraying the table with a mixture of milk and oatmeal and maple syrup.

"Enough of that, son," exploded the Captain.

But Hollis wouldn't stop and got red in the face and raised his own small voice and shouted, "He's getting drowned. He is. He is. HE IS."

This behavior was rewarded by his father jumping up from his chair, grabbing the boy, rushing him upstairs, dumping him on his bed and slamming the door.

It was a pensive Captain who returned to the house an hour after he'd left on a morning which was to have been spent reviewing accounts with his brother. He kissed Oleander, then took her by the shoulders and said, "Where's Hollis? I've done the boy a terrible injustice. The McKiver boy, Christopher, was fishing off the breakwater at Cape Elizabeth this morning and a wave took him and swept him out to sea. His brother saw it happen. They're out searching for the body now. Odd thing on such a fine day. How could Hollis have possibly known?" He left the question hanging.

It happened again in late October. Hollis woke his parents in the middle of the night frantically pulling at the bedclothes and shouting: "They're burning in a fire. Go save them, Papa. Go save them!" He was told he was suffering from a bad dream and ordered back to bed. The morning papers reported that a family of five had perished in a fire at a farm in nearby Hampton. "Alerted by their piteous cries, neighbours were unable to save a single soul owing to the ghastly intensity of the flames," read the story in part. Two weeks later the little lad heard the death pleas of a farmer nine miles away who fell into a silo of grain and suffocated. By then, Hollis's acute hearing became almost the sole subject of discussion between his parents. What should they do? Their chief concern was to protect their son. The papers were full of stories about the unfortunate fellow in England with a disease that horribly altered his appearance and who had been dubbed "The Elephant Man." They feared that if news of their son's unique talent got out, he risked being labeled a freak and forever after hounded by reporters and curiosity seekers. The Captain delayed his departure and sent the ship south under the first mate.

The first week of December, the family was in Boston at the office of Dr. Peter Smythe, who had a large practice and was a graduate of the Harvard Medical School, as attested to by the prominent framed diploma in his waiting room.

"Have you noticed any pattern to these, ah, shall we say, predictions?" said the skeptical physician as he peered over his spectacles at the specimen of a small boy.

"The weather is usually fine," offered Oleander, feeling silly.

"I was thinking of something more, ah, shall we say, biological," said Smythe.

But they couldn't think of anything more to say, biological or otherwise. A thorough physical exam failed to find anything unusual.

"A bit of wax in the ears, that's all," said the doctor as he showed them out with a tonic he had recommended. "Give it to him three times a day after meals. It's got a bit of a bite but he'll manage. Be right as, ah, rain, in a week or two."

Two months later, Hollis was still hearing things. After the experience with the doctor, they decided not to discuss the matter with anyone else. The Captain spent several long days in the library going through medical texts but could find nothing. Instead they concentrated on their son, who had become reluctant to talk about the voices. They asked him to tell them each time he heard them, without fail, and there would be a reward; each day they poured over the local papers and noted any accidents or violent deaths. And they looked for a pattern.

It was Oleander who found it.

"It's the clouds," she exclaimed one evening as they were going through the day's newspapers in the parlour. And she leapt up and danced around behind her husband's chairs singing, "It's the clouds, it's the clouds! That first time, when you were at sea, we'd been looking for shapes in the sky. I've just been remembering the weather every single time Hollis says he hears something. It's always a fine day."

She'd got it right, as subsequent events proved. Succinctly put, Hollis could hear things — his parents determined the maximum range to be about twenty-five miles — if the sky contained a mass of fluffy white clouds but was otherwise clear, and if what was being said carried a heavy emotional charge. After three consecutive confirmations, they were certain and the Captain penned a stiff letter to Dr. Smythe. "He was rude to you and I wish to rub his nose in it," he told his wife who thought it was, perhaps, not a good idea.

The new evidence had a catalytic effect on the doctor. He wanted the boy back in Boston to conduct studies "under laboratory conditions." The parents thought not, but they did invite the physician to Portland, as their guest, to confirm their son's remarkable gift. He arrived toward the end of May 1849 and spent a week. Oleander put him in what she called "the yellow room." She had carefully chosen wallpaper with an exuberant pattern of roses. She felt the cheery atmosphere could have nothing but good effect on the taciturn, self-important healer.

Away from the office, Dr. Smythe turned out to be a more compassionate individual. He was an intelligent man, after all, and one who loved to fish and liked a brandy after dinner. He and the

Captain went down to the beach every morning at dawn and cast into the waves for bluefish. In the evenings they went through the papers and chatted over cigars and a glass or two of port. On only the second day the doctor was there, Hollis heard the moans of a fisherman in a ship out on the bay, who had been accidently run through with a harpoon — the evening's paper carried a graphic account. The child heard nothing more during the remainder of the week but the incident and "the obvious sincerity and, ah, sanity" of the parents convinced him of Hollis's remarkable ability. The Captain persuaded him to keep it to himself, in the interests of the child's welfare, until Hollis was older and better able to handle the attention which they knew would inevitably follow, once news of their son's talent reached the general public. Dr. Smythe agreed, asking only that he be allowed to keep Hollis as a patient and might be permitted, from time to time, to make suggestions regarding the boy's well-being.

And that is how, in the Fall of 1852, at age seven, Hollis found himself enrolled in the Cambridge Military Academy outside Boston. Dr. Smythe thought it would do the boy, who was a slight and dreamy child, "good and, ah, shall we say, make a man of him." And he added that the boy's gift might, at some future date, be of help to the nation. Oleander thought it the very worst idea she'd ever heard, but by then Hollis had a sister, and there was another baby on the way, and the Captain, for once, went against his wife's wishes and insisted on it.

School was a nightmare for Hollis. He hadn't been there a week when an older boy, Brent Pittsfield, who became a U.S. Senator during the McKinley administration, dubbed him Hog-Ears and it stuck. Worse, being close to populous Boston, on days when the weather was right, he was plagued with the screams and shudders of dozens of accident victims.

The only person to be told about his special abilities was the headmaster and he'd been sworn to secrecy. In any case, he only half believed it, while granting that, "if it proved out it might, at some future date, have some usefulness from a military viewpoint." Early on, Hollis had tried to speak to him about the pain the voices caused but the headmaster's only response was that they would cease to bother him: "once the school has toughened you up." Hollis never mentioned the matter again.

Hog-Ears became a lonely boy who lived for the rare visits of his mother. Whenever she could get away, she came down to Boston and took a room at a nearby inn where the two would spent Saturday night and all day Sunday together, "being silly," as she put it.

The boy was saved from utter misery during his time at the Academy by the chaplain, Father Moose. Father Moose, born Peter Beldewellen, was a legend at the school. His nickname came from a luxuriant goatee he sported and his wild hair which sprang from the sides of his large head like antlers. He had fought with the Dutch at the Battle of Waterloo, and was a kindly, open-hearted man. For more than fifty years — until he suffered a stroke while performing communion in 1873 at age eighty-two — he was the protector of those young cadets who fell outside the raucous norm and struggled to find a place for themselves in the student hierarchy. He would have these students over for lunch on Sunday. His wife would serve a chicken or a goose or a roast and on afternoons when the weather was good, they'd play field games like Kick-The-Can or Run-Sheep-Run or, in winter, go skating on the pond or build snow forts. Always after these outings, they would gather around the fire in the living room and Father Moose would read to them. He chose his texts widely, from the stories of the Greek gods and goddesses to the latest serialized episode by that new British writer, Charles Dickens.

Hollis had never been a good student; he didn't like sports, and, after almost nine years, he still stumbled through the endless drills performed in all weathers on the parade ground. Yet in 1861, at age fifteen, less than a week after the surrender of Fort Sumner to the Confederates in the Charleston, South Carolina harbour, he was singled out by the War Office for a posting to Washington, D.C. His fellow students were astonished. "They want Hog-Ears," exclaimed Brent Pittsfield when he heard the news. "Now that the war's coming, they must be short of bacon!"

Hollis arrived in the Capital with the 6th Massachusetts Volunteers. By this time, Washington was ringed with states that supported the South and the regiment was jeered and stoned and shot at while changing trains in Baltimore. The Mass 6th fired back and twelve civilians were killed. When the squad marched down Washington's Pennsylvania Avenue on April 20, they found howitzers in front of the Treasury building and the Mint and the entire city barricaded and sandbagged. Hollis was billeted, along with his new comrades-in-arms, on the floor of the U.S. Senate, where he dreamed about his mother and the beaches of Cape Elizabeth.

Over the next month, Hollis, along with everyone else, waited for the war to begin. Apart from a brief meeting at the War Office the day after he arrived, where he was told he would be given "special assignments," he had no idea what he was to do. Day after day, more and more troops poured in. Then, in mid-June, he was suddenly reassigned to a group of Pennsylvania volunteers who were camped in Virginia, just across the Potomac, under the command of a Colonel Lew Wallace. Wallace had been told of the lad's gift and had been instructed to use it. After a brief interview, the Colonel told Hollis he suspected "your ballyhooed hearing is a bunch of hooey."

Still, he signed a requisition for a tent and two weeks' supplies, ordered him to camp on Russell Ridge and told the lad to "let me know if you hear anything."

That was fine with Hollis, who had been bedevilled by the echos of the pain of others on an almost hourly basis since his arrival. Fine day had followed fine day and the thousands of green and bungling troops who now occupied Washington were forever having accidents; at least one of them was killed in some dumb mishap or other every twenty-four hours. Away from the centre of activity, Hollis hoped he might get some peace. On July 3, 1861, he set up his tent among big oaks and birdsong on a ridge which felt as though it were a thousand miles from anywhere. Alone at last, he was as happy as he'd been since the last Sunday at Father Moose's house.

Nothing much happened for the first ten days. He was good at solitude and contented himself by walking in the woods, re-reading his mother's letters and writing her every day, letters he kept neatly folded in his journal waiting for the day he'd get a chance to post them. He took great pains in cooking his meals and tried to invent new ways of preparing army rations. After dinner each night, he read from the Bible, the only book he had with him, frequently coming across things that he found highly amusing. The endless squabbles, the gossip, the backbiting, the vengefulness — just like life at school, he thought. As soon as it was dark, he rolled himself up in his army blanket and seldom slept for less than ten hours. The voices in his head were mostly quiet.

Then, in the very early hours of July 15, he woke to whispers of fear murmuring in his skull. It sounded like frightened men and boys praying and pleading. He sat up in the dark tent and tried to make them out.

"Oh Mama, Mama, don't let them..." he heard.

"May the blessed Lord Jesus save and pro..."

"Dearest Mary, Mother of Our Saviour Je.."

And louder, "No, no, I cannot...." and mixed in with this, other sounds also packed with emotion, "We'll give 'em hell..."

"I'm gonna get me ten yank..."

"Be the best fun I ever had."

Shouts of "On to Washington" and "Hang Lincoln..."

Hollis leapt up in the dark and struck his head on the tent pole. My God, he thought, the South is on the march! Must warn Commander Wallace! He dressed quickly with the voices of fear, desperation and mock courage ringing in his ears and started down the mountain. There was no moon and he stumbled and fell many times and lost his way in thickets and thorns. It was a scratched and bleeding Hollis Toggsham who limped into camp at sunrise gasping for directions to the Wallace tent.

"Commander's not here, sonny," one grizzled Sargeant told him.

"But I've got to warn him. Enemy's coming! They're almost here!"

"You don't say," chuckled the old soldier leaning on his musket. "I suppose they're just over that hill," he said.

Hollis nodded furiously, "I can hear them. They're coming!"

"Well, go get yer rifle, fella. We got some shootin' to do." He laughed hoarsely until it brought on a coughing fit.

Now that Hollis looked around, he could see that the whole company was in full uniform and moving out. "Get yer gun boy. Look lively. You look like you already been in the fight and it ain't begun yet," called a corporal.

By agreement between the generals of both sides, the Battle of Bull Run had been scheduled for more than a week but Hollis, up on the ridge, was perhaps the only person in the North or South, soldier or civilian, who didn't know. All his equipment was back in the tent. His regiment could be anywhere. He had no idea what to do so he let the flow of his men and equipment sweep him forward into Hades.

It was an altered soul who staggered back into the Capital over Long Bridge the next day in the pouring rain along with the thousands of others of the defeated Union Army.

He had seen the right hand of a boy beside him blown away as he reached for a canteen. He had seen human entrails hanging from the burning branches of trees. He had tried to stop the flow of blood from the terrible wound in a man's thigh while the man murmured, "More light, comrade. More light..." And worse, for him, the horses, gored and bloody, their sides torn open, gashing at their wounds, legs splintered, eyes bursting. Sometime in the afternoon, a bullet grazed him in the temple and he was knocked into a ditch where he lay for many hours with no thought of trying to get up, his head exploding with his own pain and the magnified terror and suffering of thousands of others that thundered in his skull. Over eight hundred were killed, more than twenty-five hundred wounded. Hundreds of the Union Army deserted. William Tecumseh Sherman, whose own troops held the Confederates back to protect the retreat, would call it "the best planned and worst fought battle in history."

Fortunately, his injury turned out to be a minor one, but Hollis had had enough of war. He ached, voices screamed and beat in his head without letup; he couldn't eat or stop his body from shaking. Three days after the battle, dazed and humiliated, he requested a discharge. Wallace, out of compassion or because of Hollis's young age or, more likely, to be rid of the troublesome kid who had mysterious connections in the War Office, dispatched him, not home to his beloved Maine, but three thousand miles away to the New Mexican Territory, where it was feared there would be an attack by the South out of Texas. "Keep an ear out for Indians," grimaced Wallace as he signed the paper and handed it to the pale and trembling boy with the big ears. One day Wallace too would be sent west to become the reluctant governor of the same territory, but that was years in the future.

Hollis arrived in Santa Fe in mid-August with a contingent of volunteers from Kansas and was immediately sent on sixty miles north to Taos to join his new commander, the famous Colonel Kit Carson. Hollis, still homesick but a little recovered from the disaster of battle, was pleased with this turn of events. While at school he had read a penny dreadful about the exploits of the fur-trapping mountain man who, it seemed to Hollis, was the one true living hero of the frontier. At age fifty-two, Carson was a stocky, gruff man with shoulder-length grey-blonde hair who, when not in Union Army uniform, wore buckskin leggings and a beaded vest sewn for him by a Ute woman.

Carson was as curious about his new assignee as Hollis was about him. In reviewing his transfer papers, Carson had noted that

A few of Hollis's company prior to the battle of
Bull Run. He was one of the few soldiers who didn't
know the battle was scheduled for July 15, 1861,
and was severely ridiculed for it.

the lad was said to have exceptional hearing abilities over long distances. Carson knew many native shamans and had often been astonished by their powers. "About time we had one on our side," he muttered to himself.

The day after Hollis reported for duty, Carson proposed the two-day ride out the short distance to Taos Pueblo which had been a Tewa settlement for eight hundred years. As soon as the horses entered the dusty plaza between the ancient, rambling multi-story adobe structures, Hollis felt at home. Carson made introductions. When he came to the medicine man, he said to Hollis, "This here fellow can see beyond the mountains." Hollis bowed slightly and wondered what far-off horrors might visit the poor man at night.

Carson, who hadn't yet mentioned the boy's special talent, suggested they ride up the mountain behind the village to visit Blue Lake, a sacred spot to the Tewa. They were making their way through the thick grey-green sage brush that covered the lower slopes when the scout reined in.

"You tell me about it now," he said as Hollis drew up.

"What, sir?"

"Your damn magic hearing. What else? And don't call me sir. Call me Kit."

"It's a gift, sir. And a burden."

"Kit."

"Yes, sir. Kit."

"You can call me Sir Kit," the burly man grinned. "What do ya mean, a burden?"

"I hear mostly people in pain. Things I don't want to hear."

"How's it work?"

When Hollis had finished his brief explaination, Carson looked up at the sky and said, "Like today?"

"Yes, sir, er, Kit, sir."

They rode on in silence for almost an hour, Hollis turned in the saddle and looked back from time to time out across the wide

Taos pueblo where Hollis spent his happiest time
while serving in the army. The shaman treated
him like a son.

plain cut by the zigzag trench of the Rio Grande. Off to the left he could see down the vast smoothed teeth of the Sangre de Cristo range almost all the way to Santa Fe, sixty miles distant. Then, as they rounded a massive boulder which had long ago broken away from a cliff higher up and come plunging through the trees, Hollis heard a soft anguished cry. Then a moan. Then silence.

"Sir, er, Kit," he called, "I, er, just heard something."

The two reined in and Hollis listened. For the next ten minutes nothing, then another moan and a few scrapes of language which Hollis repeated as best he could.

"It's a prayer to the red-tailed hawk spirit," said the frontiersman. "The man's dying. Where's it come from?"

Hollis pointed north and west high up on the slope of the adjacent range.

It took them almost two hours to reach the outcropping where the sounds originated. As they picked their way among the pines through shale and rock slides, the voice grew progressively weaker and often lapsed into silence. A thin trail made by goats or deer led upward to a massive overhang. They tethered the horses and went the last few hundred yards on foot with Hollis leading the way. For half an hour he had heard nothing. The boy had no sooner stepped on the huge slab of rock which hung above the valley, than he lost his footing and began to slide back in toward the cliff face into what appeared to be an opening in the rock about fifteen feet across. Carson just managed to catch an arm and haul him back to safety.

"He's down there," said Hollis, catching his breath. Both men inched to the edge of the hole on their stomachs and peered down. There, at the bottom of an almost circular chasm thirty feet below, lit by pale, slanting light which filtered in though a crack in the rock about three-quarters of the way down, lay a deer, a broken spear in its chest, its neck bent at an unnatural angle — and a man. The deer was dead. Small dirt-coloured birds pecked at the dull eyes.

215

The famous frontiersman Kit Carson
at fifty-two. He befriended Hollis and
believed in his special powers.

"Manuelito. Jesus. It's Manuelito," exclaimed Carson peering down. And the man's head moved.

It took them an hour to bring him up using a length of rope the mountain man kept in his saddle bag. The Indian had a broken leg, a deep gash on his forehead and another in his side. He was weak with loss of blood but a sip of water revived him enough to insist that they also bring up the deer. Without saying anything, Carson threw Hollis the rope and motioned that he would lower him into the pit down to retrieve the carcass. It took another hour to settle man and beast on the two horses. Manuelito rode in front of Carson; Hollis followed with the deer slung over the mare's rump.

On the way back, they pieced together what had happened. Manuelito had gone out hunting on foot at dawn. By mid-morning he had tracked a family group of four animals, a doe, two fawns and a buck, to beneath the overhang. He took a shot but the powder and lead ball, which he'd packed himself, exploded in the chamber and the animals took off up the ridge. He decided to circle around with his spear and meet them from the opposite direction. He arrived at the overhang first and positioned himself out of sight behind a rock slightly above. The buck led but, cautious, moved out to the edge of the outcropping, too far away for a sure kill. The doe was closer and he caught her in the chest but as she went down she slid in the loose rock toward the pit. He rushed forward and managed to catch the end of the spear and hold her impaled, half over the chasm when the buck charged. An antler caught him in the side, sending both him and the doe to the bottom. He'd struck his head on a rock in the fall. The deer had broken her neck.

"I made my peace," he said to Carson.

Riders came out to meet them as they neared the pueblo. Carson told them their brother had been saved by the ears of the white shaman and there was as much fuss over Hollis as there was over Manuelito. Word had gone through the village even before they arrived and everyone poured into the plaza. They took the reins of Hollis's horse and led him around like a hero. The kids ran after him and tried to touch his boots.

In early September, Colonel Carson was ordered to Santa Fe to head up a regiment of volunteers against Confederate General Henry Sibley. Sibley was moving up the Rio Grande with over three thousand mounted Texans, hoping to seize the territory and cut off the routes to California. Carson left Hollis behind.

"Don't need no magic to chase those boys back to Texas," he said the day he set out from the Taos Plaza, just down the street from his home and the trading post he had operated for more than twenty years.

The next twelve months were the best of Hollis's life. He practically lived at the Pueblo. He was welcomed and his special powers revered, and he was invited to many ceremonies. The small frontier population meant he was not often plagued by the cries of the wounded, the sick or the dying. And he met and fell in love with Rebecca Moonlight, the daughter of a shaman. Often that fall, the two of them rode up into the golden aspens on the slopes of Sacred Mountain and came back only when the sky burned with a skein of stars. On Christmas Eve he was invited to take part as a warrior in the parading of the Virgin from the mission church, and marched proudly between dozens of huge bonfires which lit up the plaza, firing his army pistol into the air in advance of those who carried the elaborately gowned statue on a bier.

In February of the next year, 1862, the Texan force was defeated in Glorieta Pass. It was the start and finish of the Civil War in the Territory. With the war out of the way, Brigadier General James Carleton took over administration of the territory and set about ending raids on the Rio Grande settlements by the Mescalero Apache tribes to the east. Colonel Carson, who would have preferred to remain in Taos with the love of his life his wife, Josefa, the mother of his seven children, was again pressed into service and this time he took Hollis with him.

The note he sent requesting Hollis to report for duty read, in part, "you say you can hear voices full of emotion, you probably heard me and Josefa carrying on all the way from Blue Lake. I hear you been up to few things on your own."

Hollis was tanned almost black and had grown his hair until it was longer than Sir Kit's famous locks. "See you've gone Tewa on me," said Carson when they met, "Ain't nothin' wrong with that."

The campaign against the Apache was a short one. It began in September, and by February 1863 most had either gone into hiding in the White Mountains or fled to Mexico. An unfortunate four hundred were rounded up and forcibly resettled as farmers on the Pecos River at Bosque Redondo near Fort Sumner, two hundred and fifty miles to the southeast. It was Carleton's idea. He was a well-intentioned man and had a vision of turning the nomadic tribes who had plagued the Spanish and Anglo settlements for over two hundred years into gentle, God-fearing farming folk. They told him the Pecos was alkaline and couldn't be used for irrigation but he wanted the new reservation there to protect against Comanche raids and he was, after all, the head honcho.

The campaign had been hard on Hollis, mostly because of his sympathy for the other side. It didn't help that Carson also thought it was a wrong-headed scheme. "Thing is," he told the seventeen-year-old on a brilliant evening in late October when they were on patrol near the Mexican border, "these people ain't never stayed in one place for more'n a month. They ain't no farmers and I can't see one reason on God's earth to make 'em into farmers. The way I see it, we got too many farmers already. Now, I'm not sayin' the General ain't smart ...." he let his voice trial off.

After he was released from active duty, Hollis returned to Taos while Sir Kit was ordered to direct Ute and New Mexican militia in raids against the Navajo-Dine people, hundreds of whom were taken prisoner and sold to Spanish families as slaves. In Taos, Hollis and Rebecca resumed their rides but little more. She seemed distant, less in the here-and-now.

By July he and a surly Sir Kit were together once more, this time at Fort Canby, a hundred miles west of Taos, rebuilt on the ruins of Fort Defiance, which had been destroyed by the Navajo three years before. Carson had almost a thousand men under him. They were to spend the summer and fall destroying Navajo crops and sending any Dine they caught to Bosque Redondo on the sour Pecos. More farmers.

"Tell you what," Carson said to Hollis as they watched from their horses as a field of Navajo corn went up in flames. "Them women and children scrubbing Spanish floors and doing Spanish washing are a damn sight better off than these ones up here who'll soon be starving."

"Why can't we just leave them alone?" asked Hollis.

" 'Cause the general wants 'em caught is why and he's smarter than both of us put together. It's not up to us to like it or not like it."

By November, when the first snows came, the troops had destroyed every field within a fifty-mile radius of the fort and seized more than two million pounds of grain from secret hiding places where the Navajo had stashed it for winter.

"And in the whole damn summer and the whole damn fall," demanded a tipsy Carson dressed in a Buffalo robe and swigging whiskey from the bottle, "How many Navajo did we see? They've got the power, Hollis. Like I said, they can disappear like that," and he spat a slug of whiskey into the fire which exploded in a jet of blue flame. "We got the power too, don't we, boy?"

Snow fell nearly every day for a month and mean winds screamed over the empty plain. They were at over seven thousand feet and right through December the temperature never rose above freezing. In January new orders came from Santa Fe and Hollis was summoned to the Colonel's quarters.

Carson, away from his wife, on a mission against Indians he'd known all his life, was in a foul mood as he paced the small, drafty room. The army had always stayed put in winter when conditions made travel risky. Now Carleton wanted them to scout Canyon de Chelly, reputedly the heart of Dine country.

"Scout it?" roared the mountain man. "Hell, we can't even find it." Army maps showed only the vaguest outlines of the canyon. As far as Carson knew it had never been seen by a white man.

They moved out on January 4 under an iron sky with temperatures in the low twenties, more than eight hundred men. Then, as now, successful wars were won on the quality of the supply lines, a fact brought home to me the other night as I watched a documentary on the 1991 Gulf War and the massive build-up of personnel, ships, aircraft, armaments, missiles and electronic equipment which preceded it. Over five hundred thousand troops assembled in the deserts and on the seas around Iraq against the Baron of Baghdad. Feeding them alone required the mother of all strategies, one reason, perhaps, why Sadaam thought it would never happen.

A hundred and thirty years before, on the high plains of Dine country, they used oxen to tow the supply wagons, more than sixty of the powerful beasts — augmented with a couple of hundred pack mules. The snow was deep over the washes and gullies that fanned the plain like the lines of a hand; a bitter wind gusted and swirled out of the north. Every day Carson had to send out sappers ahead of the wagons and mules to break trail. Still, they lost twenty-seven oxen in the first four days to exhaustion and broken legs when they slipped on icy rocks and hidden crevasses beneath the snow and had to be shot. Hollis rode with the officers. Carson, uncertain about their destination, wanted his shaman nearby in case he heard anything.

"How many Navajo you seen since you come out here this summer?" he asked on the third day as they rode under a white sky.

"Eight," said Hollis.

"There's ten thousand, maybe twenty thousand of them out here. You'd think they hear us coming."

Hollis shrugged.

"They damn well don't. They see us coming, know what I'm saying? Met a Comanche medicine man once who they said could be screwing his wife ten miles away at the same time he was right in front of you talkin'? That'd be a somethin', wouldn't it, boy? Ridin' around out here freezin' yer nuts off and at the same time be back in the big double bed with Josefa..." He chuckled for a moment and grew serious, "You think they can make themselves invisible?"

Hollis said under his breath that he hoped they could.

"You hear anything yet?"

Hollis shook his head and pointed to the sky, a cold, uniform white blandness, horizon to horizon. Carson pulled up his collar and spurred his horse ahead.

That night, January 9, they were camped on the south side of a mesa trying to stay out of the wind. The sky cleared and the temperature plunged. Sometime in the dark, Hollis woke. A painful moaning, a dirge whispered in his head. Navajo! And not far away. He struggled into his frozen boots and coat and went to the Colonel's tent. The sky was a deep midnight blue awash with stars. A delicate silver moon rode through the clouds like a princess.

"Thank the body of the blessed Santa Rose de Lima," mumbled a groggy Carson after Hollis shook him awake and delivered the news. "How far?" he asked sitting up in the mound of buffalo skins that covered him. Hollis reckoned eight, maybe ten miles northeast.

Just after lunch, one of the advance party returned with news that there had been a skirmish with a group of Dine at the mouth of the canyon. Eleven warriors had been killed and perhaps fifty women and children taken prisoner. They were in bad shape, said the soldier, sick and hungry. It was one of these women Hollis had heard keening in the night.

That evening they camped at the mouth of the canyon and, after his own meal, he helped hand out a ration of grain and meat to the captives, who made no effort no escape but wanted only to stay near the source of food. The children, swaddled in blankets and sheep skins, had hollow eyes and big bellies. The women were listless and uncommunicative. He had picked up a little Navajo and tried to speak with them. The only phrase he could be certain he made out was a curse on his ancestors.

The cold snap continued into January 11. Carson, under the impression there was a single canyon, divided the force into two groups, one scouting the north rim, the other taking the south, believing the two would meet. In fact, Captain Pheiffer, with four hundred men including Hollis, went up an off-shoot named the Canyon del Muerto by the Spanish two hundred years before, while the Colonel proceeded along the main canyon with his contingent. When they failed to meet, both returned to the entrance. Pheiffer had taken another nineteen prisoners.

Overnight, Hollis, buffeted by the agonies of an entire nation as it slowly starved to death, lay on his back in numb purgatory, gazing at the wind-whipped canvas of the tent roof. Some time before dawn the clouds moved in and the wind fell. The voices stopped and it began to snow.

Before he rode out with Pheiffer for the second time, he said to Carson, "They're suffering, Sir Kit."

"And we're not?" said the Indian fighter.

"You know what I mean."

Carson was in a black mood that wouldn't lift for months. "And things ain't gonna get much better for 'em neither," he said and mounted and pulled down his hat. An aide threw a second fur robe across his shoulders. The snow picked up as he moved off into the thin grey air.

The great walls of the canyon soared to a thousand feet and embraced them as they made their way slowly along the icy river bed. The soldiers gawked at the natural magnificence as though they were on a tour of the Vatican. The exhausting work of breaking trail continued all day, with the Captain replacing the lead teams every half-hour. That wasn't the only reason progress was so

Canyon de Chelly, the Navajo's final refuge. The forced walk to Fort Sumner, during which thousands died, began here in 1864. Hollis felt his gift had betrayed them.

painful. After going less than a mile, they were jeered by Navajo who swarmed along the trails and in the mouths of the caves high up on the cliff face. They cursed and pelted rocks and fired shots. All day one old woman hobbled along a narrow trail two hundred feet above them, screeching like a witch. Finally, one of the troops could take no more and brought her tumbling into the valley with a single shot as though she were some huge and fallen crow. They camped eight miles in, protected by an overhang which projected out near a bend in the river. They tore down old wooden lodges for their fires and were warm for the first time in a week. The next day, it was over. The Navajo, richest tribe in the southwest, terror of the pueblos and settlements along the Rio Grande for two centuries, began to give themselves up by the hundreds. Carleton's burning of the fields had left them without food. A huge number of troops had invaded their most ancient, most secure stronghold. They knew Colonel Kit Carson as a fair man and trusted him to treat them well. It was over.

"It's finished," Carson said to Hollis and they rode back through the gates of Fort Canby a week later, "And I don't like it." By the end of the month the man who solved the Indian problem was back in Santa Fe with his beloved wife. The papers wanted the story. He wasn't talking.

Hollis returned to Taos to find Rebecca great with child, the birth only a week or two away. She said it was Manuelito's baby. Hollis was nineteen years old and he felt a hundred. He kissed her on the cheek and held both her hands. "It's better like this," she said softly in Tewa, "We were not ready for each other."

"No," was all he could manage.

They went for a walk along the stream which flowed out of Sacred Mountain and was covered with a crust of ice. When he left the plaza she walked with him to the gates near the mission and took his head in both her hands and kissed him on each ear as she had done when they were lovers. He smiled and mounted the army mare that had been with him all the way to Canyon de Chelly. He felt suddenly hungry, as though he hadn't eaten in a week. He rode into the Fonda Hotel in town and ordered a big dinner of steak and fried potatoes and pie for dessert and he ate by himself in the corner near the fireplace.

Carson had no more need for his "ears" for the time being. In May Hollis was ordered to report back to Washington for reassignment. General Grant's massive attack on Lee's forces south of Washington had begun. It would be the longest and bloodiest campaign of the war. The General urged the Army of the Potomac on and on despite staggering losses on both sides. The Union lost fifty-four thousand in little more than a month.

Hollis set out on May 10 with two families from Arkansas who had had northern sympathies in a Confederate state and journeyed out to the New Mexican Territory hoping for a new life. It hadn't worked out and now that the Union army had swept through their home state, they felt the war would soon be over and so were headed home. Part of their route passed though Indian Territory and they were glad to have the young soldier along. Hollis didn't hear a thing the moonless night when the Comanche stormed over their five wagons just east of the Texas panhandle and took all nineteen prisoner. He was rescued six months later, on November 15, by a squad of troopers lead by a Captain Thompson who had been with him at Canyon de Chelly and who had spent much of the previous August in the canyon cutting down five thousand peach trees, the final act in General Carleton's scorched earth policy.

Hollis never spoke of his time with the Comanche except to say to a Santa Fe reporter that he was "grateful to be alive." Asked to speculate why he thought he was allowed to live when eleven others had perished, he would say only, "The Comanche have a point of view. It's one I can appreciate." Also mentioned in the article, which appeared in the *New Mexican Gazette*, January 27, 1865, was Mrs. Winifred Toggsham (nee Simpson). The two had been rescued together and had been married at the Cathedral two days before.

The war was winding down at last. Sherman's Army was in

Savannah and a peace delegation from the South, albeit an unsuccessful one, had met with President Lincoln at Fortress Monroe, near Washington at the mouth of the Potomac. Hollis requested a discharge and this time, after two months' delay, it was granted. By then the young couple had already made plans to go back east with a large party going via the Santa Fe Trail.

The evening before they left, on a damp cold day in early April, they dined at the Carsons' on a fine roast of venison and beans and rice with green chile, followed by Rosita's light-as-a-feather sopapillas with honey for dessert. At the door Hollis shook hands with Carson.

"How many came in?" he asked.

"Eight, nine thousand," Carson replied.

"How many died?"

"Maybe two thousand."

"And how many stayed in the canyon?"

"I reckon about half of 'em," Carson smiled.

"They gonna make farmers of those that did come in?"

"No. They ain't," he said and closed the door quietly

Carson was right, the experiment soon failed and the Navajo were allowed to return to their traditional lands just three years later. Before Hollis died in 1947, at one hundred and two, he would see Navajo lands expanded to eighteen million acres and the tribe living much as they always had. But by then his first-born son had long since inherited the family gift and passed it on to his son.

◆ Eric Toggsham, my grandfather, was born to Hollis and Winifred in 1880. His two older sisters, Sofie and Flora, doted on him. Like his father, Eric was a delicate child with refined features except for the ears which were unusually large and stuck out. Hollis suspected he had "the gift" the moment he laid eyes on the newborn in the bedroom of the big house in Portland the couple shared with his mother. The Captain had died in 1862.

Eric loved to be read to and his sisters were more than willing to oblige. They read him every Victorian children's tale — short on plot and long on morals — they could find in the Portland Library and The Edward Book Shop on Charles Street. Eric listened to everything with rapt attention but his favourites were Bible stories and his favourite Bible story was the one about Samuel and Eli. No matter how many times he heard it, he would clap his hands and laugh and laugh at the part where young Samuel, working in the temple for Eli, the high priest, is woken in the night three times by a voice he takes to be Eli's calling him. "Here am I," Eric would whisper, echoing Samuel's words each time he presented himself to Eli. Finally the lad, following Eli's instructions to Samuel, would bellow, "Speak, for thy servant heareth," when the Lord called. Then he would fall silent and listen intently to one of his sisters read God's astonishing reply: "I will do a thing in Israel, at which both the ears of everyone that heareth it shall tingle." At the end of the story Eric would ask, "My ears sometimes tingle. Do yours?" And again he would fall into peals of rapturous laughter.

When he turned four, Hollis took his son into the heavily curtained parlour, and sat him on his knee and asked him if he sometimes heard things that were not there.

"Yes, father," said Eric solemnly.

"When I was a little boy, I heard them too. I want you to promise me, son, that you will never tell anybody about them except me. Will you do that, son?"

Eric nodded.

"If you ever hear anything that, er, you think you should tell somebody about, come to me. Is that clear?"

"You mean if someone is calling for help or hurting, father?"

"Yes, son."

"I've heard people doing that but I thought it was my 'magination."

"You tell me next time, son." And he held him close and gave him a kiss and sent him off to play with a pat on the behind.

Hollis had used his own powerful hearing a few times since returning to Portland. He'd sent the fire squad here or a rescue team there but he never did let on how he knew of the emergency, making up some fanciful tale of smelling smoke on the east wind or simply acting on a hunch. He didn't want to hear the voices. He blamed them for ruining his childhood. His whole youth had been churned up and destroyed by the wailing and keening of the sick and dying. After age thirty his special abilities began to decline, slowly at first and then more rapidly. Peace gradually seeped into his life. By age thirty-five his hearing was no more acute than anyone else's. At ninety, he was stone deaf and considered it a great blessing. "I live in silence," he used to tell his great-grandchildren, and break into a wide toothless cackle.

He had wanted nothing more than a quiet life when he returned from the west, and soon apprenticed himself to a plumber. Eventually, he opened his own shop. The life of a tradesman suited him and he inherited enough money to continue to live in the big house. Early on, his son Eric set his mind on going to college. He was not terribly good at school but he studied hard. Harvard wouldn't take him, but McGill University in Montreal would. So, in the fall of 1896, at the Portland Railway Station, he kissed his mother, his grandmother and his sisters goodbye and shook hands with his father who, in parting, clapped him on the back, and he boarded a train headed north. He arrived to find a big, booming city on the St. Lawerence River. The mansions of timber lords and mining barons were going up on the hill around the university and the harbour, called "the world's largest inland port," was crowded with ships. At first, when the weather conditions were right, Eric was tortured with the cries and moaning of the large population. Someone, somewhere within his magnified earshot was always in trouble. He learned to deal with the near constant noise by keeping busy on days when his circuits were fully open and carefully scheduling his study periods when he needed to concentrate on dull and overcast days or at times when there wasn't a transmitting cloud in the sky. He was unknowingly helped in these efforts by Edith Pepper, a slim, attractive and exceptionally bright girl with a will of steel whom he met in the middle of second year. Edith decided Eric was the man for her at a Tea Dance at the Student Union and there was nothing to be done about it. She graduated in 1901, one of the first women to do so at McGill. Eric followed a year later with a Masters in Divinity. They celebrated their honeymoon on board a ship out of Boston, bound for Bombay. Eric had a teaching post at a boys' school run by the American Bible Society in Madras, South India. Edith hated the sub-continent even before they had even lowered the gangplank.

"This is a filthy place," she said to her young husband while they were still several miles out at sea. "I can smell it from here."

The train ride south, in the comfortable European Only, first-class carriage, suggested to her that with attention to detail she might one day manage to carve out a clean well-lighted place for herself but her intense dislike of the flies, the dirt, the beggars, the disease, the heat, the stench of that first day never her left her. She would tolerate India because that was her husband's wish, but she would not like it.

Eric, on the other hand, loved it. For the first several weeks after the couple installed themselves in the comfortable red-brick house on the school's New England-inspired quadrangle, Eric couldn't wait for dinner to end so he could go out into the town for "a bit of fresh air." The more crowded the streets, the more gaudy the displays in the markets, the richer the aromas, the better. Lepers, beggars, supplicants, prostitutes, the destitute, the well-to-do, the criminal. "All of life goes by you in an hour," he enthused to Edith.

"And a lot of it leaves itself on you, I'm sure. Wash your hands before you touch anything," she cautioned.

On several of these nocturnal rambles during his early days in Madras, he noticed a scrawny, impoverished fellow wearing a soiled white *dhoti* who always stood silently on the same street corner. With him was a large, sleek, well-fed reddish brown dog. One evening, grandfather, ever curious, stopped to talk to him. Normally a highly tactful man, Eric surprised himself by saying to the chap, "See here, what's a skinny undernourished man like you doing with a plump, well-fed dog?"

"Goodness gracious me," began the fellow in English, "I was thinking you would never be asking. The dog is looking so well because he is all the time taking nourishment from the world of the spirit."

"What do you mean by that," asked a now highly curious Eric.

"I am meaning, sir, that the dog is meditating at every single moment on the abiding peace and love of the Lord Supreme."

"But that's remarkable," said Grandfather, now totally absorbed.

"You can be seeing for yourself, can you not? Why do you not look into the dog's eyes?"

Feeling it was the most natural thing in the world to do, Grandpa squatted down and peered into the dog's face.

The dog didn't blink. Grandfather, spellbound, stared into its brown and golden orbs for a good two minutes without blinking either. When he came back to this world his heart was full of peace and he felt as deeply contented with the world as he had for some time.

"What is this meditation?" he asked the man as he stood up.

"You are a man of God, I can see that. I am thinking that every-day you are praying to the Lord Supreme for this and that." Eric smiled, the man continued. "When you pray, you talk to God. You are all the time asking Him for good health, for money, for help-ing people, for what you are needing in your life. When you med-itate, you are listening for what God is giving you. So much peace and joy and light He is giving and giving. Otherwise they are same thing. Meditation is the obverse of the prayer coin."

"What's the dog's name?" asked Grandfather gently patting the animal's head.

"I am calling him Vivekananda."

Benares in 1905, about the time that it was visited by Eric at the height of his interest in India's holy sites.

Vivekananda, the meditating dog. Madras, 1902.

"I know Vivekananda! I heard him speak at the Conference on World Religons in Chicago in 1895. He was very powerful. He talked about his master, I can't remember his name."

"What can it matter?" said the man, and they parted.

When he got home, Grandfather undressed, put on his cotton pajamas and slipped under the mosquito net which covered the large cherrywood bed like a silver cloud in the moonlit room. When she had listened to the tale, Edith turned her lovely, white lace nightgowned bottom to him and said, "These fakirs talk such nonsense. Go to sleep."

In the morning, Grandfather said his prayers for the day with Edith, as he always did, and then retired to his study and listened silently to God for twenty minutes before breakfast, a practice he continued for every day of his life. When asked about it, even decades later, he would smile and say, "It's a habit I picked up in India from a dog."

After his encounter with Vivekananda he took a great interest in all things Hindu, especially temples. On his days off, usually a Sunday, he would visit those in the area, first introducing himself to the chief priest who often showed him around. They made an incongruous pair, these Indian holy men barefooted in white or saffron or blue *dhotis* and Grandpa in his black suit, straw fedora and tightly laced oxfords. He found himself particularly drawn to a nearby temple dedicated to the elephant god Ganesha. He visited it numerous times and became a life-long friend of the young head priest.

For all his delight in the country, India was difficult for him. Eric had a tolerance and compassion for human suffering which had been finely tuned by his gift. How many nights did he lie awake, tortured by the cries of the injured, the sick, the dying? At times it would seem that all the pain of humanity concentrated itself in his skull and become a single anguished note, a high pitched tone that sounded as though it emanated from the very soul of humankind. On nights like these he did not sleep and appeared exhausted and red-eyed in class the next day. If it persisted during the day, he would sometimes be forced to apologize to his students and dismiss the boys for the day. He continued to act on his father's advice and did not discuss the cause of these "headaches" with the school's principal, which led the other teachers to regard him as something of a "weak sister." In another way he was fortunate to be where he was. Weather patterns in South India were such that most summer days were peerlessly blue, without a cloud in the sky. On many winter days a thick, humid blanket of grey hung over the countryside. The seasons of his greatest affliction were autumn and spring and it was on one such day in late April 1906 that he broached the subject with his friend at the temple of Ganesha as they strolled in the columned courtyard.

"I would like, sir, to discuss a personal matter," began Grandfather tentatively.

"I am all ears, as you English say," replied his holy friend.

Eric smiled at the inadvertent reference to his gift. "No, sir, it is I who am all ears. Let me explain." And he went on to give a brief summary of his condition.

"So let me understand. You are hearing faraway voices in your head. Yes?"

"Yes."

"I am thinking this is a great blessing. God has a great work planned for you, it is clear as the eyes in your head but in the meantime it is torturing you like anything. Yes?"

"Yes."

The priest thought for a moment and then suggested that he return that evening and that they pray to Ganesha. "Elephant has very big ears. He will have an answer, surely to God he will."

That evening the two sat cross-legged on small blue silk pillows — Grandfather somewhat uncomfortably — set out on the stone floor of the deserted temple and, for almost an hour, prayed to and meditated on the looming statue of the beneficent pachyderm. At one point Grandfather thought he saw the left ear of the beast move. After what felt like an eternity to Eric, the priest chanted the sacred word "Om" seven times, drawing out the "mmm," and they bowed to the altar with folded hands before heading out into the moonlit courtyard.

"And so, my good friend, did my elephant speak to you?" he asked when Eric joined him.

"I...I couldn't be sure. I did think I heard something."

"You did not hear clearly? That is why the elephant is speaking so clearly to me and asking me to tell you what he said. What is it you were hearing?"

"Ocean," said Grandfather.

The priest beamed and did a kind of joyous jig. "Oh yes, elephant is speaking to you as he is speaking to me. He is saying you must throw all your hearings into the ocean of the universal God-consciousness where they will be gently absorbed and dispersed even as the ocean absorbs and disperses a tiny drop of water."

"Throw the voices into the ocean of God-consciousness?"

"Oh yes, yes, exactly right."

"But how?"

"Elephant will explain next time you meditate."

And, in a curious way, he did. Grandfather found that he could, indeed, accumulate the voices as though they were water in a bucket and could then empty the full bucket into the vast universal sea of the silence-washed shores of his meditations. On bad days and nights he sometimes had to empty the pail five or six times but, from then on, when the weather changed and the voices came in all their pain, he manned the bucket brigade. It gave him considerable respite.

He become doubly absorbed in all things Indian, particularly those that had to do with things of the spirit. He took to photographing the ornate carvings and classic pillars and courtyards of the temples, taking careful notes in a precise thin hand in blue-black ink. Later he wrote up his research and submitted articles to American publications. Many appeared in religious newsletters and journals and one illustrated essay was picked up by *National Geographic*.

Edith also plunged into her new life, despite herself. Always a quick mind, she could soon could speak Hindi and read and write Sanskrit, neither of which Eric ever mastered despite his greater sympathy to the people and culture. The former Miss Pepper ran a tight, distinctly British ship, carefully instructing the three women who worked as servants on the proper way to make a bed and prepare fish and roast beef and even Yorkshire pudding. Domestic life, however, was not enough to keep her active mind occupied so she decided to teach her charges to read and write — an outrageous idea in turn-of-the-century India. At first, the women — little more than girls actually, two were under seventeen and the other two had barely reached twenty — said they could never do it. Then that they would not be allowed to do it. Edith visited their homes and announced to their astonished husbands that either they would attend her classes or they would be let go. The men, who relied on the extra income for the small luxuries it allowed them, hemmed and hawed and finally gave in. The servants of other households soon joined her lessons and, before the year was out, every day between four and five, as many as fifty women and girls would gather, in their bright saris, under the huge mango tree in the square for lessons. She called them "my flowers."

Robert was born in January, 1903. The baby almost died. Edith had toxemia; the labour was extremely difficult. She bled copiously and suffered from anemia ever afterward. In her weakened state she contracted dysentery. Slight to begin with, she lost weight and her recovery was slow. She came to regard India as her enemy, the very force that was preventing her from regaining her health. Still, she hung on for another three years; by then even Eric recognized that they must leave.

Their ship docked in Boston in September, 1906. It was too late to land a teaching job and so, in a tough job market, Grandpa took what he could find — a post as minister of three rural parishes in southern New Hampshire. The manse consisted of a four-room white clapboard house with dark green trim in the town of Hopkington. The small stable attached to the house contained a buggy and a sixteen-year-old mare called Joan. Every Sunday, Eric would deliver his first sermon at eight o'clock in Hopkington's neat stone church and then hitch up Joan and trot off to Langton, four miles away, for the eleven o'clock service. After church he lunched with one family or another and then set off around two for Shawville, five-and-a-half miles distant, to be in the pulpit by four.

It was a quiet life after the excitment of India. Grandpa used the time to develop his inner resources. He prayed and meditated daily, often while staring, eyes half open as he'd been taught in India, at a small gaudily painted statue of an elephant he kept on a low table along with a candle in a heavy brass candlestick and an incense burner which he'd purchased in the Madras bazaar. Edith considered it a pagan practice that she said, correctly, would have shocked his straight-laced New England congregations. She had no truck with mumbo-jumbo. Instead she worked at regaining her health by taking long walks with young Richard in the deep New England woods, three seasons of the year. In 1907 she started a reading group for local women which met every Wednesday evening in their tiny parlour and, in the course of three years, read aloud all of the novels of Jane Austin. In February 1908, the morning after the circle met, she gave birth to Rebecca, their second child, who was to grow into a brilliant, strong-minded young woman who, at age twenty-two, much to her mother's consternation and her father's secret pleasure, would convert to Judaism and marry a rabbi.

On an unseasonably cold and overcast May morning when Becky was three months old, Eric put down his teacup at breakfast and said, "Edith, would you mind awfully if I went down to Boston and looked for another position?" She smiled and said nothing, so that afternoon he drove the carriage into Concord and caught the train to Boston. Two months later they moved to the capital where he had taken work with the American Bible Society on the understanding that he would accept a position overseas as soon as it become available. In October 1909 the young family sailed for Turkey. At age thirty-two, Grandfather was to be the new headmaster at the Episcopal Boys' School in Maresh.

Eric, who on his father's advice had not disclosed the nature of his gift even to his wife, watched his own son Richard closely for any signs that he had inherited the family's sensitive hearing. His fourth and fifth birthdays passed without any sign that his hearing was any more acute than that of his playmates, much to Eric's relief. Then, on a glorious sunny morning, two days out of Boston, Richard, who shared the small cabin with his parents and sister, woke his father at first light to say that they must alert the captain that a nearby ship had struck an iceberg and was sinking. He "could hear the poor people screaming to God to save them," he told his sleep-logged father, who, on waking, also heard the terror of the sailors as their ship foundered. Leaving the women in bed, the men of the family dressed and went to inform the Captain. He was a gruff fellow in his fifties who had, not so many years before, run his own whaler out of Nantucket and he thought the father and son who insisted that he meet them while still in his night-shirt were "ready for the loony bin."

"Let me understand this," he roared as the three stood on deck outside his cabin. "You want me to turn this ship north and go off on some cockamamie search for a boat you say is sinking?"

Grandfather nodded.

"There are one hundred and seventy-four passengers and crew on this ship," he shouted over the bright, brisk wind which blew the morning's fluffy clouds across a washed sky. "You expect me to start crisscrossing the ocean looking for some phantom vessel as though I were chasing a wounded whale?"

Grandfather nodded.

"You're telling me you can hear the sailors on board some ship that's going down ten or twenty miles away calling to God to save them?"

Grandfather nodded again.

"That's the craziest damn thing I every heard," exploded the Captain and went back into his cabin, slamming the door.

The frightened steward, whose unpleasant job it had been to wake the captain, grunted and headed back to the dining room where he had been directing the setting of tables for breakfast. Father and son spent the next hour walking the deck as Grandfather explained the Toggsham gift, how it seemed to affect only first-born males, and its implications. The two, each tortured by the cries from the doomed fishing boat beyond the horizon, spent a difficult hour and it was a red-eyed little boy who sat down to his oatmeal that morning. The weather had, by then, turned colder still. The sky was overcast and, without the clouds for sound to bounce off, blessedly silent.

Even before the ship docked at Patras, the port on the southern Turkish coast closest to Maresh, Edith did not like what she saw. It appeared to be a makeshift town hemmed in between a range of menacing mountains and an oily sea.

"We're going to be happy here," said Grandfather as the ship's cables were secured to the unsteady pier.

"If you say so," she replied and busied herself loading Aunt Becky into her pram — whose upcoming ride down the gangplank was to be the last she ever enjoyed in her baby carriage. It had to be left in a leaky warehouse in the pinched port city, along with about a third of their luggage when, early the next day, the family set out for their new home fifty miles back in the hills. When grandfather told his wife that their mode of transportation would be mule train, she retorted only, "I'm not surprised." She was surprised, however, unpleasantly so, at the contraption the porters rigged up to carry her children. It consisted of two large wooden tea crates tied together with hemp and hung one on either side of a mule. A child was placed in each box. At first attempt, Richard was so much heavier than Becky that his tea chest simply slid to the ground the moment he was placed in it, dragging the chest with his sister in it up on to the poor animal's back and almost spilling the sweet little girl out on top of him. The situation was remedied by settling several large stones in with Rebecca to act as ballast. The trip took four days, much of it with one child or the other hanging over a precipice with nothing between them and a long fall except the flimsy bottom of the crate. Grandmother said afterwards that it was this excursion above all else that convinced her of the existence of a higher force.

The school turned out to be another surprise, this time a pleasant one. A solid series of well-built brick buildings stood just east of the town, protected by a twelve foot wall. Inside the compound, the school, the administration building, teachers' quarters and the headmaster's home were arranged around a compact grassy common in which several shade trees grew, including a massive oak. If you stood by the fountain in the centre of the common, it was possible to think that you were in Boston on some hidden lane in Beacon Hill instead of lost in the hostile mountains of Turkey. The commodious house had fireplaces, walnut floors and fine plaster work. Edith thought she might be happy here after all. Grandfather gave it a quick once over before excusing himself to go off and explore the town.

He headed straight into a maze of streets which took him through a series of mounting cobblestoned alleys hedged in by high, four-or-five storey buildings. It was twilight and many of the merchants, in *jolobas* and yellow leather slippers, were packing it in for the day. Still they bowed and salaamed as Grandfather passed like a shadow, dressed in his pastor's black suit. The place seemed especially exotic, which was just the way he liked it. When he emerged near the top of the town, he found himself in a small square fronted by what he thought at first was a mosque but which, in the dying light, looked more like a Christian church. No one was around and he decided to try the heavy, carved oak door. It swung open easily and he was immediately greeted from the depth of a high narrow room by a voice which said, in a deep, raspy almost-but-not-quite, Indian accent: "Goodness gracious me, it is my dear headmaster who is just arriving."

As his eyes became accustomed to the darkness, whose opacity was hardly disturbed by the light of a single candle guttering on a distant altar beneath an enormous wooden cross complete with a life-sized depiction of Christ in his final agony, he made out the large figure of a bearded man in white and scarlet robes fairly galloping toward him.

"Dear one, dear one," he said, pulling alongside and taking my grandfather's hand gently in both his own. "I am so happy I am making your acquaintance. Alexander Toumian at your service."

He was in the middle of vespers in the empty church and invited grandfather to join him in finishing the service, which he conducted entirely in Latin. That done, the two repaired to his study where they shared a glass of wine. "The regime is not liking the consuming of alcoholic beverages," explained Toumian as he topped up the glasses. "That is why I am making my own wine in the basement, for religious purposes, you are understanding, dear one."

Toumian "You-must-be-calling-me-Alexander" was Armenian and took care of the spiritual needs, and often the secular needs, of a community of some five hundred souls in Maresh and in the surrounding countryside.

"Not always easy, dear one," he said pulling at the magnificent black nest of a beard. "We are having some not so interesting conflictings with the Turks," he went on. "They are not always liking us. I am not being able to think why not."

"I had expected to find a mosque here," Eric volunteered.

"Maresh is having ten mosques. Some very beautiful. I will take you, dear one. I am being friendly with the Caliph."

Eric asked about the curious accent. "You speak as though you learned your English in Calcutta."

"You are being correct. Calcutta, yes. Hummmmm." And he seemed to drift into a reverie.

"I was in Madras in south India for four years. Loved every minute of it."

"Ah, yes, India. The home for every sort of soul we have in this world. You would be agreeing, dear one?"

For almost an hour the new friends chattered on about the sub-continent and the delights and mysteries they had encountered there. Alexander had been sent out from Egypt as a young priest. Eric felt so comfortable with him he told him about his gift. The priest took him at his word and plied him with questions. He thought it was marvelous, a manifestation of God's power, a miracle.

When he arrived home, Edith was fretting at being left alone so soon after their arrival and said, in a shocked voice, "Eric, you've been drinking."

"Yes I have, dear one," he confessed, and went on to tell her about his new friend with such enthusiasm that she forgave him.

The family settled in well. Grandfather, a man of huge energies, quickly reorganized the school's curriculum and began to work closely with the teaching staff of six to ensure that they taught the way he felt they should. The school had been little more than a distraction to the previous headmaster, who preferred to ride and hunt birds and small game in the surrounding hills, and the staff welcomed Grandfather's firmer hand. He had the common cleaned up, the slate roofs of the buildings repaired and the chimneys repointed. His wife busied herself in teaching the housegirls to cook and keep house in the English way. After six months she could speak Turkish fluently and had, once again, begun her reading and writing classes for all who wanted them, this time including many of the men who worked around the school. For his seventh birthday, Richard was given a horse with four white feet, whom he named Calaban, and soon spent most of the time that he was not in school, eating or asleep, off in the hills with a bunch of local boys and their mounts.

The winters in these mountains were often misty and overcast, summers were hot and dry with only the occasional late afternoon thundershower to disturb the domed blue of the sky. It was bad transmitting weather and Eric and his son were grateful for it. Only for a couple of months a year and the odd day here and there did the sky fill up with friendly looking clouds, bringing the wails and cries of the population to their ears. The episode with the ship's captain had convinced Richard that his father was correct in keeping quiet about his special abilities. Eric had discovered, as his father Hollis had before him, that for the most part nothing could be done to bring relief to those who called out for help. They were too far away, too difficult to locate; on the occasions when he did try to intervene, his help often came too late, after the event had resolved itself. On a walk in the mountains a year after arriving in Turkey, Richard told his father he had developed a facility for "not hearing them" and getting on with his life much, I suppose, as we have learned, these days, to carry on normally in a room where the television is blaring.

Eric turned thirty-five in 1910 and found that his special powers were gradually declining, for which he was again grateful. Then, in the small hours of a splendid May night as a crescent moon rode though silver clouds strewn across a deep navy sky, Eric woke to a terrible shrieking and Richard came running into the room as if he'd been visited by a revenant. But this was no ghost. Eric was able to make out a few ghastly pleading words and they were Armenian. He ordered his son back to bed, went out to the stable, saddled Calaban and rode up to the church to rouse his friend.

The cries came from below the town where several Armenian families farmed and kept sheep. They were industrious and did well selling vegetables and eggs and sheep yoghurt, cheese, mutton and wool in the thriving Maresh market. The road was steep and rocky, little more than a double path and, in the dark, the horses had to pick their way carefully forward. It took more than an hour before the two arrived at the first of the Armenian houses which were strung out down the valley. It was shuttered and locked and they continued on without knocking. The same was true for the next two farms which were closed so tightly, with the heavy shutters drawn and bolted, that they looked uninhabited. The door to the fourth, however, hung open on one hinge. They dismounted and went in. At first they saw nothing. They could only hear the moans of a woman. She was in the second room, drawn up in a heavy black blanket. When they came toward her she cringed and turned away. The priest spoke a few soft words in Armenian and she began to wail. She opened the blanket to reveal two small girls, no more than six or seven, huddling against her. They appeared to be unhurt. The men helped her up and they fetched water and she cleaned herself and the children and put them back to bed, cooing and telling them they were safe. Eric bustled awkwardly around the kitchen, lit a fire and after some time presented them with tea in a handsome brass teapot. The three sat at the substantial dark wooden kitchen table which was set — incongruously given the circumstances — with a large lace doily and a luxuriant bouquet of new spring flowers. The woman was calm, almost too calm, Eric thought, as she told them of how they had come and smashed in the door, beaten her two sons and her husband and tied them outside while they raped her in front of her daughters who, she thanked the blessed Virgin, they had not touched. They took her husband — she called him her beloved — and the boys with them when they left. She released one terrible sob and was quiet again.

"Soldiers?" questioned the priest.

"You know it," she said without emotion.

Eric wanted to take her into town and put her up at the school but Toumian said no. "We are not wanting to attract attention, are we, dear one? I am saying it is better for her to stay here."

Eric went back up the path to the closest house and after much pounding on the door and calling in English and the repeating of an Armenian phrase Alexander had written down on a paper, he could hear the bolts being slid back and the door opened. It was, by now, almost four-thirty and the sky's deep blue quivered with light in the east. A man came and two teenagers and another much older man with thick matted grey hair, and they went back down the hill and brought up the woman and the little girls to stay with them. The priest and the teacher rode back to Maresh with hardly a word between them, Alexander to climb though the crooked streets to his church, Eric to return to the early morning noises of his own cozy home as it stirred with sleepy life in the early light. As they parted Alexander said, "It is the beginning." And Eric nodded.

He feared he couldn't rely on his own fading hearing and would miss the start of some atrocity that might be averted by quick action, so he enlisted the help of his son. The boy was no longer to ignore any cry. Each would be followed, no matter how faint. Richard was told to be triply alert if he heard any Armenian words. Eric also cautioned his son that it would be difficult, that he would hear some dreadful things but that he must be strong, they had to help, he was certain God wanted them to. Every morning in his prayers and meditations, Eric asked for God's compassion and light to fall on their community.

Summers were usually virtually cloudless but the summer of 1913 turned out to be unusually damp. Day after day, night after night, the sky filled up with perfect tranmitting clouds and the voices came in as clear as distant sirens. Father and son often heard the first glimmerings of a raid, sometimes as far away as thirty miles. On nights when they knew the army was active, they sent runners to contacts Alexander had organized among the Armenian community and they put out the warning. Before long, human forms would arrive at the gate in the high wall which surrounded the American school, some in pyjamas and nightgowns, others hastily dressed. As many as four hundred would crowd silently into the compound where tents and shelters had been set up along the

This photograph was acquired by Eric Toggsham at
a Turkish market during the Armenian pogroms.
(From his private collection.)

walls. When the last had entered this safe haven, the double, iron-studded doors would swing shut and the massive oak beam would again be slid into place, barring the entrance.

The military knew Armenians were being sheltered at the American school and were puzzled by how they managed to get so much advance warning of raids. At first they stepped up their campaign in the city, striking suddenly and at odd hours, even risking the occasional daytime incursion. It did little good. A single incident would spark a quick and massive retreat to the school. The colonel in command of the district filed reports with Constantinople, protesting that "the alien population is seeking refuge in the school operated by the United States Christian Bible Organization" and asking most urgently for permission to post troops around the school. Permission was never granted. Official government policy was clear on the Armenian question: no pogroms were taking place. The Turkish Army surrounding foreign property for no apparent reason? Absolutely out of the question.

So Grandfather and Uncle kept theirs ears open and sounded the alarm at the first hint of trouble. Gradually, the number of raids in Maresh and its vicinity declined, though other Armenian communities were not spared. The continued attacks angered and frustrated my grandfather. He protested vehemently each time he heard of one, first to the mayor and ultimately to the local army colonel himself. He also wrote long detailed letters to Bible Society headquarters in Boston describing the events. The former had no effect whatsoever nor, in the short term, did his letters. In the long term, however, they did serve a purpose. They were kept on file and eventually turned over to Armenian groups in the U.S. where they are still used today as proof that the oft-denied atrocities took place.

Grandpa had promised Edith that they would return to the States "not a minute later than January 1, 1915." The family had bookings to sail for Southampton in September 1914. Then, on July 28, 1914, not so very far away from Maresh, in Sarajevo,

Bosnia, Archduke Francis Ferdinand, heir to the Austro-Hungarian throne, was shot by a Serbian revolutionary. The Hungarian foreign minister insisted that Germany back him in severely punishing the Serbs who had long been a thorn in the Empire's side. Kaiser Wilhelm II and his government had no real enthusiasm for the task but reluctantly agreed, in the full knowledge that Russia would take Serbia's side which would risk bringing down the whole delicate web of European alliances. What they could not have known is that the action would set off a war like no other the world had ever seen. Turkey sided with Germany. While the U.S. remained neutral until the final year of the conflict, a naval war surged in the Mediterranean and any thought of going home for the Toggsham family was out of the question.

It was school as usual in the compound at Maresh. Even the colonel was instructed that nothing was to be done to offend the Americans, who both the Turks and their German allies were anxious to keep out of the war. Gypsies and Armenians continued to be harassed but, for a time, it seemed that the population at Maresh would be spared entirely. Then, on an August night in 1917, Richard, now a mature lad of fourteen, came running into his father's bedroom, yelling, "Father, Father, come quickly. It's Reverend Toumian."

Man and boy raced though the night streets to the cathedral and burst into the tight square in front of the church. Three men stood on the steps of the church, smoking cigarettes and passing around a bottle of what, even from this distance, Eric could see was one of Alexander's special supply of wine. Overcome with emotion he rushed forward and tried to grab it. One of the men laughed and pushed him away, leaving a bloody hand print on grandfather's nightshirt. At the sight of the blood he drew back and turned toward the church. The door hung open. The altar cloth was on fire. Flames were already singeing the feet of the Saviour. The painted flesh had begun to blister and pop. In the broken light of the flames he could just make out his friend, slumped in the aisle where he had fallen, still brandishing a massive brass cross. Grandfather turned him over gently. His chest was a mass of blood.

"You have been coming," said the priest. "I am knowing you would. That is the kind of person you are being, dear one."

He tried to lift a hand but could not. Eric took a pillow from a pew, put it under the cleric's head and went to help Richard with the fire. The lad had already managed to douse most of it with sand which Alexander, who had always feared a fire in the wooden interior of the structure, kept in buckets concealed in the choir loft and behind the pulpit. When he returned to Alexander only a few moments later, the priest was dead.

The next day, as Grandfather returned, still white with rage, from an interview with the mayor, he was intercepted by a lad, one of his students, who said he must go immediately to the market in the next town.

"They are selling the silver from the church," explained the boy. Eric rode directly into the market to the merchant's stall. The man was gracious, a businessman, he explained, one who bought and sold, no questions asked. That morning he had had a chance to acquire, at a very good price, a pair of silver candlesticks and a silver goblet. He had, unfortunately, already sold the candlesticks, to whom it would not be correct to say, a personal matter between buyer and seller, but he did still have the goblet, would the honorable headmaster be interested? He named too high a price and Grandfather, without a word of haggling, paid him and took the chalice, wrapped in a purple cloth, and rode home along the rocky path, weeping.

I've seen the chalice, held it in my hand. I was in attendance in 1974 when it was presented by my Uncle Richard to the Armenian Archbishop of New York in a special ceremony honouring my grandfather's work in Turkey, sixty years before. We had a wonderful meal in the church hall afterwards prepared by the ladies of the congregation; the small flat spicy meat pies were especially good.

By then Uncle Richard had been retired from Great Northern Telephone Co. Ltd for nine years. The family had returned to New England in 1919. My mother was five years old at the time, a blond, blue-eyed little charmer, the darling of the war-weary troops returning on the same ship out of Southampton. I came across a photocopy of her passport recently, issued in London a week or two before they set sail. It was among the papers shown to me by an Armenian rug salesman in Montreal. He had copies of the whole family's passports in a filing cabinet in his office along with all of my grandfather's letters to the home office.

"Proof it really happened," he said. Half the Armenian community had copies, he said. I'd mentioned my grandfather — and the grail — in the hope he'd knock a few dollars off a Kilim I admired. Have I no shame? He shook my hand and sent a boy out for coffee and was prepared to talk for an hour, but a deal on the carpet? "Honestly, I have to tell you, for a carpet of this quality, I can't..."

Edith was homesick for Canada when they returned and insisted they all spend a few months with her family in Montreal. They never left. Grandpa soon found work as a school principal and went on to become a deputy minister of education in the province. He also authored half a dozen history books on the *ancien regime* in *Nouvelle France* but that's getting ahead of myself.

Richard enrolled at McGill University in the fall of 1920 but dropped out right after Christmas to take a job in the telephone company labs. He hoped to discover the scientific basis for his gift and make a significant contribution to communications. Since he would not reveal the nature of his research to his employer or co-workers, he was obliged to do much of the experimentation at night and developed a reputation as a tireless worker. Unfortunately, nothing ever came of it. The family's special hearing was entirely of organic origin and could not be translated into wires, crystals or later, vacuum tubes. He lost interest in the matter entirely after age thirty-five, when his powers began to erode and, at his retirement party in 1963, was honoured principally for his work on the development of Halo Lite, a flourescent tube fitted into a translucent panel around the screens of television sets in the mid-1950s. Ophthalmologists of the day mistakenly believed it was harmful to the eyes to watch television in an unlighted room and Halo Lite, which came on automatically when the set was turned on, was judged a clever and easy solution in an era which worshiped convenience. The invention made the set a best seller in Canada in 1956.

Uncle Richard married Aunt Zinnia in 1929, ten days before the stock market crash. Their first and only child, Andrew, came into the world at Montreal's Royal Victoria Hospital in February 1931. Richard watched carefully for signs of the family gift in the young lad but they did not seem to appear and he came to believe, with some relief, his son had been spared. Then, one wintry Saturday afternoon, when cousin Andy was seven, Uncle and his wife, Aunt Z, famous among the menfolk of the family for the size of her bosom, whiled away an hour or two at the Chateau de Ramsey, a seigneur's home, built in 1690 in what was by then the heart of Montreal. The family had just left the salon of the original chateau with it's birch logs flaming in an ancient Franklin stove which, by the permanent look of it, had been set into the fireplace eons ago. As they were about to leave the room, Andrew squeezed his father's hand and asked, "Who's that talking?" Save for a guard or two, the building was deserted.

"I don't hear anything," said Uncle Richard without thinking.

"It's a man talking about the first issue or something," said the boy innocently. "He's happy about it but he speaks in a strange way. Is he in the next room, Daddy?"

He wasn't in the next room. What was there, framed and hanging on the wall, was the front page of the first issue of the Montreal Gazette, dated July 27, 1775. An editorial urged readers to "join your neighbours to the south in throwing off the yoke of the

British oppressors." The name of the author and founder of the paper appeared underneath: Benjamin Franklin.

"He said a bad word, didn't he, Daddy?" said Andy to his baffled father.

"What did he say son?"

"You know," the boy teased and blushed.

"No, Andrew, I didn't catch it," said his father suddenly serious, "What was it?"

"He said 'Bastards'," replied the lad, burying his face in his mother's fur coat.

Richard tousled his son's hair and said nothing. An hour or so later the family went across the street to Murray's Restaurant, an early Montreal chain, for Welsh Rarebit, Andy's favourite.

"That was a funny place," said the boy as his parent lingered over a second cup of coffee. "You could hear voices. How did they do it, Dad?"

Richard said nothing but that night, as he tucked his son into bed, he broached the subject. "You heard voices this afternoon?"

"Yes, it was swell. Was it a phonograph?"

His father sighed, "No, son. I think they were real voices. You heard them but nobody else could. Nothing to worry about. It's something special that runs in this family. I used to hear them too when I was your age. We'll talk about it tomorrow with your grandfather." As he switched out the light, he added, "Don't say anything to your mother. It's a special men's secret."

The next afternoon, Andrew, his father and his grandfather went for a long walk along Sherbrooke Street. A thaw had set in and it was mild and slushy. The wind carried the first faintest hint of the smell of damp earth. Andrew walked and listened and said nothing until the older men had explained all they could. A wet snow began to fall and they went into the Queen's Hotel Cafe between Drummond and Stanley and ordered tea and a hot chocolate for Andrew.

For the next twenty minutes they explained the nature of the gift to a puzzled looking little boy.

"The man who said the bad word wasn't having an accident," said the lad creaming the melted marshmallow of his second cup of cocoa.

"We think you might hear voices from the past," said his father looking serious.

"Yes," enthused his grandfather, still as bouncy and enthusiastic as he'd been in India thirty years before, and who was well into writing his fourth book on the history of the province, this one titled *Stories of Old Quebec*, "Isn't it exciting? We're going to have a lot of fun with this, Andrew. Lots of fun."

And so they did. Over the next few years, Andrew and Grandfather spent many weekends together travelling to significant places in the European history of *Nouvelle France*: the ramparts and old churches of Quebec City; sites of Indian wars along the St. Lawrence River; the old loyalist towns on the U.S./Canada border; the Richelieu River and upper reaches of Lake Champlain where the fur trade began. Andrew listened and repeated what he heard and Grandpa took massive quantities of notes on index cards in a fine spidery hand.

As a teenager, Andrew's interest in history faded. The many, many weekends of intense listening and the effort to repeat the old French, bad English and incomprehensible Huron, Abnaki and Iroquois he heard while his grandfather tried to write it all down — including the bad words — took its toll. During his final years in high school, he developed two new passions: girls and literature. He begged off excusions with Grandpa.

By his final year at McGill, his preoccupations had narrowed to a single girl, Elspeth Peterson, and a single literary era, Paris of the 1920s. Of all the writers of that fabled place and time the one he admired most was Ernest Hemingway. During the last dance of the Graduation Ball, held on Saturday, May 27, 1951 at the Ritz Carleton Hotel, Elspeth whispered tenderly that she would always think of him fondly but she'd been seeing a fellow in fourth-year

Law — he could hear the capital "L" in her voice — and she thought it would be better if they "saw other people" during the summer. The next morning he left on the train for Sudbury, Ontario, where he spent the next five months working as a labourer at the Inco nickel mine during the day, drinking Molson beer at night; missing Elspeth all the time — and plotting his new life in France.

He quit the job on October 7 with almost two thousand dollars in his savings account. On October 10, he was on a freighter out of Montreal bound for Le Havre. He arrived in the City of Light by train ten days later as a pearly twilight spread across the city.

Andrew left his bag in a locker at Gare du Nord and took the Metro to the Cardinal Lemoyne stop on the Left Bank. Hemingway, he'd read, had lived near there when he first came to Paris. He walked down Cardinal Lemoyne and into Place Contrescarpe in a daze, enchanted beyond imagining at finding himself among the elegant and ancient buildings; the cobblestoned streets bathed in the pale, rosy light and soft, luminous air. He was dazed, too, by the sighs and whispers which echoed in his head as though he held a seashell to his ear. Instead of playing back the sounds of the ocean, he heard a vast welter of voices dating back to the origins of the city. Montreal had been as quiet as a forest glade compared to this. He came into an ancient square and sat down on a stone bench for a moment to see if he could make any sense of what he heard but so many voices came tumbling over one another that after a few minutes he gave up, relegating them to an irritating but tolerable background buzz. He came to think of Paris as The Human Hive.

It was almost dark now and he was famished. Across the square he spotted a small restaurant with an enclosed terrace. Bright incandescent lights illuminated the white table cloths. He stood for a moment and examined the table d'hote menu held by two metal nymphs which suggested, he supposed, that the food came directly from the gods. A waiter, dressed formally in the old French style with a white linen napkin draped over his arm, showed him to a table. By European standards it was early, hardly eight o'clock, and he was the only diner in the room. The waiter made it his task to introduce this obvious naif to the glories of the French table. First he fetched a glass of light country wine and a bottle of icy mineral water. After giving Andrew several minutes to puzzle over the menu, he returned and proposed that he begin with oysters and leave the rest to him, a suggestion that delighted Andrew. After a half dozen plump, exquisite malpecs, a small plate of wild mushrooms sauteed in butter and red wine arrived with a flourish. A mild-fleshed river perch followed, which his mentor deftly filetted at the table. Next a green salad, singing with vinagrette. After that, steak Bernaise, a golden basket of *pommes de terre frites*, and a *pichet* of wine, this one a hearty red. For the finale, creme caramel and a silky goat cheese served with walnuts and sweet muscatel raisins dried on the vine. The meal would end, *naturellement*, with *café filtre* and a digestif. But Andrew had reached the limits of pleasure with the cheese and the crusty baguette which accompanied it. So happy he feared he might cry, he begged for the cheque and after many mercis and bows, he escaped into the velvet night.

Utterly sated, and content for the first time since Elspeth's poisoned whisper, he strolled up the short hill into the huge, heart stopping sweep of Place du Pantheon, then ducked down rue Coujas, across Boulevard St. Michel, and into the warren of streets at the north end of Luxembourg Gardens that, eventually, gave way to the Seine. He was aware at every moment that he walked where his hero Ernesto had walked. Long about eleven he slipped into a crowded cafe and ordered a coffee, reminding himself that he should retrieve his bag and find a place to stay, but the magic of the quarter held him like a new lover and he couldn't tear himself away. He continued to wander wherever his heart took him. Around midnight he found himself in a brightly lit bistro and soon fell into conversation at the bar with two British girls from Manchester who had also arrived in Paris that day, students at the

Ecole des Beaux Arts. When the bar closed, Enid and Rosemary ordered two bottles of wine and the three of them went off together to the quays along the Seine where they sat and talked and talked and watched until dawn turned the swift, dark water first a pearly grey and then pink washed with faintest gold. He invited them to breakfast at the Closerie des Lilas which, he assured them, was one of Hemingway's favourite cafés, but by then they wanted only to sleep.

At 5:30 am he found himself alone at the Lilas. A waiter swept the terrace between the tables with a wet broom. He took a table inside and ordered a *café au lait*. For the first time, he felt tired. He was about to take his first sip of coffee when he heard a new voice rise about the background murmur he carried around in his head. It was a raw, nervous, worried voice. A reedy baritone. A doctor's voice. A familiar voice. The same voice he'd heard that summer back in his bunk in Sudbury reading from *A Farewell to Arms* on CBC Radio. Younger and less hoarse but unmistakably the same! It was Ernest Fucking Hemingway.

The master was obviously going over a work in progress. Andrew listened, scarcely breathing for fear even his own breath might upset the transmission. He was about to hear one of the seminal works of modern fiction at it's conception. What astonishing luck! And on his first day in Paris! He blessed his father, his grandfather and the gift. As he leaned forward slightly, all attention and concentration, he heard the author speak in a low voice: "Her fetid eyes blazed red and hot and angry and filled with biting, hurtful tears, as though each terrible year with him had turned to molten lava and was now running down the smooth, pale skin of her perfect cheeks leaving hideous pock-marked trails of grey ash to mar the much admired landscape of her flawless face..." A long pause followed, as though the writer were contemplating his work, then suddenly an angry despairing burst that set Andrew back in his chair: "Oh God. No. No. I'll never get it right. Never. I can't..." groaned the disembodied voice. Another pause and, then, in a louder, bolder voice, *"Jean, un rum St. James. Vite, s'il vous plait."* Then silence.

Andrew buried his head in his hands. This must be a nightmare, some twisted trick the past was playing on him. It couldn't be Hemingway he was hearing. Must be some minor gothic scribe of the previous century. The master could never written like that. Impossible. The prose was so convoluted, so overwrought, so just plain bad. He leaned forward again to catch another word but all he heard was the swish of the plane trees in a light early morning drizzle.

On the odd chance that it was Hemingway, how could he help him? For ten minutes, he concentrated with every fibre on the Hemingway style he knew and loved, in the desperate hope that he could pass on a few writing tips from his vantage point in the 1950s. He was beginning to think he needed a rum himself when the voice came again, soft and musing, "Maybe if I took out some of the adjectives."

"Yes, yes," whispered Andrew under his breath. "Take out some of the adjectives. Do it. Lord, please do it now."

A long silence and then, a few minutes later, haltingly, the voice read again: "Her eyes blazed hot and filled with biting tears as though each year with him had turned to molten lava and was running down her cheeks to mar the perfect landscape of her face." Another pause, then a long musing "Yes. That's better. Cleaner." The voice had more confidence now.

"Don't stop," urged Andrew under his breath. "Make it simpler. Please." For a long time he heard nothing then, perhaps thirty minutes later, the voice said to itself in a satisfied way: "This is something new, Hem. Something fresh. Clean."

"It's him. God, it really is him. Thank you. Thank you." Andrew stood up suddenly and knocked over his chair. The waiter hurried over. "Is monsieur alright? Could I bring him something?" Monsieur had never been better, said Andrew and he could bring him a rum St. James.

The bar was beginning to fill with people stopping for coffee before work. Shop girls ordered croissants "pour emporter" and took them away on white plates covered with starched white napkins. He wanted to rush up to one of them and tell her that Ernest Hemingway, the famous American writer, was there, right now, in this bar, writing stories. He restrained himself. They'd take him away and lock him up. Or indulge him, perhaps. "*Une autre fou americain.*" He felt half crazy. He waited another hour but heard nothing more. The bar was crowded and noisy. He needed to sleep. He asked the waiter to recommend a hotel and was promptly shown to a room above the café.

He awoke in a panic. Hung over. Disoriented. Grey late afternoon light pressed at the window. Slowly it came back. Paris. The Meal. The Girls. Ernest Hemingway! It was him. But what was the story about? He thought he'd read everything his hero had written and he couldn't remember anything about a tortured heroine pining for a cruel lover. It sounded more like a nineteenth century pot boiler. Could he possibly have missed it? How could the man who transformed the way English was written scribble such pap? He dozed off again.

Dinner smells drifted up from the café below. Andrew sat up in bed and looked out at the tops of the plane trees and finally got out of bed and pulled on his clothes. After a long negotiation with the desk clerk, a shower was arranged for him in the building across the street. Clean and freshly shaven, he set out for the Gare du Nord to retrieve his bag.

He spent the evening back in his room over the Lilas trying to devise a strategy. Unlike the special talents of his male kin, his acute hearing operated independent of weather and emotion, though there was some weird filtering system he suspected might have to do with sun spots or the phases of the moon. He seemed to be more sensitive at some times than others. Proximity was essential, as it had been for Hollis, Eric and his father.

He pulled out his notes of known Hemingway haunts gleaned

from biographies and magazines and newspapers articles and poured over them, working with a map of the 5th, 6th and 7th *arrondisements*. By midnight he had marked up the map and made a list. At the top was the Closerie des Lilas, next a small café on Place St-Michel where Ernest was said to have done some of his early work (No name. Still there? Andrew noted beside it); Hotel du Pantheon (E.H. rent hotel room for writing. This hotel?); Jeu du Paume (Tuilleries Gardens, looked at the paintings here); Gertrude Stein's house, 27 rue de Fleurus (Can I get into her old apartment?); 74 rue Cardinal Lemoine (Lived here with Hadley when first in Paris?); La Pêche Miraculeuse (Restaurant built out over the Seine. One of couple's favourite); Place St-Sulpice; Sylvia Beach's bookshop, Shakespeare & Co. at 12 rue de l'Odeon (Still there?); Brassrie Lipp; Deux-Magots; 113 Notre Dame des Champs (Lived here?); Nègre de Toulouse (Restaurant); the Rotonde, Dome; Select (Big cafés. All on Blvd Montparnasse. Settings for *The Sun Also Rises*).

Next morning he was the first customer downstairs. He had scarcely ordered a *café crême* when he heard, "Work it over. Work it over like a fighter in the ring. Soften up the opponent." A few minutes after that the author read the same sentence he'd been working the day before. He heard the author's mid-western accent: "Her eyes blazed and filled with tears. Each year with him had turned to lava and was running down her cheeks." There was a pause. "Good. Good. And clean. Good and clean. You're getting somewhere, my boy. It's working." Back in 1922, the writer was still struggling.

In 1951, as Andrew took his seat in the Lilas it was one-ten in the morning at the famous writer's *finca* in Havana and Hemingway was taking a piss on an oleander bush in the back garden. He'd been celebrating the sending off of the manuscript for *The Old Man and the Sea*. He looked up at the stars and shivered as he buttoned himself and thought, for the first time in a long time, of the early days in Paris and of Hadley and of how much he had loved

259

J

her. That he probably still loved her. And of how hard he'd had to work at his writing in those days. And those very early stories. Jesus. He shook his head and said to the sky and the feral cat that pressed and purred against his shins, "What a screw up I was. Still am, huh, puss." And he went back into the quiet house. His third wife, Mary, had been asleep for hours.

Andrew spent the afternoon nursing a demi-blonde at Lipp's. He caught bits and pieces of the author's voice once or twice, but he was only chatting with the waiter about olive oil, the best time to pick the olives, when and how to press them. Interesting, but not literature. Around five he called Enid. She and Rosemary were just getting up. The three of them met for supper at The Polidor off Boul-Mich near the Luxemborg gardens. A big lamb stew and vegetables sopped up with pieces of crisp baguette and washed down with a couple of liters of robust country red. Andrew was hardly aware he was eating, his attention was entirely taken up by the warm pressure of Enid's thigh against his as they sat together on one of the restaurant's rustic benches.

He went to bed that night without Enid, who kissed him a long goodnight in the French manner while her friend was in the loo. The girls wanted to do the clubs; he wanted to be up early. "Soon," she had whispered as they parted. He couldn't sleep, and lay awake and thought about Enid and then Ernest and then Enid and then Ernest again. Was he hearing the writer's earliest fiction? Why wasn't it about fishing and camping in Michigan? Why was it so bad? If he could hear Hemingway, could the writer somehow pick up his thoughts? Could the work be somehow guided?

The next morning it rained. After a fruitless hour at the Lilas, he decided to try the Hotel du Pantheon to see if he could locate Hemingway's old writing room. He hiked up the hill to the wet, windy plaza and asked the crone at the desk if she knew the American writer Ernest Hemngway.

"*Non, mais ma seour le connait bien,*" she replied. The way she said it made him wonder if Hemingway had been her sister's lover,

---

perhaps even recently, after the war, but the woman said it had been a long time ago when they were both young. Was she still alive, her sister?

"Of course," the woman cackled. "Do I look like I have a sister who could be dead of old age? Get out of my sight, you nasty young man," she teased. "If it's my sister you want, you'll find her on the other side of the square in rue Clovis. She runs my parents' old hotel. Hotel Clovis, it's called, very original. She's not dead but she's no spring chicken, I tell you. Much, much older than me. She's been there since the last century."

He found the hotel. Behind the desk was Suzanne Rainville, a handsome woman in her fifties.

"Hemingway? Of course I knew him. Like a brother, and not like a brother," she winked. He came to see her whenever he was in Paris. Known him for years. Used to rent a room on the top floor when they were kids. "Not the last war, mind you," she sighed. "The one before that."

"Could I rent the same room?" he blurted.

"You some kind of writer too? You think the walls will inspire you?"

"Could I see it?"

"Of course you can see it. I'm in the business of renting rooms, aren't I? Pay me for a night and you can do more than see it, you can sleep in it, you can entertain your girl friend in it. Mind you, I'll charge you the double rate if she stays more than a night or two."

The room cost eleven dollars a week. From the window he could see the back of Notre Dame and Isle St. Louis. There was a bed, a desk, a chair, even a tiny fireplace. The room was cold and damp as a wet mitten. He wrapped himself in the bedspread and the single thin grey blanket from the bed and sat at the table and tried to read *The Brothers Karamazov*. He wondered if Hemingway had really rented this room: he suspected Mlle. Rainville would say anything at all if she thought it would bring in a few francs. Also,

Paris hotel where Andrew stayed in
1951 during his research into Ernest
Hemingway's early writing habits.

he was plagued by the feeble mutterings of an old man — one of the room's ancient inhabitants, no doubt — who seemed destined for the dungeon, the guillotine, or both. Then, a little after four, he was startled by a grunt and suddenly the voice he'd heard at the Lilas said, "I can't believe how bad this stuff is. It's shit. Utter shit. A writer? I'm a fraud. A bullshit artist. Yeah, a Goddamn bullshit artist. An idiot. Look at this stuff. Shit. All of it. I wanna write like Edgar Allan Poe..." the voice trailed off.

Edgar Allan Poe! Andrew leapt from the chair. Sweet Mary Mother of God, the greatest prose stylist of the twentieth century wants to write like that verbose thrill-seeking nineteenth century dope fiend? "Impossible," he called out over the dripping slate rooftops.

"This one," continued the slightly nasal baritone, "she's such a perfect heroine. How she loves Rupert and yet can never love him. Her terrifying nightmares and insomnia. Her long, unbraided hair, the silk dresses with the jet beading. The way she plays the organ..."

Andrew concentrated, focused on a single point. "Write about your own experiences. Your own experiences. Your own experiences." He repeated the phrase to himself until his head ached. This was nuts. How could he put ideas in the head of a writer three decades earlier?

A little later he heard: "This one is about Anna. I knew Anna better than anyone, we practically grew up together." Could he possibly be getting through? "When I came back from the war, she spent hours sitting by the bed sharing her deepest thoughts. I'll never forget her icy fingers. The way she touched my wound as though it were a bruised flower, a lily that had been crushed. She was my own, my whole, my other...I knew her." Pause. "But I can't write about her to save my ass."

"Write about yourself, the things you like to do. Write about rivers and the bush and fishing. Fishing. Fishing. Fishing," Andrew repeated intensely.

263

"This one should've worked," came the voice, "this story about that old Italian count in the villa near San Pietro where we holed up. I can still hear his footsteps in the crypt where he raped and murdered those innocent country girls. Why won't it work? Why?" After a short pause the voice continued, "Or this one. The girl with the violet eyes and ivory skin who's bitten by an apse and goes into a coma and is buried alive and when her grief-stricken lover kills himself and is buried beside her and she can hear the spade digging his grave. This is powerful stuff."

Silence.

Suddenly very loud. Very angry. "BUT WHEN I WRITE IT, IT COMES OUT AS BULLSHIT!" A groan. And then, resigned, exhausted: "I'm goin' fishin'."

Andrew walked over to Enid's hotel in the rain but the girls were out. He looked for the Negre de Toulouse restaurant, asked a few people about it, but no one could remember it so he crossed it off his list. On the way back to the hotel he stopped at Lipp's and drank two *formidables*, each over a litre of beer and ate a fat knockwurst, split in two and slathered with Dijon mustard. He was asleep, head spinning, by midnight.

At the moment Andrew's head hit the pillow, back in Cuba, Hemingway was navigating *The Pilar*, his black Chris Craft, into Havana harbour after a day on the gulf stream fishing for marlin. As he manoeuvered into the dock he thought about fish and what an important part they'd played in his life and in his writing. What the hell is it with me and fish, he wondered?

It rained again the next day. Except for the mumblings of the lunatic nobleman, Andrew heard nothing. He spent the day reading Hemingway's Nick Adams stories out loud. He figured it couldn't hurt. By four he felt he'd spent the day on a river in Michigan casting for trout himself. He telephoned Enid and arranged to meet for dinner at nine.

La Pèche Miraculouse, another spot on his list, hung out over the river like a pirate ship moored in the mist and fog and lit by lanterns. They began with lobster bisque. He ordered the eel. She, the sole amandine. He noticed a few ancient vintages on the wine card and began to tell her about the flood in 1904 that ruined many of the city's best cellars. She talked about the fashions at the *prêt-à-porter* shows that were in all the papers. They didn't begin to click until she told him about the Jeu de Paume and some of the wonderful paintings there. Hemingway had gone there and written about them, he said. They drank a litre of white wine. When the waiter came with coffee he also brought two glasses of Calvados, the fiery apple digestif, on the house — a salute to "les deux amoureux." And at that very moment he heard Hemingway say, "Let's sit by the window." A female voice replied, "Do let's. The lights on the river are so beautiful." It's his wife, Hadley, thought Andrew, tremendously excited. "Aren't we the luckiest people Tatie?" Tatie? Her nickname for him? Her husband said they were and ordered a Beaume wine and Crabe Mexicaine for both of them.

"Andrew, what's the matter?" he heard Enid say. "You're a million miles away."

He said he suddenly felt sick, the eel perhaps, and asked if she'd she mind if he sent her back to the hotel in a cab.

"Just like that?"

"Yes but it's not you it's, ah...it's not you. It's Ernest Hemingway."

"Can I ask you something, Andrew?"

"Sure, Enid, anything but let's go. OK?"

"Are you a poofter?"

"A poofter?"

"You know, queer. A homo."

"No."

"You might as well be," she said. "And forget the cab. I can find my own bloody way home."

The waiter hurried over and began to clear the table. "Another Calvados," said Andrew. He sighed and sat down again just in time to catch Ernest saying, "When my writing isn't working, I wonder

The Polidor restaurant in Paris near the Luxembourg Gardens. Andrew often dined here.

if I deserve to be so happy."

"It will work. I know it will," said his wife. "Happiness is the most important thing, isn't it? As long as we stay happy, the writing has to come."

"Maybe I should try to write about something else."

"Oh, Tatie, I would love to read about some of the times you've told me about when you were at home camping out in the back country. You have a way of making me see it just right, the way it really is." A silence followed broken by Hadley saying in a small voice, "Let's go straight home and after dinner make love."

Hemingway worked every day now. Andrew scarcely dared leave the room until one or two in the afternoon. The stories were going better, the author himself seemed to feel. To be sure, he was cleaning up the prose, but the subjects were the same. Andrew sat in his room and read E.H's early stories aloud over and over again until he'd practically memorized them. At other times he concentrated on the phrase "Write what you know," or chanted "Fishing" or "Michigan" until he felt absurd.

On a Tuesday in the third week of November, before lunch, Hemingway said, "Screw it, I'm going to that Shakespeare bookstore. I need some air."

Andrew got to Shakespeare & Company first. He heard Hemingway come in and make some comment to Sylvia Beach, who ran the place. The young writer wanted to borrow some books but he had no money. She told him to go ahead and choose whatever he liked; he could pay her later. He asked if she had Bram Stoker's *Dracula* or *Frankenstein* by Mary Shelley. Andrew felt his stomach churn. "Choose Chekov or Twain, somebody straightforward, for God's sake," he wailed out loud in pure frustration. The young American woman behind the cash gave Andrew a sour look as he heard Miss Beach back in 1921 say, "I'm afraid I don't carry those books. Too lurid for my taste. What about a Russian author? Say Turgenev or Tolstoy?"

"Thank you. Thank you. Thank you," exclaimed Andrew again

too loudly.

The girl stepped out from behind the counter looking very annoyed. "Thank you for what? Are you all right? Have you tried the Catholic bookstore at the corner? Maybe they can help you."

He was excited to be here in this famous shop, that was all, he'd be quiet, he stammered. She had nice legs. Andrew fled the bookstore fifteen minutes later with a copy of Turgenev's *Sportsman's Sketches*. Ernest took that and *Sons and Lovers, War and Peace* and *The Gambler and Other Stories* as well. Sylvie said she didn't expect to see him for some time if he was going to read all that.

Elated, Andrew walked all the way to the Jeu de Paume in the Tuilleries Gardens, thinking he might get lucky again. Crossing the Seine at Place de la Concorde, he tossed a franc into the water and made a wish. At the gallery, he looked at the Degas's and Monets and the Renoirs and stood for a long time in front of Cezanne's *Le Circle*. He decided Cezanne beat the rest of them hands down. Very hungry now, he left the gallery, crossed back to the left bank and went to a café he'd discovered called La Palette in rue de Seine and ordered half a baguette with ham and Camembert.

Hemingway came to the room only a couple of times during the next ten days. He didn't say much and Andrew assumed he was reading. In the evenings, Andrew fell into a routine of visiting four of the big cafés all of which he knew Hemingway — and every other writer and painter in the Paris of the '20s — frequented. The background buzz was so overwhelming the chances of overhearing something significant from thirty years before were remote but he didn't mind taking a chance and occasionally he did pick up a tidbit. One evening he heard a man in his cups declare that he could never write in Paris and that he was going to Nice. A voice, which Andrew thought was Hemingway's, replied that he could go anywhere he liked but "you won't write a line unless you leave your wife behind."

Andrew would start at Deux Magots on St. Germaine, have a glass of wine and a saucer of salty black olives and continue on to

Boulevard Monparnasse, often stopping at the Polidor for supper. He'd visit the Select, the Coupole and the Dome, finishing with a nightcap at the Lilas. He allowed himself a single glass of wine at each watering hole and a brandy at the Lilas.

One night he'd just sopped up the last of a wonderful *cassoulet* at a new place over near L'Opera when the girl from the bookstore came in. She was seated by herself near the window and he assumed she was waiting for someone. In the rich light of the restaurant she emanated a mysterious quality, and it suddenly struck him that she might be the most beautiful girl in the world; when she ordered and it was clear she was dining alone, he went to her table and asked if she would join him.

"Do I know you?"

"We met at the bookshop."

"Yes, I remember. You took the Turgenev."

"Yes."

"I don't normally...."

"I just wanted to say I think you're the most beautiful girl in the world," he interrupted, surprising himself.

"You were a little crazy in the bookshop too," she smiled.

The waiter moved her things to his table. She had also ordered the *cassoulet*.

She was stunning. Auburn hair piled up, greenish eyes, long pale hands, those lips. She came from Akron, Ohio. They talked about books. He felt safe. He went on and on. She went on and on. They had apple pie for dessert — *à la française* with a glaze instead of a top crust. The one food in Paris not as good as the American version, they agreed. They had cheese and grapes. He suggested the Lilas for a digistif. They kissed on the corner of Boulevard Marparnasse. At the Lilas at one in the morning he started to tell her about the voices in his head but stopped mid-sentence to kiss her again and a very few minutes later they were climbing the worn staircase behind the bar to his old room.

Their clothes were strewn on the floor when he woke at six.

Ernest Hemingway, Paris, 1922
(Courtesy of Mrs. S.J. Lanahan)

Isabelle slept gently on her side. She moved and smiled. He whispered he'd be back in a little while with a breakfast.

Downstairs alone in the bar, he ordered an espresso just as Hemingway called for a *café crème*. From the sound of his voice, he was in a fine mood. Andrew found himself saying automatically "Keep-it-simple-write-what-you-know" over and over very quickly.

After almost twenty minutes silence he heard: "Good. Yes. I can do this. Yes." This was followed by an agonizing ten minutes of nothing, interrupted, finally, by, "Hummmm. Yes. Let's see." The now familiar voice cleared its throat and began to read, "I can remember everything about the river near my grandparents' place up in northern Michigan." He paused, "Except the frigging name of it." And continued, " My parents used to take us kids up there a couple of times a year, sometimes more often. It was so quiet the only thing you could hear was the generator they used because they hadn't put through the power lines yet. The river ran fast and I used to watch my father and his father fish." Pause. OK. OK. Not bad. Needs work, but that's OK. I can feel it. I can do this."

For the young Hemingway it was OK. For young Andrew, it was a miracle. Tears came to his eyes. He ordered another coffee and had a tray prepared for Isabelle with croissants and butter and apricot jam and a bowl of coffee and a pot of hot milk. "He's bloody doing it. Writing about Michigan and frigging fishing," he said to Patrice as he took the tray. Isabelle kissed him and sat up naked and ate and drank coffee and they laughed and cuddled and made love in the croissant crumbs. He was too happy even to think about being happy. He would always remember the sound of the rain on the old slates.

She had to open the shop at 9:30 am. He walked her there and was back at the Lilas by ten. The café was now filled with smoke, the smell of damp clothes, coffee, then the voice read again, "As a kid I remember everything about the Two Hearted River." Pause. "Poetry, Hem, real poetry. It went on, "My grandparents owned a

This rare composite photograph, assembled by Eric in 1949, shows all four generations of Toggshams who possessed the gift of special hearing. From left to right they are: Hollis, 98; Richard, 44; Eric, 71; and Andrew, 7.

property up there and two or three times a year my parents would take us up there. Silence, except for the generator humming in the background, was great. The river flowed fast as I watched my father and grandfather floating past our trailer as they fished." Pause. Andrew was on the edge of his chair, it was like hearing the first chords of a great symphony, the lapping of waves on a new island that had just emerged from the sea.

First week in December. He was lying in bed late in the morning. They were living half the time at her place in a microscopic apartment on rue des Grandes Ecole and half the time in his room in rue Clovis. It was a Tuesday, overcast with flashes of watery sun. She was at work. In the last three weeks he'd heard bits and pieces of three new stories, every one a classic. He was grateful. Delighted. Relieved. In love. Ecstatic. Hemingway hadn't been by for a week. Now there was someone in the room. "These are dreadful," Andrew heard. A woman's voice! After a long pause, "My poor Tatie." He recognized Hadley's voice from that night at La Pècheur Miraculous. "Coffins and dead people and pain and blood. The sweet dear. He's been a different man these last few weeks, writing about being back in the States. I have to help him. It will be my Christmas present." A long, long silence. Then, "It's better this way. I'll tell him I left them on the train."

Another week or so went by. Isabelle's parents were coming to England for Christmas — her mother came from Leeds — her grandparents had a big traditional English Christmas planned, the first since the war. He went with her to the boat train at Gare du Nord, they kissed and held each other and she started to go and came back and they kissed again and again tried to part and couldn't until the train began to pull out and they felt like lovers in a B-movie, racing along the platform, she clambouring aboard at the last moment, him standing on the platform, turning up the collar of his trench coat. Then he was alone on the empty platform. He lit a cigarette and tossed the match on the tracks.

Christmas week Andrew woke suddenly in the night at Hotel

Clovis. His first thought was that he was in the middle of a nightmare. Hemingway was in the room screaming, throwing things, shouting. "The silly bitch LOST THEM ALL. No carbons. No copies. No nothing. I'll kill her." Then he began to sob. "Ten fucking months of work. I'm no writer. I don't know why I thought I was a writer. It was all a load of crap. She did me a favour. That silly bitch did me a favour. I stink." Andrew heard him taking swigs from a bottle and after a long time the voice said, "She isn't a silly bitch." And later, "I see a big white hand. It's coming to comfort me."

At the same moment, the famous author was actually in a Havana bar sipping a pre-luncheon daiquiri. "Oysters," he was saying to the barman, "That's how you could tell Christmas was coming in Paris. Even the working-class cafés would fill up with husbands and wives eating oysters and drinking champagne. I remember one year watching them in a cafe across from a hotel where I had a room for writing. They seemed so warm and happy. We all deserve to be warm and happy."

Isabelle came back in January and in the spring they went to Spain together.

DE

The
schnauzer kid

◆ In 1933 my Norwegian grandfather on my mother's side, Gudmund Olmstad, a ship builder in the town of Trondheim, decided to leave his native country to seek his fortune in America. Along with his wife Kirsten and their young children, two sons and a daughter, Gunhild, who would later become my mother, they endured steerage class on the Norwegian-American Lines flagship *King Haakon* to New York. After being inoculated, deloused and processed by the authorities on Ellis Island, the Olmstad family moved in with distant relatives to rather cramped quarters on the west side of Manhattan, in the area known as Hell's Kitchen. After a stint of plying his finely honed shipbuilding skills at a collection of mind-numbing dishwashing jobs, Gudmund was fortunate to land a position as a draughtsman at the navy's Brooklyn dockyard. At that point the family had seen enough of the cramped life in Hell's Kitchen and went looking for an apartment of their own.

As luck would have it, they managed to find a lower four-room apartment in a run-down tenement building near eleventh street in the borough of Queens. The rent was cheap, the landlord ruthless and the neighbourhood, though a bit too colourful for Mama

Olaf and his sister Gunhild in Tyrolian get-up. Taken a week before their departure for America in 1933.

Kirsten's Lutheran tastes, was ideally suited for the raising of a family. The ethnic make-up of the neighbourhood was a stimulating brew of Italian, Greek, Jewish, Black and Puerto Rican, no doubt the sort of thing Americans have in mind when they refer to the melting pot. For Papa Olmstad their new home had the advantage of being a short subway hop from the dockyards. But most interesting of all, at least for the children, was the fact that their house was a mere stone's throw from the thriving Schiff-Waldhof Motion Picture Studios. For afternoons on end the neighbourhood kids would hang about the studio gate, peering through the wire fence, trying to catch a glimpse of the Masked Phantom who was spotted from time to time as he emerged from the soundstage in his get-up to sneak a quick piss and a smoke in the lane next to the stagedoor. At that time the studios were a busy factory branch of the Hollywood Dream Machine and on a given day the four soundstages would be humming to full capacity, turning out any number of grade-B romances, wacky comedies, cliff-hanger serials, jungle movies, fight pictures, pirate flicks and gangster epics. Over time the Schiff-Waldhof Motion Picture Studios trademark product became a certain kind of hard-edged New York gangster flick, the kind that usually ended in a slow dolly shot of a dark prison corridor, with the bad guy in chains being led off to the chair. "Tell Mugsy I ain't scared." Music up. Fade out. The end.

Gudmund's oldest son Olaf, who had just turned eleven, was, along with his siblings, enrolled at the local school, where in a surprisingly short time he acquired a firm grasp of the American vernacular. In less than a year Olaf had lost all trace of his native Norwegian and had mastered the finer linguistic embellishments of the local patois which the inhabitants of the borough of Queens proudly referred to as The Queen's English.

One morning as Olaf's mother was shopping for salt-cured herring fillets on Queens Boulevard, she came across a poster at the fishmonger's shop urging locals to register with the casting department of the Schiff-Waldhof Motion Picture Studios for work as

The Brazilian Spitfire. From
the movie "Harem Girl." It
was said she had the "gams
of a racehorse and the mouth
of a mule driver."

extras. The following afternoon, armed with photographs of her three children, she went to the studio and signed them up. The woman in charge of the office was most complimentary.

"Your kids are so adorable. All day long we get nothing but dark children. Italians, Greeks, Jews, Arabs, Negroes. You should see some of them, so dirty, and they don't even speak English. Never nice-looking blond children like yours."

Within the week Olaf was asked to appear at the studio for a crowd scene in a motion picture entitled *The Fight of His Life.* The accompanying pay scale promised five dollars for the day's work, with additional pay for speaking parts or overtime.

At seven o'clock of the appointed morning Olaf arrived at the studio where he, along with fourteen other stagestruck kids, was herded into the costume department. An army of technicians set to work transforming this lot of extras into the movie version of a ragtag Brooklyn gang. Olaf was outfitted with a checkered and neatly torn shirt, a roomy pair of knickerbockers and a newsboy cap. Smudges of burnt cork were applied to his face, arms and hands.

The group was next led onto the sound stage. At the far end was a brightly lit mockup of a front door and a grand staircase as well as part of the outer wall of an elegant mansion. Standing at the top of the stairs in a pool of light was a middle-aged gentleman, impeccably attired in a tuxedo, chatting with a beautiful dark-haired woman dressed in a worn and dowdy gown, while two hairdressers and a girl from wardrobe did little touchups on them. An assistant director arranged Olaf and the extras in a semi-circle at the bottom of the stairs.

The sequence they were about to shoot was part of a standard wrestling epic featuring Buster "Boozy" Wallace as the wrestler and a young Mercedes del Rico, the "Brazilian Spitfire," in her first screen appearance, as the homie babe. The story, such as it was, revolved around a punch-drunk former champ trying for a come-back in order to win the purse for his mother's life-saving opera-

Mr. European sophistication, Adolphe Verdoux. He was in fact born Mortimer Parker in Toledo, Ohio, and never visited Europe. In private life he was a passionate collector of Japanese erotica.

tion. Along the way the wrestler encounters a leggy Mercedes del Rico in the tenements and, together with a spunky gang of kids, they do battle with a ruthless landlord played to evil perfection by "the man you love to hate," Adolphe Verdoux. With his insufferable European airs and his stylish acting Mr. Verdoux was guaranteed to bring class to even the most hackneyed formula picture. His presence in any movie was like money in the bank, for audiences loved nothing as much as to watch the eventual comeuppance of this suave villain. Comic relief would be provided by a lanky and bug-eyed newcomer, "Gloomy" Fritz Mandelbaum, who invented and perfected the "slow burn" for this film.

Olaf's scene would come near the end of the picture as Mr. Verdoux, on his way to an elegant party, is confronted by Mercedes del Rico and the slum kids.

The director Bram Halliday, a hack veteran of any number of grade-B flicks, including some of the early silent Tarzan pictures, swept onto the set. In every respect, his outfit conformed to the strict dress-code so fashionable with movie directors at that time. Jodhpurs, riding boots, suede windbreaker, white foulard and a cattle-herder's fedora. He blew a kiss in Miss del Rico's direction and waved at Mr. Verdoux and the crew in the Italian manner. Then he turned to the kids.

"Okay. We are trying to make a major motion picture here. As long as you take orders we are going to have a good time, you understand? What we want from you is that you watch Mr. Verdoux up there at the top of the stairs as he speaks. Miss del Rico will be standing down here, with you spread out around her. Now remember this: I don't want no horsing around, and absolutely no talking. The camera will be positioned behind so it can shoot over your shoulders." Bram Halliday was forming a frame with his two hands. He peered through it and panned as he continued. "All you have to do is to stay put on the marks and not move around. Do you understand?" The kids nodded.

Next Mr. Halliday, who seemed to be all business, had a short conversation with Adolphe Verdoux, while wardrobe did last-minute adjustments to his bow-tie, cummerbund and moustache. Olaf caught a few snippets of their conversation.

"Yeah, old Boozy Wallace is indisposed again." Bram Halliday was chuckling. Adolphe Verdoux leaned his head back and pointed his thumb at his open mouth while making gurgling noises as if drinking from a bottle. Bram Halliday laughed. "Don't worry. We'll shoot around him and do pick-ups when he gets sober." They both sniggered.

Finally everything was ready. A brief buzzing noise of the siren. The camera started up. The slate marker yelled, "Scene seventy-nine, take one." Clap. The set went silent.

"Aaaaaand action," yelled Bram Halliday. All eyes focused on Mr. Verdoux at the top of the stairs. He looked swell in his tuxedo.

Slowly Mr. Verdoux scanned Miss del Rico and the group of ragged kids, his eyes narrowing menacingly. His hand went into his coat pocket and he extracted an elegant gold *etui*. He flipped it open and took out a cigarette. Tapping the end of the cigarette on his thumbnail he began:

"Now, what have we here? Something the cat dragged in? Or is it a mob ready to lynch me?" He hissed and lit the cigarette. "Ha. Ha. Ha. You make me laugh. You are so pathetic." He took a long deliberate drag, savouring the smoke. The man was a total pro. He could do this kind of role in his sleep with both hands tied.

"Maybe you think it's funny coming here to my house and disturbing me. Only I ain't laughing, see? I'll make sure that your names are collected and you and your parents are evicted from your apartments." He stabbed his cigarette at each of them.

"The buildings belong to me and I will do with them as I wish. That's the law of this land, that's the American way and I will not stand for any of your communistic ideas." He ran a hand over the cigarette case and flipped the lid up and down a few times.

"You are poor, and you will always remain poor, and you know why?" There was long pause as Mr. Verdoux took another deep drag on his cigarette.

"Do you know why?" he repeated. "Because you are nothing. Nothing. You are trash, and you don't deserve to live in this great land. Crawl back to the vermin-infested holes from where you came." He slammed the cigarette case shut. "Now beat it before I call in the guards." With that he descended the staircase, and went out of camera range.

"Aaaand cut," yelled Bram Halliday. "And print it." The crew applauded. It was a totally convincing performance, a thespian *tour de force*. No wonder they called him "one-take Adolphe."

"I think that will do very nicely," beamed Bram Halliday. "There won't be any need for a re-take. If all actors could be just like that. Now let's set up for the close-ups on the kids." He turned his charm full throttle on Mr. Adolphe Verdoux and Miss del Rico. The three of them were laughing uproariously as the crew moved the camera into a new position and the electricians adjusted the lights.

Olaf was flabbergasted. He just couldn't believe it. In his short life had he never felt so humiliated and it wasn't just what Mr. Verdoux had said; it was the way his beady little eyes had singled him out. And just look at him now, standing up there carrying on as if the whole thing was just one big joke.

Olaf was interrupted by the director and a flunky.

"He'll do just fine," said Bram Halliday, peering at Olaf through the frame formed by his two hands. "Just turn around a bit, sonny, I wanna see you in profile." He put a finger under Olaf's chin and turned his face from side to side.

"I like his blond looks. Kind of cute. Have makeup fix him up, he needs a bit more dirt on his face." As smudges were applied to Olaf's cheeks and his hat adjusted, Bram Halliday leaned over and confided in a reassuring voice:

"It's really very simple, sonny, nothing to get nervous about. We are going to do a medium close-up line on you. You get extra for that, you know. You speak English, do you?"

Olaf nodded.

"Good. All you have to do is to stand there, next to Miss del Rico, and look up at Mr. Verdoux like this, kind of innocent. When the camera moves in close, I'll give you this signal." Bram Halliday pointed a finger at Olaf. "Then you say your line: "Please, please, mister," in a sort of pleading voice. That's all there is to it. Do you think you can do that?"

Olaf nodded and said the line, but his heart wasn't really in it. Having spent the first part of the morning being subjected to the invective of Mr. Verdoux, Olaf was not only good and mad, he was royally steamed.

"That'll do fine," said Bram Halliday. "Just the right kind of edge. I like it. Maybe a touch more oomph. Okay?"

By the time the camera was lined up and the lights arranged, Olaf was seething, and it didn't help any that Mr. Verdoux was standing there looking down at him in that same menacing way.

A short burst from the siren. The slate was ready. "Scene eighty, take one." Clap. The set went silent.

" Aaand action," yelled Bram Halliday. The camera started up, then it slowly dollied in on Olaf's face. The director pointed his finger. Olaf was ready. He glared straight into the beady little eye-balls of Mr. Verdoux.

Then he let it rip. "Hey, you big chump. Why don't you just take this," he stabbed his fist into the air, while letting out a Queens version of a Bronx cheer, "and shove it up your schnauzer." His fist executed a brutal barroom sucker-punch into the open palm of his hand.

It was a perfect take, delivered in beautifully articulated Queens English. Nuanced yet muscular. Any actor would have been proud.

For a moment there was stunned silence on the set, then Bram Halliday exploded. "Cut!" he screamed. "Get this fucking kid out of here. He's never to be allowed back, understand? And someone find me another blond kid like him." Meanwhile Mr. Verdoux and Miss del Rico and most of the crew were buckled over with laughter.

That marked both the beginning and the end of Olaf's brief but memorable screen career.

Some weeks later, while assembling the first rough-cut of the movie, Miss Helen Faber, the film editor, decided in her infinite wisdom to include Olaf's performance although the script did not call for it. Max Lemmeler, the producer, an old pro who knew a good thing when he saw it, was more than charmed. He ignored Bram Halliday's protestations of "it's not in the script."

"The kid's a natural. For Christ's sake, look at him, use your goddamn eyes," yelled Max: "It's fresh, it's saucy, it's unexpected, just the kind of thing this fucking snoozer needs."

On a Friday night in October 1936, *The Fight of His Life* was given its first test screening at the Rialto Variety Theater in Bayonne, New Jersey. Bram Halliday, Max Lemmeler, Anton Kopperstein the writer, along with two flacks from publicity were at the rear of the theatre as they watched the audience slumber through the first two-thirds of the movie. Only when Mercedes del Rico sang and hoofed her way through the cleverly staged rhumba extravaganza "Love that Wrestling Man" did the audience seem to abandon their lethargy, and there were even a few scattered laughs as Gloomy Mandelbaum ogled her fabulous gams and did the slow burn. But it was only momentary. They were soon asleep again. By the time Adolphe Verdoux started his harangue, members of the audience were wandering up and down the aisles while the bathrooms and candy-counters were doing box-office business. Max Lemmeler was right; this snoozer was going to lay an egg. But as Adolphe Verdoux's tirade went on, the audience seemed to perk up; there were a few "boos" here and there, always a good sign, and by the middle of his harangue hissing had started. As Adolphe Verdoux continued the audience grew noticeably agitated. The anger was getting palpable; it was sweeping like a tidal wave through the theater. They really hated him. Max Lemmeler was rubbing his hands. This was good, really good. As Mr. Verdoux finally descended the staircase, the screen cut to the

Dear Fan – Shove it up your schnauzer! Your pal, Willie

Olaf's publicity picture.

shot of Olaf. The camera slowly dollied in. You could have heard a pin drop.

When Olaf delivered his line, the theater went wild. Some intangible blend of Olaf's sweet angelic looks and the saucy delivery of "Why don't you shove it up your schnauzer?" in combination with the raspberry and the pugilistic finesse, hit just the right button. All over the theater, Bronx cheers could be heard as fists executed brutal overhead barroom sucker-punches into open palms. The pandemonium was deafening.

For the remainder of the movie the behaviour of the audience took on a life of its own. From time to time fisticuffs would break out and at each appearance of Adolphe Verdoux the audience would let out a resounding raspberry and scream in unison: "Why don't you shove it up your schnauzer?" It was clear they were having a choice entertainment experience. Today this kind of response is referred to as "interactive audience participation."

Four more test screenings in the Midwest produced almost identical results. At the final screening at the Roxy in Kentwood, Illinois, the audience got so carried away that they caused over eight hundred dollars worth of damage to the leatherette upholstery. In the ensuing melee a third-year theology student was knocked out cold by a brutal overhead sucker-punch. When he came to an hour later in the emergency room of the Goddard-Stinson Hospital his first words were: "Damn, that was a hell of a fight picture."

Some days later the representative from The Hays Office, one Hubert Meadows, a lacto-vegetarian and former dance instructor, screened *The Fight of His Life* to ensure it adhered to the rigid Motion Picture Production Code in effect at the time. He questioned the use of "schnauzer" but was reassured by the flack from publicity that the term merely referred to Mr. Verdoux's nasal appendage, much the way one talked about Jimmy Durante's "schnozzle," Will Hampton's "beak" or Eddie Conway's "snotter."

"That's precisely what I thought," muttered Mr. Meadows,

Olaf and his wife Sigrid, Oslo 1956. At the time
of this photograph, he had just been appointed
assistant loan-officer at Nordiske Merkantil og
Handelsbank.

pocketing a small envelope from the studio flack and retreating to the commissary for a light snack of warm sardines and cold buttermilk. Within four days the film received the Hays Office seal of approval. As *The Fight of His Life* was about to go into general release across America, the studio flacks geared up. This was going to be good. No, more than good, since here finally was a "B" flick with an "A" promotion budget. A Manhattan songwriting team, Sheela and Roger, was hired to turn out a hummable ditty, "Shove it up your schnauzer," and negotiations were under way to have Olaf and Adolphe Verdoux appear on "The Jimmy Durante Radio Hour." But the publicity department had bargained without Olaf's consent. By the time the studio had lined up a further radio interview with Sidney Gardiner and an extravagant photo spread for "Silver Screen News," a gangly, surly and newly zit-ridden Olaf insolently refused to cooperate. Puberty, in all its destructive power, had hit like a freight train and ravaged the once sweet and saucy demeanor of our Norwegian teenager.

In any event, Papa Gudmund's employment at the navy dockyards had not panned out as expected and the Olmstad family had already made plans. They packed up their meagre belongings and returned, sadder but wiser, to Norway. In the haste and confusion of their departure the Olmstad family forgot to leave a forwarding address. By the time the ocean liner docked in Trondheim, the movie was put into general release. Over the next two years the picture cleaned up at box offices all across America and, unknown to Olaf, his screen appearance was being imitated by teenagers from Maine to California while his memorable line soon entered the American vocabulary, much like "So is your Aunt Tillie and a razz-a-ma-tazz" had a decade earlier. In the studio's mail room, the fan letters piled up. Tens of thousands of them. Most were addressed to "that Schnauzer Kid." But there was no Schnauzer Kid to forward them to and, alas, no signed eight-by-ten glossies available. So, what does a great studio do to satisfy such overwhelming demand? They fake it. The photograph Mama Kirsten had originally brought to the casting department was blown up and airbrushed a bit, while a young man from publicity, in a neat cursive hand, signed the picture: "Dear fan. Shove it up your schnauzer. Love. Your pal, Willie." The studio never really got Olaf's name straight, but it didn't seem to matter. At any event, after some time the demand for signed eight-by-ten glossies tapered off and eventually it stopped.

By the early fifties the Schiff-Waldhof Motion Picture Studios went into steep decline. Television was gaining wide popularity and there was little appetite for tired formula movies. Audiences preferred to stay at home to watch Milton Berle in drag, and who could blame them? The studio's once glorious inventory of hits languished in the library, all but ignored by the public. To make up for sagging profits, Schiff-Waldhof started retrieving the silver nitrate from some of their old films. Thousands of movies were destroyed in this manner. On an August evening in 1952, mere weeks before a bankruptcy hearing, several sound stages and production offices went up in flames. When the fire hit the vaults with its flammable nitrate filmstock, the place literally exploded. The conflagration destroyed the entire archives along with the original negatives and all known prints of *The Fight of His Life*.

As for Olaf, he never saw the movie, for it wasn't released in Norway. In suburban Trondheim he soon got over his difficult adolescence and with time forgot all about his short-lived foreign movie career. He grew up to be a regular Norwegian lad whose only lasting impression of America was that their brine-cured herring fillets were far too salty.

It was only in the late eighties, when Argentinean film archivist Jorge Mendera came across an almost pristine print of *La Batalla de su Vida* in a film vault in Montevideo, that Olaf's screen debut again saw the light of a film projector. As it turned out, the film was a Spanish-dubbed version and, as is so often the case with dubbed movies, lacked most of the muscle and punch of the original as it attempted to straddle almost impassable cultural-linguistic barriers. Olaf's memorable line, translated from the Spanish, went like this:

"Hello mister. I would like to push this (ayeee, caramba!) into the nose of your German dog."

TS

Borge's Gambit

◆ When the German *Wehrmacht* invaded Denmark in the early morning hours of April 9, 1940, most of the country was not only soundly asleep, it was more or less comatose. This included the Danish military high command which at the time was on a low status alert, having no particular reason to expect an armed incursion from the south. As for me, being only five at the time, I was conked out, sleeping the sleep of the innocents. My uncle Borge, on the other hand, was wide awake. From the window of his third-storey Copenhagen walk-up he watched the endless columns of field-grey uniforms march by as the German troops moved into position all over the city. Uncle Borge was not a happy man. This unexpected development could only mean one thing: the disruption of his orderly bachelor life.

He had spent the night with his cronies playing chess at his favourite hangout, Café Metropole, a downtown Copenhagen establishment which catered to layabouts, idlers, communists, socialists, anarchists, artists, chess aficionados and whores. As he was biking home in the early hours through the empty streets, he had been startled by groups of Stuka dive-bombers flying in formation overhead and dropping leaflets that demanded unequivocal surrender and obedience to the new masters. The invasion of the little kingdom was accomplished in a matter of hours with little bloodshed.

By noon of that day, both the king and the government had capitulated and the Germans taken control of all strategic positions.

Things soon went from bad to worse. Curfews were imposed. Coal for heating and electricity, along with long lists of foodstuffs, were put on the restricted list. But most galling of all, at least in the eyes of Uncle Borge, was the curtailment on the sale of cigarettes and coffee. Borge, as a dedicated night owl, liked few things as much as sitting in a café in the early hours over a chess game, smoking and drinking endless cups of java. With the new curfews in effect, all nightlife ceased at seven p.m, which was usually about the time Borge started his day. A further indignity was imposed when off-duty German soldiers dropped into Café Metropole from time to time for a friendly game of chess. This is where Borge drew the line. On the few occasions when he did play against the enemy, it would invariably result in the total destruction of the opposition in a few well-chosen moves. It should be noted that Borge was a superb player who, in 1938, ranked twenty-eighth in the European tournaments in Bern.

From time to time Borge would drop by our house to play chess with my dad, who was considered a good player, but certainly not in Borge's class, although my dad usually gave him a good run for his money. The two of them would huddle in the gloom of the dining room, illuminated by the faint glow of a ten-watt bulb, cursing the Germans as they pondered their moves. For coffee they resigned themselves to an insipid brew concocted from finely ground chicory, flavoured with a dash of vanilla and liberally spiked with home-grown Beulah-grass extract "to round off the corners and add some much needed *zaft*." For cigarettes they manipulated an assortment of cured and diced foliage, flavoured according to a secret Hungarian recipe and wrapped in pages from an illustrated family Bible. This paper with its crisp texture and fragile weave was found after some industrious experimentation to be best suited for the task. The two of them would invariably cross themselves before they lit up their "Stinkadoros Infamosos." "War makes men do ungodly things," Borge would intone piously, notwithstanding the fact that he was a devout agnostic. The stink was awesome.

Although well into his forties and not known as a vain man, Borge was nevertheless beginning to show signs of apprehension about his incipient baldness. From a Dutch animal husbandry journal he had learned that frequent and robust massaging of the outer dermis could regenerate hair follicles and stimulate vigorous hair growth in certain breeds of Holstein cattle. As a firm believer in the principles of evolution set forth by Darwin, he assumed that what would work on the hide of a Holstein cow should also work on his scalp. Thus, he would recompense me handsomely for riding astride his shoulders during chess matches, kneading and massaging his balding pate with my grubby fingers as he pondered his moves. From that vantage point, perched over his shiny crown, I acquired not only the rudiments but also some of the finer points of chess.

Prior to the outbreak of the war Uncle Borge had made a comfortable, if erratic, living as a portrait painter, a *métier* at which he excelled. His portraits, which were painted somewhat in the style of the early Dutch masters, were much sought after by "egomaniacs with wallets matching their overblown self esteem," as my uncle put it. It is curious to note then, that his paintings were celebrated for their meticulous rendering of reality and total absence of flattery, which at times tended towards the grotesque. Double chins, warts, receding hairlines, bad teeth, obesity and any physical malformations were faithfully transmitted to canvas with an eerie and almost clinical precision. Why anyone would willingly submit to this aesthetic punishment and pay a whopping fee in the bargain was a constant source of wonder to Borge. He would often have the subjects themselves choose the pose, attire and setting since, he reasoned, "when they themselves select these ingredients they reveal subtle clues as to the magnitude of their vanity." At that point he would snap a roll of film and work from the photos, having no further use for the subjects' cooperation.

With the onset of the German occupation, business dried up. To make ends meet Borge would from time to time engage in the odd black market deal. At one point he obtained a quantity of sub-standard Polish bicycle tires which he turned into sub-standard shoe soles and automobile brake pads, reaping a handsome profit in the process. Leftover bits of rubber were ground into a sticky chewing-gum base and flavoured according to the same secret Hungarian recipe he applied to his ersatz tobacco. Although the gum was lumpy and not particularly tasty, it sold very well in a country deprived of all the normal amenities of civilized living. During this time Borge got embroiled in a colourful assortment of marginal, illegal and highly disorganized communist and anarchist organizations. They valued his skill as an artist and frequently employed him in the forging of fake I.D. cards and food-rationing stamps. Later he supplied anti-German cartoons to a number of underground communist newspapers. The one cartoon he did of Hitler running away from an onrushing tank that resembled Stalin earned a measure of fame when it somehow found its way to America and was reprinted anonymously in most of Hearst's newspapers.

As the war dragged on, the coffee and cigarette situation worsened to the point where obtaining even chicory and Beulah-grass became a problem, by which time the Old and New Testaments including the illustrated Apochrypia had faded into memory. It was during this godless period a rumour started circulating around Copenhagen that the Wehrmacht had stored huge quantities of captured American cigarettes, coffee, foodstuffs and war paraphernalia in a large well-guarded shed in the port area.

Uncle Borge was a man who liked to keep his nose clean and mind his own business, but in this particular instance he decided after some deliberation to make the shed and its contents his own business. The way he saw it, the "liberation" of some of the coffee and cigarettes might deal a devastating blow to the German war

Rationeringskort for Kaffe og The
15. April – 30. Juni 1940

Kortet tildeles **ikke** Børn under 6 Aar.

Navn: _____

Adresse: _____

Denne Del af Kortet opbevares til Brug ved event. Uddeling af nye Kort.

Hvert af Kortets 10 Mærker giver Ret til
Køb af det anførte Kvantum Kaffe eller The.

Juni 1940	Juni 1940
100 gr Kaffe	100 gr Kaffe
eller	eller
50 gr The	50 gr The
Juni 1940	Juni 1940
100 gr Kaffe	100 gr Kaffe
eller	eller
50 gr The	50 gr The
Maj 1940	Maj 1940
100 gr Kaffe	100 gr Kaffe
eller	eller
50 gr The	50 gr The
Maj 1940	Maj 1940
100 gr Kaffe	100 gr Kaffe
eller	eller
50 gr The	50 gr The
April 1940	April 1940
100 gr Kaffe	100 gr Kaffe
eller	eller
50 gr The	50 gr The

Børge's fake rationing cards. They soon proved to be worthless.

machine. Endless hours were spent at Café Metropole with his fellow chess players as they hatched one harebrained scheme after the other, at one point even discussing an armed frontal attack on the shed. This plan was eventually dropped for being unnecessarily dangerous, especially considering that they didn't possess a single firearm among them. It was while Borge was engaged in a chess game with a local idler and was about to execute a variant of the Obliganov gambit that inspiration struck. I know this firsthand because I was present at the time, having been pawned off by my mother for an afternoon of babysitting. Uncle Borge's short stubby fingers started drumming the tabletop as he slowly inhaled his stinkadoro. His eyes narrowed into tiny slits. The usual coterie of hangers-on gathered around the table.

"This little variant," he mumbled, pointing at the chess board, "is called the Obliganov gambit and is named after a great Russian player who not only understood the game of chess in all its delicious refinements but also had a profound understanding of human nature. And what is the secret of his gambit?" Borge took a long deliberate drag on his reefer. "Greed. In other words, to checkmate your opponent, serve up something he can't refuse. A queen for instance. As he's reeling from his success you hit him with the wily knight. Your opponent is off his guard, heady with impending victory. Then, like a bolt from the clear blue sky, check and check again." With that Borge toppled the black king. Dead silence.

It was an amazing performance, given that Borge was not a man to make public pronouncements. Even I, who was only six at the time, knew that something extraordinary had just taken place. But exactly how this statement could in any way relate to a shed in the port area was unclear to everyone, including, I suspect, Uncle Borge. Nevertheless, in the ensuing debate the considered opinion of most present was that a conservative and innocent-looking opening gambit was needed, something that would pique the Germans' interest and engage them in the game.

That opening gambit was unexpectedly provided a week later by a notice in the newspaper. "Luftwaffe Marshall Göring to inspect German troops in Denmark," ran the headline. Borge had a sketchy familiarity with the lardy German commander from newspaper stories and news reels, and one thing he recognized was that even by luft-marshall standards, Herr Göring was an acutely vain one. As a painter of portraits, Borge was a bit of an expert when it came to vanity. "We have found our adversary's Achilles' heel. Now the wily knight will strike," Borge announced grandly. He had at this point only the vaguest idea of how to go about all this, yet the tiniest wisps of a plan were beginning to percolate in Borge's caffeine-deprived mind.

During the next few weeks Borge was not to be found at his usual haunts. In fact he was nowhere to be found at all. He was holed up in his atelier with all the usual paraphenalia of a painter as well as stacks of illustrated German news magazines and history books. For seventeen straight days he laboured on a 96-cm by 53-cm canvas. The final result, unveiled at Café Metropole, was a spectacular tapestry of recent Germanic history unfolding in a sort of neo-kitschy style, reminiscent of certain late nineteenth-century Italian artists. When the painting was fitted some days later with a gold-leafed and richly carved Venetian frame, you could almost swear you were looking at the work of an Italian Master. Yet "there is a very modern sensibility suffusing this Nordic *chef-d'oeuvre*," one German art critic would later declare. In other words, the painting entitled "Freunde" was a brilliant collage of contemporary German historical icons right up to and including the Anschluss of Austria and the invasion of Poland. Panzers, Luftwaffe, U-boats, Blitzkrieg — it was all there. And right in the middle, the Reich plenipotentiary to Denmark, Dr. Werner Best, in his *obersturmführer* uniform, smiling while shaking hands with a blond yet somewhat callow youth dressed in what appeared to be a Hitler-*jugend* uniform with the Danish ensign on the sleeve. Not only was the execution flawless but the sentiments were easily understood. There was initially some grumbling among the clientele at the Café Metropole, who wondered exactly how this painting which glorified the despised enemy could in any way help liberate a shed brimming with coffee and American cigarettes. After a few hours of heated debate, Borge managed to convince the sceptics that it was part of a larger scheme which doubtless would leave the enemy reeling.

The painting was delivered by Borge himself via bicycle to the German embassy a few days later with a short note expressing his respects to the Reich plenipotentiary Dr. Werner Best.

The following morning Borge received a telegram from Dr. Best, who seemed much taken by the gift and wished Borge to be present at an embassy party some four days hence for an evening suffused with "Sauerbraten, Rothkohl, German *gemütlicheit* and humouristicality." As an added bonus the telegram promised an introduction to Luft-Marshall Göring who would be arriving at that time for his inspection tour.

Borge came to our house a few days later. He badly needed an appropriate outfit for such an impressive occasion. A tuxedo or "smoking," as the Europeans call it, would nicely fit the bill. My father had one, inherited from an uncle, and it fit after a fashion once my mother made a few alterations. He looked splendid.

The party was, according to Borge, a dazzling affair. The Reich plenipotentiary had thanked him warmly and introduced him all around as a Danish friend of the German people and the genius who had painted the work of art prominently displayed in the centre of the room. Göring, fancying himself an art connoisseur and famed as a collector of plundered art works from all over occupied Europe, was impressed. *"Das ist doch prima,"* beamed the obese Luft-Marshall as he peered closely at the canvas. Both Herr Göring and the Reich plenipotentiary thanked Borge profusely on behalf of the German people. Such vision, such understanding of the German destiny and the thousand-year Reich, such appreciation of the tapestry of history, and so on. Borge thanked them

Göring moose hunting in
Denmark. Since moose are
not native to this part of
the world, the Luftwaffe
high command thoughtfully
stocked a game reserve with
the Norwegian variety.

both very much indeed and took the opportunity during a lull in the festivities to line his various pockets with an assortment of complementary American cigarettes and Belgian chocolates which were arranged on small trays around the room. He also managed to put away eight cups of excellent coffee. His spirits soared. Whatever else one could say about the Germans, they certainly knew how to brew a mean cup of java. The combination of nicotine and caffeine in his anemic bloodstream almost led to him passing out on the Boukhara. Before he left the party he managed to conceal what amounted to fourteen packs of Lucky Strikes and three boxes of Excelsior deluxe chocolates in various parts of his specially altered tuxedo.

Never in my young life had I tasted anything as enchanting as Belgian chocolates. It is said that the sense of taste is the most evocative of them all, that it can unleash a deluge of memories. Just look at how a simple Madeleine opened the floodgates to twelve volumes of recollections by Marcel Proust and in the process spawned a veritable industry in doctoral theses. In my own case a taste of Belgian Excelsior deluxe is all it takes to make me six years old again.

Two days later Uncle Borge received yet another telegram from Dr. Best, asking him to drop by at his convenience to discuss a matter of some urgency. At four o'clock Borge met the visibly tense plenipotentiary at the heavily guarded embassy. After some preliminary hemming and hawing Dr. Best got around to the point: the splendid gift had caused some unpleasant friction between himself and Herr Göring. Dr. Best confided that when the Luft-Marshall first saw the painting prior to the party, he had for a moment put the problems of the Luftwaffe and the Eastern front on the back burner in order to throw a king-size fit, angrily demanding an even bigger painting of himself. As he ranted and raved he had, according to the Plenipotentiary, shouted, "I will not be upstaged by a Bavarian lard-ass like yourself!"

It was fast becoming apparent to Borge that this was not just a courteous request for a portrait but a command from the very highest German authority. Obviously there was a great deal at stake here for Dr. Best: either produce a painting to Herr Göring's satisfaction or end up as cannon fodder on the Eastern front.

"I will be more than flattered to execute such an undertaking for the sheer honour of it," beamed Borge, "and as for payment, don't give it a second thought. I would be delighted to do it for free as a present to the Luft-Marshall. There are, however, certain materials which I require and which are unobtainable for ordinary citizens such as myself. Things such as canvas, paints, oils, thinners and brushes, and of course cigarettes and coffee for inspiration. I work far faster and better that way."

"Well, of course," retorted the visibly relieved Reich plenipotentiary. "Who doesn't need a little stimulant from time to time? Anything at all that you should require from German stores will be made available. All you have to do is ask for it. Even better, I will provide you with a open requisition form. It will let you procure anything you need by simply presenting the document to the supply officer at any of our military depots."

Borge departed with the freshly signed requisition order in his wallet after warmly shaking hands with the plenipotentiary. Within minutes Dr. Best was on the hotline to the foreign office in Berlin where Herr Rippentrop expressed great relief at the outcome of the meeting.

With the precious document in hand, Borge now set about to acquire the needed supplies. In a hired taxi cab he went to the German storage shed in the port area and presented the requisition form to the supply officer. It worked like a charm. Oils, paints, canvas, thinner and brushes piled up.

"Oh yes, I almost forgot. I'll need some cigarettes. Lucky Strike, two cartons."

Due to Borge's rather rudimentary command of the German language he unintentionally asked for two crates, which didn't seem to perturb the supply officer in the least. In short order both crates were wheeled in, each containing two hundred cartons.

"And maybe some coffee. Java, ten kilos, and one of those smoked hams hanging on the hooks over there. No, better make that two."

And he really needed a new pair of good leather shoes, and of course six boxes of Belgian Excelsior deluxe chocolates. When he left one hour later in his brand new wool suit he needed three taxis to transport all the goodies to his *atelier*.

That night they celebrated at Café Metropole. It was almost like before the war. The windows had been carefully blackened out and the noise was kept to a minimum in order to avoid detection. By midnight the smoke was so heavy that two participants passed out and had to be carrried outside for fresh air. The aroma of coffee and cigarettes wafted down the street like waves onto a beach, making pedestrians come to an abrupt halt as they were led by their noses to the café. In no time at all word had spread around the neighbourhood and by one a.m. the place was mobbed. As the first workers biked to work in the grey dawn light, the last of the coffee and cigarettes had gone.

The following afternoon Borge set to work. He sent out word that he was looking for Vera Skavenius, a thirty-six-year-old Lithuanian chemist who had lived illegally in Denmark for some years and during that time made a name for herself as the preferred bombmaker of the resistance movement. Her ability to concoct explosives from readily available materials made her expertise indispensable. The fifty-kilogram bomb that sank the torpedo boat Prinz Wilhelm as it was moored at the Copenhagen pier was a potent concoction of soda and fertilizer concealed in an innocent-looking paint drum with a time-delay fuse cobbled together from two alarm clocks. Vera was also responsible for the huge explosions that ripped apart a large munitions factory in the countryside near the town of Odense and left it burning for days. It is interesting to note that the German censors demanded that the story be reported in the papers as a failed British air raid that hit only a shed and killed a few cows. Some days later a Copenhagen daily headlined their front page: "Two days after botched RAF raid, six cows still burning." Vera was also the inventor of a trenchant stink bomb which was used on numerous occasions with great success to break up German military parades and rallies. The outstanding feature of this bomb, besides the plethora of foul aromas, was that it was almost impossible to detect the source of the stink. Using only an electric Krupp food processor, Vera would cook up a rich brew of oil-coated, pungent molecules, whose eye-watering qualities were only released as the outer oil coating evaporated. By the time the bouquet reached nauseating levels, the molecules had wafted too far from the source for it to be found. Today this little marvel of chemistry is known as TRA or time-release action and is most commonly employed in underarm deodorants.

Vera and Uncle Borge now retreated to his *atelier* and set about the task ahead. After some weeks my father and I went to visit. It was wonderful. The place resembled the workshop of some deranged alchemist. There was stuff everywhere: tubes of paints, stacks of drawings, books, magazines, paint samples, bottles and jars, chess sets and coffee cups. Dominating the room was a huge easel propping up an enormous canvas with a very rough and somber charcoal outline of what appeared to be a vast city in total ruin. But more interesting than the canvas was my uncle's strange behaviour. Though I was only six I knew for certain that Borge and Vera were very much smitten with each other. Small secret gestures and glances didn't escape my attention. It was fascinating to notice how Uncle Borge seemed to have changed since I last saw him. He looked better fed, his clothes, which in the past he had never paid much attention to, were neater, he laughed more easily; in short, his whole appearance exuded an extraordinary sense of well-being and happiness. Even his once derelict hair follicles seemed to me to have gained new initiative.

That was the last I saw of my Uncle Borge and Vera for some time. During the following two months they rarely left the *atelier*, except for Borge's expeditions to the shed in the port area. Besides his usual supplies he got quite adept at wrangling the most unusual merchandise from the quartermaster. Over time, Vera and my mother were outfitted with hats, coats and dresses from Paris, nylon stockings from America and shoes from Italy. I would regularly receive my allotment of Belgian Excelsior deluxe.

Periodically Borge would dash off a short telegram to Dr. Best, assuring him that all was coming along just fine, and that the painting would be ready for Göring's birthday. Other than that Borge and Vera kept to themselves as they laboured around the clock devising just the right blend of pigments and oils for what was to become Borge's *chef d'oeuvre*, and which the handful of German art critics who were lucky enough to see it would acclaim as "the essence of Nazi art," "the very apotheose of Teutonic kultur" and "the visual distillation of the Third Reich zeitgeist." Even propaganda minister Joseph Goebbels who had coined the phrase. "Whenever I hear the word art, I reach for my revolver," was forced to concede that this was indeed art. It was magnificent. A vast canvas, four metres by six metres, depicting a glorious panorama of German history in that heroic style so beloved by the Hitlerites. Sculpted youthful torsos tilling the virgin soil, wielding swords, striding hand in hand into the golden sunset. Frederick the Great on a magnificient white stallion. *Der Ehrlkönig, Die Lorelei.* The perfidy of the Versailles treaty. The cowardly bolshevik masses fleeing the victorious swastika. It was *sturm und drang*, *heimat und sehnsucht* and *götterdammerung* with a dash of the quest for *lebensraum* all rolled into one with not the slightest hint of *schadenfreude*. And there in the centre of the picture: Göring, larger than life, firm jaw, aquiline nose, weighing at least fifty kilos less than reality dictated, with not the slightest hint of male-pattern baldness, beribboned in his air marshall's uniform, staring determindly yet benevolently into some unspecified yet glorious future. It was grand.

Three days later an army truck escorted by six armed motorcy-

Göring with his art advisor. The bit of framed painting in the upper right hand corner is the only image that survives of Borge's masterpiece. From the military magazine "Signal."

cle outriders arrived at Borge's *atelier* to pick up the completed, but not quite dry, masterpiece. All traffic was halted as the convoy snaked its way through the city. When it arrived at the embassy the plenipotentiary was almost in tears of relief. "The Luft-Marshall will be ecstatic," he announced. "But there is no time to waste. Even as we are speaking a Heinkel cargo plane is waiting at the aerodrome. In a few hours the painting will be in Berlin and all our worries will be over. I am going to deliver it personally to Herr Göring. We will speak upon my return and I shall give you a full report on the Luft-Marshall's reaction." With that the convoy sped off.

That same afternoon Borge made his final visit to the storage shed in the port area. He stocked up on the usual necessities and exchanged what appeared to be a mislabelled crate of cigarettes.

The following evening Vera and Borge went into hiding. They spent the remaining years of the war holed up in a picturesque fisherman's cottage on a small island some thirty kilometres off the Jutland peninsula. With time Vera became not only an accomplished chess player but she also taught Borge a few surprising variants on the Obliganov gambit. When their little stash of goodies finally gave out, Borge quit cigarettes and coffee for good.

And now for the rest of the story. The crate of cigarettes that Borge had returned to the German supply depot contained one of Vera's signature concoctions. After two days a putrid odour started emanating from the shed, and as the days wore on the stench grew more intense. The building was evacuated and that same evening a spectacular explosion that could be seen as far away as Lund in Sweden reduced the shed to a heap of ashes. For days a piquant odour of American cigarettes and roasted coffee beans hung over the port, giving the area a short-lived reputation as a tourist attraction.

Oh, and about Herr Göring's painting. Here Vera had worked her alchemist's skill in an amazing way. She had manipulated a variety of stable and unstable paint molecules in such a manner

Eighteen tons of java and fourteen million American cigarettes go up in smoke.

that Time Release Action would cause a gradual instability in the pigments. In other words, with time they would become transparent. And to top the whole thing off, just a hint of her signature stink bomb was added. Not much, just a subtle unpleasant odour that would linger for years. As for Borge, what he had done was to execute a series of sixteen paintings, one superimposed upon the other. Over time, as each layer of pigment turned transparent, the layer underneath was revealed. The process was so gradual that no one noticed changes from day to day, but over weeks and months the scene would alter in subtle ways, a sort of long-term morphing. Göring would get just a little fatter and balder as time went on, his uniform seedier, the horse more decrepit, the healthy youth hollow-cheeked, the buildings sagging and in need of a paint job. As each layer slowly faded the next layer would reveal an even bleaker scene. The final painting, parts of which I had seen sketched on the canvas the day I visited with my father, showed a naked, bald and severely hollow-eyed Luft-Marshall cowering in the smoking ruins of what was once the glorious Vaterland. He was hunched over a chessboard and about to execute a move. On close inspection it was clear Herr Göring was about to be trapped in the Obliganov gambit. And there in the background, the wily knight: the spitting image of Uncle Borge in glorious armour with his sword raised over Göring's balding head, ready to strike.

It may be of interest to note that Herr Göring initially adored the painting. It was hung in his palatial Karinenhall where, for a while, it shared prominent wall space with stolen art works from all over Europe. Gradually, however, he developed a distinct dislike for the painting and it was eventually moved to a less prominent space. In April 1945, just before his last-ditch escape to the National Redoubt in the Bavarian Alps, a distraught Göring ordered all the stolen art works crated and transported to safe-keeping in an unused Austrian salt mine. As the convoy sped off he personally ignited the one-hundred-eighty kilos of dynamite that blew up his beloved manor along with the remaining contents,

Vera and Borge, 1958.

including Borge's *chef d'oeuvre* which had been specially wired with eight kilos of TNT. It is rumoured that Göring muttered "I couldn't stand the stink anyway," as he pushed the plunger.

TS